Suspect Attraction

Brenda Margriet

Published by Brenda Margriet Clotildes, 2025.

SUSPECT ATTRACTION

First edition. April 8, 2025.

Copyright © 2025 Brenda Margriet.

ISBN: 978-1990697135

Written by Brenda Margriet.

To everyone who dreams big dreams.

Enjoy the journey, no matter where the road takes you.

CHAPTER ONE

TROUBLE WALKED INTO my office at 8:57 that Monday morning.

I didn't know he was trouble then, of course. Didn't know the skin rippling on my arms was a warning. Didn't know how different my life would be in a few short weeks.

Dismissing my goosebumps as a chill from the cool air following him in from the outer room, I gestured to the visitor's chair.

He reached across my desk. "Seth Updike. Nice to meet you."

"Regina Blynde. Welcome to Blynde Dating Agency." His hand was warm and dry and lightly calloused. Warning number two—the butterflies battling in my belly. He wasn't the first sexy silver fox I'd interviewed. He wasn't even the first I'd been attracted to. I pushed aside my reaction as the normal hormones of a healthy hetero female confronted by a good-looking male.

Besides, he was a client. And clients were strictly off limits.

He settled into the leather and chrome chair. No arrogant sprawl, no nervous perching. Just an easy confidence I rarely saw in an applicant.

My normal tactic when meeting a new client was to let them take the lead. A few moments of silence had most people jumping in to fill the void, and I learned a lot in those first minutes of babble. Seth Updike, however, appeared ready to wait me out. His broad chest rose and fell with even breaths, his hands lay loosely on his thighs, and his blue eyes watched me with lazy amusement.

Two decades plus in human resources had taught me strategies for dealing with all personality types. This man was going to be a challenge, but I was confident I could handle him. I adjusted my approach.

"Tell me what you are hoping we can do for you, Mr. Updike." I always kept things formal until invited otherwise.

"It's Seth."

Bingo. He'd taken the first step. Now we were on the path to becoming a team working to achieve the same goal. "And I'm Ginnie." I leaned into my tall-backed executive chair and swivelled gently. I knew it dwarfed me, made me look tinier than my five foot and a half inches. Even the twenty pounds of grief weight I carried was disguised by its size. It was a purposeful choice. The less threatening I looked, the more people opened up to me.

You'd think people hoping I will find them love and companionship would be eager to tell me about themselves. Not so much. We all have masks we hide behind. We all want others to see us as stronger, prettier, smarter than we see ourselves.

I am not exempt from this. My mask is stitched together with pain and sorrow and fury. It helps me see the masks others wear.

"I'm not here to find a soulmate." This was warning number three, though I didn't know it at the time. "I'm fifty years old and understand when to temper my expectations. I'll be happy with a companion, someone who enjoys the same things I do, who doesn't create unnecessary drama, who will enhance my life."

I knew he was fifty-*one* years old from the online profile he'd filled out. He might have misspoken without a hidden agenda—I often had to think hard before I remembered I was fifty-four—but then again, he might be vain enough to lie just that teensy bit. It was a small failing and I liked him better for it.

"What made you choose my agency?"

"You hooked me with the name." The lazy amusement flared into a bright spark, the crow's feet around his eyes deepening. I despaired the day would ever come when wrinkles on a woman would be as sexy as those on a man. "The fact that you're a local business reeled me in. It was your process that landed me, though."

He'd listed fishing as one of his hobbies. Along with hiking, camping, skiing, and other outdoor activities. I found it easy to believe he'd been honest about those pursuits. He had the lean honed look of a guy who spent little time in front of a TV or computer screen.

"What about the process?" I probed.

He crossed a khaki-clad leg over his knee and smoothed his palm down his thigh. It was his first sign of nervousness. "I researched other online dating services, but they felt too impersonal, too"—he circled a hand in the air above his head—"global. When I read that the online profile is only the first step in your matching system, and that you interview all applicants face-to-face, I figured I'd give it a try. I was also impressed that the references on your website are all from people in their forties and older. I have a twenty-five-year-old daughter. I'm not interested in dating

3

anyone even remotely close to her age."

Well, that was refreshing. I rejected many of the men—and more of the women than you might think—who applied because they were unwilling to consider potential partners in their own age group. Not that I insist clients stick within a certain range. But those who are adamant their dates *must* be ten or fifteen or twenty years younger often have issues that are more complicated than I am willing to deal with.

"Your application indicates your most recent long-term relationship ended about ten years ago." We didn't use the term 'married' on our forms. It was the commitment that counted, not the paperwork.

"Yes." This brevity was at odds with his earlier openness.

I poked a little more. "So why now? What encouraged you to seek our help?"

The skin at the base of my throat tingled from his stare as he contemplated his response. He continued to avoid my eyes when he finally did reply. "It seemed like the right time."

I sensed there was more to his answer, but he was allowed to keep his counsel. Unless his secret harmed another of my clients. Then I'd be all over his ass.

I pulled over the folder I'd prepared. "Here's a selection of women I think might suit. Let's get to work."

An hour later, Seth Updike left, and I breathed a sigh of relief.

It had been trickier than I'd thought to find him a match, though I couldn't put my finger on *why*. In appearance, he was eminently dateable. His honest, competent, and good-humoured attitude hadn't flagged during our session, and he had been open to most of my suggestions. Yet I wasn't happy with any of the women I'd shortlisted for him, and I was disgruntled and doubting my skills by the time we'd settled on one.

I slid out of my chair, bending and stretching to get the kinks out, and then headed to the outer office.

Blynde Dating Agency leased a small suite of rooms on the ground floor of a narrow old building on a downtown street. A dance studio occupied the second floor. When I worked late, which was most nights, the soft thuds of footfalls and faint strains of music that drifted through the ceiling kept me company.

For the first several years, I had run the agency from my own home as a solo enterprise. Two years ago, when I needed something to keep me sane after...well, *after*, I threw myself into expanding the business. Now I have three employees. We do one-on-one social coaching, advise members on how to write their profiles, and even conduct inquiries if a client wants us to vet someone not associated with the agency.

In reception, Maeve Applekamp sat at a sleek desk that faced the main door and wrapped around behind her. She was a tall spare woman in her sixties and ran the office with the efficiency of a British nanny.

"Is Piper coming in today?" I asked.

Piper Latimer is my webmistress/tech guru/cyber geek. If it involved the guts or brains of a computer, she did it. Though she had an office next to mine, she often worked from home.

"Not until after lunch. And Indra is off because of the Singles' Supper last Saturday."

I nodded. Dating events like Singles' Suppers and Welcome Weekends fell into the realm of our social coordinator, Indra Braniff.

"Did you need Piper for something?" As usual, Maeve was doing three things at once, and all of them well. Her fingers flew over the keyboard before she reached behind her to pull sheets off the printer and tuck them into a bright yellow folder.

"She wants to explain some new algorithm she's designed. I was hoping she could do that before the next client showed up." According to the clock on the wall, I had about fifteen minutes.

"Which would give you an out before your brain glazed over from all the geek-speak." Maeve's eyes glinted as she peered over the top of her wire-framed reading glasses. She knew how much I hated technology. The label maker clattered. She peeled off the sticker and affixed it to the yellow folder. "How did the meeting with Mr. Updike go?"

"I matched him with Azalea Bickersley." My brows drew together. "I'm not sure it's going to work out, though."

"Then why set it up?"

I was wondering the exact same thing. A tiny part of me worried my subconscious had suggested the match because it *wouldn't* work. That the spark of attraction I'd felt for Seth Updike had sabotaged my professionalism. It better not be that. Because no matter what my traitorous subconscious might be up to, my *real* self wasn't looking for a relationship of any kind. I'd already experienced my one great love and look how that had turned out.

I shook off my unease. "I had to start somewhere. Most matches take a couple of shots before I get a feel for the client. If Piper comes in soon, send her my way, won't you?"

Back in my office, I dialled Azalea's number.

"Hello?" Before I had a chance to respond, the high twittery voice repeated, "Hello?"

"Hello, Azalea. It's Ginnie Blynde."

"Oh, Ginnie, how lovely to hear from you!"

I'd met Azalea about five weeks ago, in mid-December, when she'd registered for the agency. Despite our short acquaintance, she never failed to greet me as if we were long lost friends reconnecting after the passage of years.

"I'm calling to see if you are available tomorrow evening. I have another match I'd like you to meet."

Her voice had that odd jumpy quality you hear when people are walking and talking at the same time. "I'm so sorry. I can't talk right now. I'm halfway out the door. The girls are coming over this evening and I have to nip out to get the goodies." Her naughty giggle had me wondering exactly what those goodies would be. She continued without pausing for breath. "I know! You should join us! The girls would love to meet you."

I winced and held the phone away from my ear. Her guileless—and often loud—enthusiasm was one of the things I liked about her. I wondered if Seth might find it charming or annoying. "Oh, I don't know—"

"I insist. You must come. The girls will be thrilled." *Thud*, as of a door closing.

I doubted it. *The girls* would be well-to-do, well-known

citizens of the city, and well outside my usual circle of friends. You see, Azalea was royalty. Not Buckingham Palace royalty, despite the coincidence of William and Kate's eldest son sharing the same name as our town. But her family had lived in Prince George for generations and she had relatives and friends scattered throughout the upper echelons of business, law, and medicine.

"I won't take no for an answer." She sounded beyond delighted to have me gatecrash. "Seven o'clock, my place. You have the address."

And before I could protest further, she hung up.

As I turned through the gates leading to Azalea's house that evening, I reflected that this wasn't the oddest thing I'd done to accommodate a client. I'd set up dates at ski resorts and on party boats, delivered "it's not you, it's me," speeches when a member couldn't get up the courage to make the break themselves, and convinced more than one love-struck person that proposing on the second date might not be the best idea.

The asphalt drive was black as pitch without a speck of ice. Azalea must employ an army to keep it clear. Or maybe the whole thing was heated. Well, she could afford it.

When I said Azalea was royalty, you probably thought I was exaggerating. I was, but not by much. Her home wasn't a castle, but it was certainly one of the largest in town. Set on a ridge overlooking the city, it might even qualify to have 'grounds' as opposed to a yard. To my left, a huge expanse of unmarred white, smooth as butter cream frosting, was encircled by a neatly trimmed, waist-high, cedar hedge. In the centre, protective burlap coddled more delicate shrubbery. Rising from their midst was a large statue of a naked man, sculpted in the Greek—or maybe Roman, I was no expert—style. He looked rather pathetic, what with the snow capping his head and shoulders, and I wanted to give him a consoling pat. Maybe on his stone-hard naked buttocks.

I parked my small blue sedan beside two SUVs—one a sleek silver Mercedes Benz, the other chunky and black with a logo I didn't recognize. Which probably meant it cost as much as my house.

Not that I'm envious. Not at all.

The double-wide, NBA-player-tall front doors were dwarfed by the storeys soaring over my head and stretching out on either side. Lamps lit the dark wood exterior at regular intervals and light streamed freely through various windows. Who needed draperies when there were no neighbours to peer inside?

Clutching the bottle of wine I'd brought as a hostess gift, I rang the bell.

CHAPTER TWO

I HALF-EXPECTED TO be greeted by a housekeeper. Maybe even a butler. But when the door swung open, the young man who stood in the opening bore such a strong resemblance to Azalea I knew at once who he was.

"You must be Carter." All I knew of him was that he owned a florist shop whimsically named Carousel. Azalea had also mentioned in passing that he had semi-recently broken up with a long-term girlfriend. I put out my palm. "I'm Ginnie Blynde."

He shook my hand, his grip cool and a touch damp, as if he'd just washed. "Yes, I know who you are. Mom mentioned you'd be coming by." He stepped back so I could enter, a welcoming yet shy smile lighting his face. "She's in the library. I'll take you there."

He wasn't as exuberant as his parent, but his brown eyes gleamed with a familiar friendliness. Other similarities were evident in the tight curls covering his head, though the shade was a more subdued straw in contrast to Azalea's golden coin. His pale brows winged up at the same angle, and his mouth was wide and full like hers. They also shared a chin dimple.

He stowed my coat in an enormous closet and invited me to follow. "So, what's it like? Running a dating agency, I mean?" He sounded honestly interested, so I answered in the same vein.

"It can be very rewarding. Humans are social creatures. We need family, whether by blood or love. I like helping people find theirs." I'd given that same reply a zillion times, and I meant it, even if my own troubles had overshadowed that joy in recent months.

The hall was so wide we could walk side-by-side. Glancing into the large, dimly lit rooms branching off it, I had an impression of lofty ceilings and killer views over the city. Shifting the wine bottle to my other hand, I wiped my palm discreetly on my hip.

"Mom seems to be enjoying herself, meeting new people. I'm glad, because I'm the one that suggested she give it a try." His mouth quirked, diffident and self-effacing. "She went through a tough time after my...my father passed. I want her to be happy."

The slight stutter told me Azalea wasn't the only one affected by the death.

We turned a corner, and an open area expanded before us. Cozy yet elegant furniture was scattered about, punctuated by occasional tables decked with vases of fresh flowers and glittering curios. I gawped like a tourist. Better to get my plebeian reaction over with before meeting Azalea's friends, to whom this would be run of the mill.

"You have a beautiful home." It was an understatement, but true, nonetheless.

"I don't live here anymore, but thanks. I had dinner with Mom before her friends came. When she mentioned you were coming over, too, I decided to stay. I wanted to meet you."

"Oh? Why?" Was he interested in registering with the agency?

We halted near a long narrow sofa table. The scent of

roses and carnations wafted from the large bouquet adorning it.

"I said I want my mom to be happy. But more, I want her to be safe." He made an expansive, encompassing gesture. "As you can see, we're rather well off. It's important that the men she dates aren't after her just for her money or connections."

This didn't come as a surprise. Azalea been honest about her reasons for hiring me. "My son is worried about gold-diggers," she had told me at our first meeting, her tone indulgent and amused. "He wants to make sure the men I date are with me for the right reasons."

I understood Carter's reservations much better, now the evidence of her wealth was right in my face. "I get it. Let me assure you, our vetting process is rigorous." His concern was touching. Carter obviously loved his mom very much. I felt a small pang that I'd never had the opportunity to share the same love with a child of my own.

"I know. It's one of the reasons I encouraged her to join your agency. Still, I wanted you to know how important she is to me."

"I promise I'll do my best for your mom." As I did for all my clients. The reservations I had about matching Azalea and Seth had nothing to do with his integrity.

I just hoped they didn't have anything to do with my personal feelings for the man.

Several doors led off the huge space. Carter led me to an open one and pointed. "They're in there. Have a good evening. I enjoyed finally meeting you."

I nodded and watched him disappear into the main hallway before stepping into the next room.

SUSPECT ATTRACTION

Once again, I was awestruck. It was like a movie set. Dark wood panelling extending to the vaulted ceiling. Bookcases filled with leather tomes and tattered paperbacks. A ladder—an actual *rolling ladder*—resting on rails on the far wall. Huge narrow windows that by day would give a stunning view of the gardens—if I hadn't totally lost my bearings on the trek here—but which at this time of night reflected the brightly lit scene inside.

"Ginnie! I'm so glad you made it! Come in, come in." Azalea rushed to greet me, the winged sleeves of her pale teal jumpsuit flapping.

I'd debated what to wear to a high-society at-home girls' night and was glad I'd gone for business casual—black trousers, soft rose turtleneck, discreet jewellery. "Thanks for inviting me." I held out the bottle of wine.

Squealing with delight over my modest offering, she tugged me toward the conversation area where two women were seated. "You're the last to arrive. Girls, I'd like you to meet Regina Blynde. You don't mind if they call you Ginnie, do you?" Her beaming grin was blinding, and only faint lines creased the skin around her mouth. Although only in her forties, I was pretty sure she'd had some work done—eyes and chin—but if so, it had been performed by a skilled surgeon.

"Of course not."

She was cheerful and sweet and loved to travel, often at the last minute on some impulsive getaway. And she wasn't as airheaded as I might be making her sound. Her flutteriness hid a pragmatic core and a glittering intelligence. I wasn't sure why she needed the frivolous camouflage, but as

I've mentioned, we all have masks. Hers was simply painted with a smile.

"Ginnie, this is Belva Ginsberg." Azalea nodded at the woman posed bolt upright as if the back of the dark leather club chair was on fire. "And Coral Loughty." The second was curled like a cupcake in an identical chair on the far side of a knee-high glass table.

When I'd accepted Azalea's invitation, I'd figured I could pop into the gathering, schmooze for a few minutes, arrange a private moment to confirm her date with Seth, and pop out again without too much fuss. That was going to be much harder with only two other guests.

"Let me get you something to drink. A glass of wine?" She scurried toward a serving cart where crystal gleamed and assorted liquor waited.

It would be impolite to refuse, so I resigned myself to an awkward hour as a fifth wheel. "Thank you. Just a small one, though. I can't stay long."

Belva Ginsberg was a thin, austere woman wearing a silky white blouse, black pencil skirt, and a string of old-fashioned pearls. To my eyes she was too formally dressed for an evening at a friend's home, but maybe she'd come straight from work. She struck me as a woman with a successful career. Maybe as a prison warden. Or a ruler-wielding piano teacher.

Coral Loughty, on the other hand, wore fuchsia yoga pants, a top with equally bright flowers scattered over it, and a matching sheer, robe-like garment. She'd tucked her feet up on the seat and glowed out of the black leather like a bonbon. The expression on her round-cheeked face was wryly amused, as if an interloper at a private party was exactly what she expected from Azalea.

Belva started the conversation rolling, if you could call it that. "Azalea told us you operate a local dating agency." Distaste dripped from each syllable.

This attitude was more common than Carter's accepting curiosity. I flipped through my mental Rolodex of standard responses and chose Option C: Naïve Enthusiasm.

"I do!" I grinned, showing all my teeth, and then flicked my gaze to her ringless hands and back up to her face. "It is so rewarding to help people find companionship. I'm sure *you* can understand how difficult it is, meeting people at our time of life."

Her eyes widened, unsure whether I'd insulted her or not, and if I had, was it a dig at her singlehood or her age?

I smiled blandly and let her stew as I continued. "Sometimes it feels easier to give up than to keep looking. I'm there to offer support and encouragement. I truly believe there's someone for everyone."

That last was nothing but the truth. I'd had my someone for a long time. Or at least I'd thought I had.

"Oh, that's so romantic." Coral sighed. "I was married once, but it didn't work out. Maybe I should sign up."

Azalea returned with my wine and dropped into the chair next to me. Her pale blue eyes sparkled. "That's a wonderful idea! You should join, too, Belva. Then maybe we can go on triple dates!"

Coral smiled in merry agreement. Belva looked horrified, which gave me more pleasure than it should.

I turned the screw a little tighter. "I would *love* to set

that up. The two of you can go online and create an account any time." Many clients preferred to keep their membership in my agency a secret, at least until they found a successful match. Azalea obviously wasn't one of them. I used her suggestion to segue into the reason for my presence. "In the meantime, though"—I twisted to speak directly to her—"I have another match for you. Can we discuss that now or would you prefer we speak in private?"

"I don't have any secrets from my girls." Azalea gazed fondly at her friends. I had no trouble seeing her and Coral as buddies, but Belva? As experienced as I was with the vagaries of personal connections, some relationships would always be a mystery.

"All right then." I gave her a brief summary of Seth's profile without mentioning his name. She might be okay with broadcasting her membership, but I didn't have his approval to do the same. "He's available tomorrow night. What do you think?"

"Third time's the charm?" Azalea's giggle made her sound decades younger.

"You mean you didn't meet your soulmate on your first date?" Belva's tone was as sour as the lemon in the gin and tonic she clutched in one hand.

The jab was directed at me, but Azalea replied with her usual cheer. "I'm so glad I didn't. I married Warren young, and I'll love him forever. Now I'm having fun meeting different men. I feel twenty again." She turned to me. "Yes, tomorrow's open."

"Great." Maeve had already made a booking for six-thirty at Da Moreno's, just in case. "I'll email you the reservation details and his file so you can review it beforehand. If you have any concerns, please let me know right away."

With my business accomplished, I could make my excuses and retreat. But the wine was good, Coral and Azalea pleasant company, and it was fairly easy to ignore Belva, so I allowed myself to relax.

As I observed Azalea, I grew more and more positive she and Seth were not a good match. Well, I never claimed to be infallible. I wished I could decipher why it seemed doomed, as the situation would be easier to avoid in future if I could recognize the signs.

Maybe I was worried for nothing. Maybe they would hit it off, be a match made in heaven.

Turns out, I had plenty to be worried about. I was just worrying about the wrong thing.

CHAPTER THREE

TUESDAY MORNING, PIPER—who I'd managed to avoid the day before—pinned me down and waxed poetic on her updated database software while I tried desperately to understand one word in ten. The rest of the day went by in a different kind of blur—meetings with new clients. I worked late that evening as I often did and managed to avoid thinking about Azalea and Seth and their date with reasonable success.The moment my eyes opened Wednesday morning, however, the couple immediately popped into my head. Even as Indra and I dealt with a minor fire involving the caterer we'd hired for Hopeful Hearts, our upcoming Valentine's Day event, a good portion of my attention was waiting for one or the other to call with a report.

Clients weren't required to check in after a date, but many did. Azalea had after both her previous matches, so I was a little surprised when I hadn't heard from her by lunchtime.

A phone call just after one-thirty was the first indication that something sinister was going on. Not that my thoughts jumped to sinister at the time. That's hindsight talking.

I was in my office reviewing matches that might fulfill a particularly picky client's very specific requests. My desk phone, the one connected with the office landline, rang. I answered absently.

"Mrs. Blynde?" The male voice was soft, hesitant, and in the higher range. "It's Carter Bickersley."

"Carter, hello. What can I do for you?"

"Have you spoken with my mother today?"

"No, I haven't." This echo of my earlier ponderings made me frown, though I kept my tone light.

"We were supposed to meet for lunch. She didn't show. I called her cell and there was no answer. The last time we spoke was just before her date yesterday." The upward lilt on the last sentence turned it into a question.

"I'm sure there's a simple explanation. Maybe her battery is dead, and she forgot about the lunch."

"She wouldn't forget. We meet every Wednesday."

Peter and I hadn't had children, for both biological and intellectual reasons. I rarely regretted that, but Carter and Azalea's relationship had me wondering how our lives would have been different if fate had made us parents. They were obviously extremely close.

"Have you been to her house?" I asked.

"I'm there now. She's not here. Neither is her car. And I don't think she slept here last night."

In an odd juxtaposition, my body relaxed while my mind tensed.

Azalea had spent the night with Seth. *She's safe.*

Azalea had spent the night with Seth. *That bitch.*

Shocked at my visceral and bitter reaction, I kept my voice even. "What makes you say that?"

"I spoke to her housekeeper Mrs. Pereira. She says Mom's bed was still made when she went to tidy her room. Also, the house was empty when she got here at ten. Mom hardly ever goes anywhere before noon."

Hardly ever wasn't exactly *never*, but the evidence seemed fairly conclusive. I guess I'd been wrong when I thought the match was doomed to fail. "Tell you what. I'll call my client and see if he's heard from her." I didn't voice my suspicions out loud. The last thing a son wanted to hear was that his mother had stood him up because she'd been distracted by a lover.

"Would you?" His relief came clearly through the speaker. "That would be great."

"Of course. I'll get back to you as soon as I talk with him." I stifled a thrill of anticipation and blinked away a disturbingly sharp image of Seth smiling at me from the visitor's chair across my desk. *Cool it, Ginnie. He's not for you.*

"Thank you." He swallowed. "I'm probably being silly."

"Your mother is a mature, responsible woman. I'm sure this is just a miscommunication."

We exchanged cell numbers and disconnected. I turned to my computer, clicked through to Seth's contact information, took a deep breath, and reminded myself to be professional. Whatever he and Azalea had done last night was none of my business. Well, it was my *business* business, since I'd set them up, but it was none of my *personal* business.

I dropped my head on my desk and thudded it up and down, hoping to knock some sense into my brain. Then I dialled his number.

"Seth Updike."

Don't ask me if my toes curled at hearing his voice. You won't get an honest answer.

According to his profile, Seth owned a construction company. From the growling and beeping and clanging leaking through the speaker, I guessed he was at a building site. "Sorry to bother you. It's Ginnie from Blynde Dating

Agency. I need to talk to you about Azalea Bickersley."

His reply was buried under an avalanche of noise.

I pressed the phone harder to my ear. As if that would help. "Sorry. What was that?"

The cacophony dulled as if he'd closed a door or moved behind a wall. "Now's not a good time. We're in the middle of a pour."

I didn't bother asking what that meant. "When will you be done?" Despite Carter's anxiety, I wasn't convinced there was reason for urgency. Azalea was probably out shopping for new, exorbitantly expensive lingerie to wear on her next date with Seth.

Catty, much?

"Can you give me an hour or two?"

I brought my afternoon schedule onto the screen and reviewed it rapidly. "Let's make it two, just to be safe. Should I call you or will you call me?" I was pleased with my briskness. No one would suspect bubbles of inappropriate lust were dancing in my veins.

"I'll call you." More commotion and shouting assaulted my ear. "Got to go."

After we disconnected, I texted Carter a quick update and got back to work.

Matchmaking was something I'd fallen into by accident.

My husband and I met at university. Peter became a high school English teacher, and I used my psychology degree to secure a job in human resources at a multinational forestry company. Over the years we introduced friends to other friends, as one does, and several of those introductions led to long and happy relationships. When I was downsized after two decades, a joking remark from one of those couples sparked the idea that would become Blynde Dating Agency.

I still enjoyed what I did but no longer experienced the innocent excitement I had when I first started. Peter's death and all that had come before had a lot to do with that.

Just shy of the two-hour mark, a knock at my door interrupted my concentration.

Seth stood in the opening. He wore jeans liberally speckled with what appeared to be dried concrete and a slightly cleaner heavy canvas coat lined with sheepskin. A grey toque was pulled low over his ears. Dirt-caked steel-toed boots laced up the ankles completed the contractor-disturbed-at-work ensemble.

I licked suddenly dry lips. "I thought you were going to call." Handling my attraction would have been so much easier through the ether. Now I was once again confronted with the full force of his...whatever it was that made me forget he was off limits.

"I decided it would be better to talk in person." He approached and I caught the scent of sawdust and frigid air clinging to his clothing. "I'm guessing you spoke with Azalea."

I scrambled to collect myself. "No, I haven't. That's why I want to talk to you."

His forehead wrinkled, brows lowering. "I don't understand."

"Maybe we should start at the beginning." I gestured to the couch tucked against the wall. This conversation could get uncomfortable, and I didn't want him to think I was using my desk as a barricade. The sofa would be more friendly, intimate.

The thought of intimacy with Seth made my breath catch. I really needed to get a grip. I hadn't ever been this discombobulated by a client. I mean *ever*.

"Can I get you a coffee? Tea?" I bounced out of my chair and headed for the door. "Water?"

"A glass of water would be great. Thanks."

I'd converted a large storage closet into a tiny kitchenette when I'd moved into the building. When I returned with two glasses of water—and a much cooler head after a minute of deep breathing—he was standing at one end of the small couch. I placed the glasses on the low table in front of it and waved him to sit before taking the other end and angling toward him. My knee almost touched his thigh. I tucked my ankles back and squiggled deeper into the corner. "You start. Why did you think Azalea was going to call me?"

He wasn't nearly as relaxed as the first time we'd met. His spine didn't touch the cushion, and he used the bare minimum of the seat. "Our date didn't exactly end well. I was certain she'd call to complain today." He swept off his toque and scrubbed his hands through his short iron-grey hair.

My cheeks prickled. "You mean you didn't spend the night together?"

His mouth dropped open and then shut with a snap. "I only met the woman yesterday. You think we had sex?"

"Hey, I don't judge. If it felt right..." A sudden flush of heat swept over me. Damn menopause. I pulled the collar of my blouse away from my neck with one hand and reached for my glass with the other. "This has nothing to do with our conversation. Blame biology," I said by way of explanation. Cool water sliding down my throat did nothing to relieve me. I fanned the air in front of my face.

He ignored the sweat beading under my nose. "I have never been that kind of guy. Even if I was, though, it wouldn't have happened. Azalea is perfectly sweet, but I'm not interested in her, and I'm afraid I couldn't hide it. I had to be honest. I had to tell her I was attracted to someone else."

Shock loosened my grip on my glass. I returned it to the table without taking my gaze off Seth. "Someone else? You met someone between leaving my office and your date with Azalea?" The hot flash retreated as quickly as it had attacked. I stopped flapping my hand and did my best to appear reasonable and sane.

"No, not after leaving your office." He lifted his chin and stared at me with an intensity that had my temperature rising again. "While I was in it."

I sat, mesmerized by the blue of his eyes. *Blue* was too weak a word. I idly considered other descriptors as I stared into their depths. Cobalt, sky, electric...

Wait. What had he said?

I bolted to my feet. "While you were in my office? If you liked someone from the selection I showed you better than Azalea, why didn't you say so?"

"She wasn't one of the choices you offered." A wry grin lifted one corner of his mouth. "She was *you*."

I've always loved the word gobsmacked. I wasn't enjoying the sensation, however.

The floor tilted under my feet. I reached for the arm of the couch to steady myself before lowering gingerly back to the cushion, keeping as much space between us as I could.

"Umm..." Intelligent, I know. But it was the best I could do.

His hands rested on his knees. His fingers twitched though his gaze remained steady. "I cancelled my account with your agency this morning. I didn't want you wasting time trying to find me a match. I felt bad enough about Azalea."

"You didn't tell her it was *me*, did you?" Please say no. *Please say no.*

"I did. I couldn't lie, not on top of everything else."

CHAPTER FOUR

SHIT, SHIT, SHIT. What a kick in the ass for Azalea, to be rejected for the very woman who had set up the date.

"You know nothing about me," I protested. "I might be married."

He hesitated before answering. "I was told you are a widow. I'm sorry for your loss."

I corralled my galloping thoughts and gagged the high-pitched voice inside me that was squealing gleefully. This was bad. Really bad. "You can't be attracted to me. You only think you are."

His eyes narrowed. "Give me some credit. I know myself. I *am* attracted to you. It's not what I was expecting when I walked in here on Monday, let me tell you."

So, the chemistry between us hadn't been all one-sided. I was both pleased and horrified. Peter had been gone more than two years, but I wasn't ready to date. Had believed I'd *never* be ready to date. The wounds he'd left were deep and not yet scabbed over.

At least I had an honest answer for Seth. "I don't know what to say." Truer words had never been spoken and all that.

"You don't have to say anything. Not right now." He stood up.

I would have copied his action if I'd thought I could trust my knees. I craned my neck to peer at him. "What do you want from me?" I hated the vulnerability in my voice.

"Nothing. Well, it would be nice if you considered the

idea, at least." He twisted his toque in his hands like a dishrag. "Once you decide...you have my phone number."

He made it to the door before I realized we hadn't talked about *my* reason for calling him. "Wait."

He turned back and the hope glowing in his expression caused my breath to stutter. "Not about that." His face dimmed. I had the sudden overwhelming urge to say something that would bring that light back but stuck to the point. "Was Azalea very upset last night?" Maybe she'd been so distraught she'd fled on one of her last-minute trips and forgotten to tell Carter.

"She said she was disappointed, but I didn't get the impression she was too bothered."

I wasn't sure whether that was good or bad in the circumstances. "Did you leave the restaurant together?"

"I walked her to her car. I assumed she was going home, but we didn't talk much."

Yeah, I wouldn't think so. "What about you? Where did you go after?"

"I drove by one of my worksites. It's near the restaurant and I wanted to check something. Then I went home." He replaced his toque and tilted his head to one side. "What's this about? Why does it matter what happened after our date?"

I did *not* want news of Azalea's disappearance becoming common knowledge. Misplacing a client wasn't a glowing recommendation for the agency. "Nothing. Just following up."

"All right." He looked skeptical, but didn't call me on it. "About what I told you...I won't pressure you. I meant it when I said it was the last thing I expected when I chose your agency. But I would really like to get to know you better, Ginnie. You'll think about it?"

That was easy to answer. "I will."

If it weren't for Azalea's mysterious disappearance, I'd be thinking of nothing else.

I called Carter. I wasn't going to confess I might be the reason his mother had left without a word. It was possible, even likely, Seth's admission had nothing to do with her current situation. Still, he deserved to know what I'd learned.

He picked up immediately. "Did you talk to him? What did he say?"

"Nothing very helpful, I'm afraid. At the end of the date, he made sure your mom got to her car, but that was it. She didn't say where she was going. He assumed home."

A tremulous sigh whooshed into my ear followed by a rather lengthy pause. "Where could she be, Mrs. Blynde? I'm getting awfully worried."

"Call me Ginnie." Despite myself, I was getting worried too. There had to be a reasonable *and* non-terrible explanation. "What about her friends? Have you talked to any of them?" Even if Azalea hadn't wanted to tell her son about her disaster of a date, it was definitely the kind of story you'd share with a girlfriend.

"I was waiting to hear from you. I suppose I could call Coral. She and Mom are really close." For an instant, his soft voice held a harder edge. "And Belva too."

"Yes, call them. And anyone else you can think of." I

clutched the straw that had occurred to me after Seth's startling announcement. "Also...is it possible your mother went on a trip without telling you? She said in our interview she likes to take last-minute vacations."

"I suppose it's *possible*." He sounded doubtful. "She'd know I'd worry, though."

"Does she book her trips online?" If Azalea used travel apps like most of humanity, I didn't know how we'd find out more. Piper might, but I wasn't ready to share this development with my team.

Thankfully, Carter's reply gave us an avenue to explore. "I know her travel agent. He was at school with me."

"Can you call him too? Maybe he can clear this up." I wracked my brain to think of what else we could do. We couldn't just twiddle our thumbs. Another idea rose to the surface, though I hesitated to mention it.

He spoke into the pause, his tone bleeding red with anxiety. "What do you think could have happened, Ginnie? Where is she?"

I steeled my resolve. "As much as I hate to suggest it, maybe she had an accident. Do you know who her doctor is?"

"Yes. She's my doctor too."

"I think you should call her, as well. She might know if your mother was admitted to hospital." Even if Azalea was unconscious, she would have had identification on her.

"Oh, my god."

"Don't panic," I instructed him sternly. "You've got to hold it together while we investigate all the options."

"Okay." He heaved in a long, slow breath. "Do you

think...should I call the police?"

He sounded reluctant and I could understand why. The Bickersleys were a well-known but very private family. Bringing in the authorities wasn't something to take lightly. "If you think that's best, then by all means. But it's only been a few hours."

"All right," he said. "I'll make the calls first. Then we can decide."

The "we" gave me pause. I would do what I could to help, of course, but this was ultimately a family matter.

Unless I was the reason Ginnie had fled.

My stomach shrank with guilt. "Let me know the minute you find out anything."

"I will. Thanks, Ginnie. I'd be freaking out if it weren't for you."

His gratitude twisted the sword of remorse in my gut. "Don't thank me. Just find your mother. That's all I want."

By the time I left the office that afternoon, Carter had texted several updates. The travel agent hadn't heard from her, and while the doctor's receptionist had been cagey—purportedly for privacy reasons—he'd assumed by reading between the lines that she had nothing to tell. He was still tracking down his mother's various friends and promised to keep me informed.

Between Azalea's disappearance and the bombshell Seth had dropped, I was vibrating with nervous tension. Luckily, it was the evening of my adult jazz class. I'd be able to work off my jitters with my best friend.

SUSPECT ATTRACTION

The dance class had been our weekly ritual for several years, even before I'd moved my agency below the studio in a convenient coincidence. Neither Lillian nor I was going to be drafted by the Rockettes anytime soon. It was simply a fun, energetic way to stay active, and learning new routines tested my physical coordination and mental focus.

We took our places in the corner of the studio, its shiny hardwood floors springy under our feet. Mirrors on three walls multiplied the dozen or so participants. It was impossible to avoid seeing myself, but I did my best. Not that I am ashamed of my appearance. Despite the extra pounds I might have tried to lose if it didn't mean giving up pasta, chocolate, and wine, I was content with how I looked in athletic wear. It's just that the graceful, skilled movements I visualize myself making never match what I see in the reflection. I prefer to remain in happy denial about how good—or bad—a dancer I am.

The instructor fidgeted with her phone and the wireless speaker system. Lillian folded forward to touch her toes and I followed suit. "How was work?" she asked.

Lillian Kelstone and I had been friends for nearly three decades. We'd met while working at the same forestry company and, though she'd switched careers well before I was laid off, we'd stayed connected. She was divorced with three grown kids, the oldest of whom was a couple of weeks away from making her a grandma.

"Interesting," I said, voice strangled by my cramped diaphragm.

"More so than usual?" She twisted her neck, and we looked at each other as we hung upside down.

Lillian's hair was cropped close to her skull and highlighted and lowlighted and whatever else it was that hairdressers did to artfully hide the grey. Mine, on the other hand, was pulled into a long ponytail, which trailed on the floor in this position. It was as dark as it had been all my life without artificial assistance, though I was plucking out random silver strands more often than I used to.

"Definitely." We rolled upright, vertebrae by vertebrae. Several in my upper back popped and clicked and I moaned at the release.

A swift glance around the room established no one was paying us any attention, but this wasn't the place to tell Lillian about Azalea. However, that wasn't the only news I needed to get off my chest.

I leaned in and murmured, "A client said he is attracted to me." I had confirmed that Seth had cancelled his account, so *client* was a tiny white lie.

"Just one?" Lillian dipped into a demi-plié in first position and rose again, grunting a little. "This can't be the only time."

"It's not." I'd had to deal with misplaced attraction before. Like transference for a psychologist, it was a hazard of the job. "It's just that..."

Her eyebrows raised. "*You're* attracted to *him*. That's what's different."

I nodded. "I *can't* be attracted to him."

"Can't be or don't want to be?" She regarded me with sympathy. "I know Peter's death and what he did put you through hell. But you can't cut yourself off from future happiness because of your past."

"Yes, I can." I scowled. Some might call it a pout, but I never pout. Lillian didn't know the entire truth about Peter, but she knew enough that I'd thought she would support my decision to stay away from Seth. "I don't want to be hurt like that ever again. You saw what I was like." How I had fallen apart.

She rubbed my back. "I did. But I worry about you, Gin. It's time you moved on. If you like this guy, why not have coffee with him? That's all. One quick caffeinated conversation. It's not a lifetime commitment."

Music blared and the instructor took her place at the front of the class. Lillian waited for my answer with her hands on her hips and her toe tapping.

Could I do this? Could I take this step away from the tragedy of my marriage? My belly bubbled with anxious heat. "You're not going to let this go, are you?"

"You've met me, right?" My so-called best friend grinned, knowing she'd won.

I sighed. "Fine. I'll ask him out for coffee." I raised a finger and shook it at her. "But I'm not promising anything more than that. Just coffee."

For the next fifty minutes, we stretched and stepped and sweat and I forgot all about rich missing clients and attractive silver foxes.

Well, mostly.

CHAPTER FIVE

IF I WAS THE night owl of the Blynde Dating Agency, then Maeve was the early bird. Our office officially opened at eight o'clock, but I knew from reviewing the key fob logs on our security system she usually arrived half an hour before, sometimes more.

When I walked in at half past eight-ish on Thursday morning, Maeve was busy at her desk. Carter, his slight body enveloped in a dark green thigh-length parka and his blond hair rumpled, sat in one of the yellow vinyl chairs lined against the wall.

He jumped up the moment he saw me. "Ginnie! I need to talk to you."

"He was standing outside the door when I got here." Maeve's tone was polite but cool. She didn't like having her routine disrupted. "I asked him to wait in his vehicle, but he refused. He also wouldn't tell me why he wanted to speak with you."

Which explained why she hadn't contacted me. We had tight protocols on what constituted an emergency. Simply saying "I need to talk to Ginnie" didn't count. Emotions often ran high, and if I was at the beck and call of every client, I would never have a moment's peace. Maeve would follow that procedure even knowing Carter wasn't a member of our service.

"I tried to call you, but you didn't answer." He shifted from foot to foot, almost hopping, his expression pinched and tight. "Ginnie. Please."

I dug my phone out of my purse and saw three missed calls. "I'm sorry. I have it set to Do Not Disturb outside of office hours." Given his agitation, his news couldn't be good. "Come on in."

Scuttling past, as if afraid I might change my mind, he began pacing in front of my desk even before I had closed the door. He gripped his curly hair in both hands then dragged his palms over his face as he reversed direction. "I've talked to everyone. No one knows anything. No one's talked to my mom since Tuesday."

My pulse sped up. Keeping my motions calm and deliberate, I placed my purse on my desk, unwound my scarf, and draped it on the coat rack. "No one?"

"No one!" He tossed me a distraught glance as he whipped by.

My long puffer coat joined my scarf. On his next pass, I gripped his forearm, forcing him to stop. The material of his parka was slippery under my palm. "It's time to call the police."

"I know. It's just...Mom hates having strangers messing about in her private life." He stared at me, his dark irises circled with white.

"I understand. But we've done all we can. We need help." Dread tightened the skin of my upper back, and I hunched my shoulders, releasing his arm. "Yesterday, I honestly thought there was nothing to worry about. But now...you shouldn't wait any longer."

Still, he hesitated. "Do I call 911?"

"I don't think so. Probably the regular line. Let me find it for you." I retrieved my phone from my purse again and did a quick search. "Here it is."

He pulled his cell from his pocket and then stared at it as if he'd never seen one before.

"Carter?"

He lifted his eyes to mine. "It just feels like...if I do this...I'll be making it real. That there will be no going back to the way it was."

"I'm so sorry," I said helplessly.

"It's okay." His chin worked back and forth for a few seconds. "What's the number?"

I read it to him. He tapped it out, held the phone to his ear, and turned his back to me.

He was right. Even if Azalea was found safe and sound, the dynamic between them would be changed forever. As for myself—I couldn't put off telling the others about her disappearance any longer. My stomach clenched.

I tiptoed to the door, opened it, stepped through, and pulled it mostly shut behind me. Maeve looked up from her computer when I halted by her desk.

"Can you find a time when you, Piper, Indra, and I can meet today?"

Her gaze fluttered to my office door and back to me, but all she did was nod.

"It needs to be as soon as possible."

She nodded again. "Indra will be in any minute, but I never know when Piper is going to show up." Her tone revealed her constant irritation at our web guru's refusal to comply with a schedule.

I didn't have the energy to smooth her ruffled feathers. "Call her. Tell her I said to get here right away."

Maeve's huffy expression melted into concern. "What's going on, Ginnie?"

"I'll fill everyone in at the meeting."

I returned to my office, shutting the door again. Carter was pacing as he talked, wearing a path around and around my desk. I listened to his end of the conversation.

"No, she's never gone away without telling me first." Pause. "Well, yes, once she forgot, but she called me before I realized she wasn't in town." Pause. "I talked to her travel agent. I've also talked to her friends and our doctor. No one has any idea where she is." Pause, and a quick, jerky glance in my direction. "No, she doesn't have any health or mental issues. I really thought she'd show up any minute."

Maybe if we'd called the police yesterday, we'd have Azalea back already. It was too late to regret that decision. The coffee I'd had at breakfast churned, an acid stew in my belly.

Carter hung up, told me the police wanted to speak to him in person, and departed my office without saying goodbye.

I trailed after him into the outer room. Indra Braniff was entering through the main door and stepped quickly to the side as he rushed past. She watched him hurry away with wide eyes, and then jerked a thumb over her shoulder and said into the unsettled silence he left behind, "Unhappy client?"

"I'll explain everything as soon as Piper is here." I turned to Maeve. "Any luck?"

"She's on her way. Ten minutes."

We didn't have a boardroom. When necessary, staff

meetings took place in my office. I returned to it and mentally prepared how I would share the news.

Indra entered a minute later. She'd taken off her bright pink wool coat and fleecy pink and green hat. Short black curls streaked with silver bounced as she plopped onto the couch.

"Piper just got here. Maeve is putting up the sign." If we had to leave the front room unattended, we always locked up and stuck a note on the glass door notifying unexpected visitors of our unavailability.

The bangles on Indra's wrist jingled as she shot the cuffs of her long-sleeved blouse, her restless energy fizzing. Not only did she implement all of Blynde Dating's events, she was our social media manager. Her vitality was a great quality for what she did, but sometimes being in the same room with her made me tired.

A minute later, Maeve joined Indra on the couch. I perched on the front edge of my desk, and Piper leaned a hip against my filing cabinet.

Today, her eyes blinked owlishly from behind large round red frames. Some days she wore contacts, others a variety of quirky spectacles. She wasn't much taller than me, favoured yoga pants and slouchy hoodies, and would have been easy to lose in a crowd except for the vibrant purple streak in her closely cropped, currently black, hair. "What's so important? Maeve said I *had* to come in."

"I said *Ginnie* said you had to come in. Don't blame me."

I was in no mood to deal with their perpetual squabbling so cut to the chase. "I have bad news. Azalea Bickersley is missing."

They stared at me with various levels of confusion and concern as I filled them in on what had happened since Carter called yesterday.

"This is not good for the agency." Maeve's stern expression grew even grimmer. She smoothed a hand over her greying blond hair, tightly bound in a bun at the back of her neck. It was perfectly in place as always. It wouldn't dare come loose from its moorings.

"No duh." Piper's scorn was a knee-jerk reaction. Her hazel eyes glittered. No doubt the computer-like brain behind them was already calculating odds and options.

True to form, Indra's first thought was for Azalea. "The poor woman. I hope she's okay."

"If the police get in touch, I expect everyone to be as helpful as possible." It was more a 'when' than an 'if.' Azalea's last known activity had been a date arranged by the agency. I didn't see how the police *couldn't* involve us.

Piper protested. "I never even spoke to the woman."

"Did you process her online application?"

"Of course. But there was nothing unusual about it."

"Then that's what you say." I met each of their gazes directly. "We assist the investigation to the best of our abilities. Azalea needs to be found, for her sake more than for the agency's. But Maeve is right. This is *not* good for business. Don't go blabbing about this to your friends. And for heaven's sake, don't tell any other clients." It was bound to come out sooner or later but later was infinitely preferable.

"Of course not." Indra pursed her lips, insulted, but I worried about her the most. Keeping secrets went against the grain of her open honest nature.

"So for now, we go on as normal?" With her curiosity satisfied and a plan for the future in place, Maeve was ready to move on.

"Yes. I'll keep you up to date if anything changes."

The three of them drifted toward the door, Maeve in the lead. She stopped in the opening and turned back, forcing Indra and Piper to halt as well. "What about Seth Updike? If nothing else, the police will ask who Azalea's date was. Should I let him know what's going on or do we let them do it?"

I'd been debating this ever since Carter had sped away. If I suspected Seth had anything to do with Azalea's disappearance, it could be a mistake to warn him about the investigation.

I refused to believe I could misjudge him so terribly. He *couldn't* have anything to do with whatever this was.

"He deserves to know," I said. "I'll tell him."

It struck me the moment I sat behind my desk and picked up my phone that I could kill two birds with one stone.

Seth answered after one ring. "Ginnie. How are you?"

There was nothing but friendliness in his smooth voice, yet my back arched as if he'd stroked my spine with one large hand. "I'm fine. But we need to talk."

"Good talk or bad talk?" Hope warmed his round full tones.

"Serious talk. Can you meet me today? Maybe for coffee?" There. I'd done what Lillian had challenged. She might not count it as a date, but I would.

"I'm on my way to Bear Lake." The small sawmill

community was an hour's drive north of town. "I'll be back around lunchtime."

I hadn't told Carter who Azalea's date had been, but she might have mentioned Seth. If she had told her son and he told the RCMP, I might be leaving Seth open to an ambush. Still, her disappearance wasn't something I wanted to announce bluntly over the phone. If I guessed wrong, I'd deal with the fallout later. "Abani's Bistro at twelve-thirty?" The sandwich shop was only three doors down from the office.

"See you then."

CHAPTER SIX

I WAS WAITING at a table in the back corner when Seth entered the restaurant. He spotted me and smiled, and a thrill flushed my cheeks. I pretended to check my phone, hoping he wouldn't notice my blush, all the while keeping a surreptitious eye on him as he strode toward me.No construction gear today. A stiff white collar and knotted blue tie peeked from the vee of his charcoal wool coat and his boots were shiny black leather. His uncovered steel-grey hair swept back from his temples and looked freshly cut.

I really shouldn't be noticing a detail like that. He wasn't going to be anything other than a client. Ex-client. But I guess I'd been paying closer attention than I wanted to admit, even to myself.

He pulled out the seat across from me. "I'm glad you called."

He wouldn't be soon. The metal feet on the legs of my chair screeched across the tile floor as I shoved away from the table. "We have to order from the counter." Thank goodness. It would give me time to regain my equilibrium. I wasn't ready to be all cozy and private with him.

He shrugged out of his coat, folded it, and laid it on one of the extra chairs before we joined the line. While ordering our sandwiches and soup, he chatted with the server and I learned he disliked chowders, never ate raw onions, and loved avocado. He accepted my offer to pay with thanks and a gracious smile and carried our tray to the table. After waiting for me to take my seat—probably making sure I wasn't going to bolt again—he lowered into his.

We distributed the food in amicable silence. I dipped honey out of the tiny plastic packet with a small bamboo spoon, stirred it into my tea, and bit the bullet. "So. The reason I called."

He crumbled a packet of square crackers before ripping it open. "I'm getting the impression this lunch has nothing to do with what I confessed yesterday."

"Not really. Well, sort of." God, I sounded like a moron. I squared my shoulders. "To be clear, I had two reasons for calling you. One, I figured it wouldn't kill me to get to know you a little better."

His smile was as dry as the crumbs he was dusting over his soup. "Thank you?"

I ignored his sardonic amusement. He wasn't getting any gushing flattery from me. A relationship between us wasn't a good idea, no matter what Lillian thought. I wouldn't pretend it was, to him or her.

Or myself.

"Two, I need to tell you that Azalea Bickersley hasn't been seen since your date."

The RCMP hadn't called the office before I'd left. I also hadn't heard from Carter. I had no idea if they were taking his concerns seriously or not. It didn't matter. Seth should know what was going on.

His spoon halted halfway to his mouth. "What?"

For the second time that morning, I ran through the events leading up to this lunch. He ate slowly and thoughtfully as I spoke and scooped up the last mouthful just as I finished.

"Eat." He gestured at my bowl. "It's getting cold. I need to absorb all this."

We finished our meals. He waited while I chewed my last bite of sandwich and then shook his head as if arranging his thoughts into a logical order. "Is this why you called me yesterday? You already knew she was gone?"

"I knew Carter couldn't get a hold of her, yes."

"I can't remember anything more than what I told you." He folded his napkin into increasingly tinier squares, his gaze unfocused. "We had a pleasant enough meal, and I liked her, but when she started talking about a second date, I had to be honest and tell her about...well...you." He slid me a quick glance.

Heat suffused my chest, and I couldn't blame it on a hot flash this time. I took refuge in sarcasm. "It was love at first sight. Sure."

"I didn't say that, and you know it." His rebuke was quiet but firm. "For a woman who runs a dating agency, you're more than a little cynical."

A sudden memory of the last time I'd seen Peter, the last words I'd flung at him, overwhelmed me. I stared into the dregs of my tea. I might be all cheerful optimism when it came to my clients, but myself, not so much. "This isn't about us. It's about Azalea. Is there *anything* you can think of that might help?"

"Not at the moment. But I'll keep trying."

He leaned across the table and wrapped his hands around mine as I clasped my empty mug. The warmth of his touch overwhelmed the faint heat lingering in the ceramic under my palms. Electricity swept up my arms and into my belly. My fingers twitched and his grasp eased. I could pull away if I wanted to.

But I didn't want to. No matter what I told myself, his blatant attraction felt *good*, as if a dry and arid part of me was finally being tended and cared for. And though I didn't believe in love at first sight, I had no trouble believing lust could be instantaneous.

How could I not, when it was eroding my best intentions every second I spent in Seth's presence?

"I don't want to make you uncomfortable," he said softly. "This is just as much a shock to me as it is to you. But here we are." His thumbs brushed my knuckles in rhythmic motions as his blue eyes blazed into mine.

Tremors of arousal rippled up and down my spine. "Ah, screw it." I deflated. "Fine. I'm attracted to you too."

A flare of triumph flashed across his face, fading almost instantly into an expression I couldn't read. Had I called a bluff? Had he been taunting me for some unknown reason? My bravado flickered and died.

He must have seen my doubts. His hands tightened on mine. "Don't. Don't regret telling me. It's good you did. Really good."

My cell vibrated against the tabletop and the tension between us snapped. Relieved to have an excuse other than cowardice to drag my hands from his, I answered without checking the screen. "Hello?"

"Regina Blynde? This is Corporal Travis Tam. I'd like to speak with you regarding Azalea Bickersley."

The Prince George detachment of the RCMP was housed in a modern building of odd angles and random materials in the heart of downtown. In the summer, the sidewalk leading to the main doors meandered through a landscaped garden that was a welcoming tangle of flowering shrubs and leafy green willows. On this January day, tombstone-grey solar lights struggled to poke out of the grimy snow, and skeletal trees loomed with sinister intent.

Or at least that's what it felt like to me.

The hushed atmosphere inside did nothing to settle my galloping pulse. I'd known this interview was coming, but had assumed it would be on my turf. Even though I had done nothing wrong, misplaced guilt and unwarranted fear made my fingertips tingle with nerves.

Corporal Travis Tam had insisted I come at once, so I'd left Seth with a hurried and distracted goodbye. The detachment was only a few blocks away and had limited public parking, which made retrieving my car from the agency's small lot pointless. I nervously speed-walked the short distance and, despite a bitter winter wind, was overheated by the time I checked in at reception.

Whether it was strategy or indifference, I waited nearly twenty minutes before the clomp of booted feet heralded Corporal Tam's arrival. During that time, sweat cooled under my arms and breasts and I grew uncomfortably damp. Now more irritated than agitated, I accepted his offered hand with equanimity.

He led me not to a sterile interrogation room with table and chairs bolted to the floor and a camera in the corner of the ceiling but to a perfectly ordinary meeting room. A three-year-old poster advertising the Musical Ride hung next to a large frame displaying a dinner-plate-sized version of the Royal Canadian Mounted Police emblem—a crown with golden arches and a red velvet cap atop a wreath of green maple leaves surrounding a buffalo head.

"Sorry for the wait." Tam pulled out a chair on the near side of the table, gestured me toward it, and circled around to the other side. Placing a blank yellow legal pad on the table, he groaned softly as he lowered into his own chair, the buttons on his dark uniform shirt straining.

I am sure at one time he had been trim and fit, but somewhere along the line his gut had expanded, his hair had retreated, and his good humour had evaporated. Not that I expected any police officer to be jolly. You couldn't pay me enough to do their job. I just hoped he was taking Azalea's disappearance seriously.

He didn't follow his apology with an explanation, but dove right in. For the third time in less than six hours, I recounted all I knew. I reported my conversation with Seth faithfully but warily, expecting a rebuke. Tam remained impassive, making notes but no comments. When I finished, he took me through the whole sequence again, prodding for more details, more impressions. He was polite and thorough, and I relaxed, assured he wasn't brushing off Carter's concern.

He laid his pen on the table and leaned back in his chair. The leather of his heavy wide utility belt creaked as he crossed his arms over his ample belly. I relaxed even more. It was almost over. I had made it through.

"Thanks very much for coming to talk with me." Tam's

voice was a deep bass and rumbled lazily up from his toes. "Have you been here before?"

"No, I haven't." And would be very happy never to be in the building again. I reached for my purse, itching to make my escape.

"Not even when your husband was killed?"

The edges of my vision blurred, leaving only Tam's jowly clean-shaven face sharp and clear. Cold, calculating eyes. Straight, uncompromising mouth. Alert, watchful expression. This sudden reversal, from calm professionalism to suspicious disbelief, was shocking, disorienting.

An infinity passed before my heart took another beat.

I gasped, and the world rushed back. The heating vent hummed like a swarm of bees, yet the tip of my nose was cold. "N-no. Not even then."

The investigator assigned to Peter's accident had been a young woman. Whether it was her age or her gender that made her compassionate I had no idea. Maybe it had been neither of those things. Maybe she'd thought she'd get better results by treating me kindly.

If so, she'd been wrong. The driver of the vehicle that had struck Peter as he'd jogged through an empty parking lot, catapulting him into the concrete base of a lamp standard and shattering his skull, *and then left him to die*, had never been found.

"I ran your name in our system. Made interesting reading." His gaze never left my face. "Why was your husband out running so late that night?"

Why ask if he'd read the report? It was all in there. Still struggling to recover from his broadside, I didn't have the wits to challenge him. "We had an argument. He went running to cool off."

"Did that happen often?"

Argue or run? I thought a little wildly. "He ran almost every day. Sometimes at night, sometimes not." Shame and self-reproach flushed my veins like poison. Cold spread down my chest and into my limbs. Could he see my turmoil?

"What did you argue about?"

I couldn't remember. No, that's a lie. I knew exactly what we'd argued about. What I couldn't remember was what I'd told the police two years ago.

My fingers knotted so tightly together my knuckles ached. I focused on the pain, used it to jump start my brain. "What does this have to do with Azalea?"

His expression smoothed out, returned to bland blankness. "Nothing. Just curious. Curse of an investigator, I guess." He pushed his chair back and stood up. "Thanks again for coming in. If I think of any more questions, I'll be in touch."

Dizzy from the rapid changes in subject and attitude, I rose and followed him down the warren of hallways to the lobby. He shook my hand and lumbered away.

I was halfway back to the office before I wondered about his last words. Had he been talking about Azalea's disappearance? Or Peter's death?

CHAPTER SEVEN

MAEVE PULLED OFF her cheaters as I walked in the door. She needed them for close-up work but hated wearing them. "How did it go?"

I'd let her know I'd been summoned to the detachment the minute I'd left Abani's Bistro. "He seems to be taking it seriously." So seriously he'd looked into my past. The past I wanted to keep hidden, dark, and secret.

"That's good." She nodded. One rebellious strand had absconded from her tight bun and nodded with her. If that wasn't evidence of the day's disturbances, I didn't know what was. "I cleared your schedule for the afternoon since I wasn't sure how long you'd be."

"That's great. Thanks. Give me a minute and we'll see what we can put back on."

Indra waved from her office but didn't come out to chat. In her seldom used space next to mine, Piper wore heavy headphones and bopped in her chair as she squinted at her laptop. I had an unexpected yet welcome sense of homecoming.

I closed my office door, which I rarely do when alone, and collapsed into my seat without removing my outerwear. I still trembled from Tam's ambush, my fingers and toes chilled from shock more than the frigid walk.

I wouldn't mention the corporal's interest in Peter to the others. Couldn't mention it. It was rather ironic, though. He was the reason they worked here, after all.

SUSPECT ATTRACTION

When I decided my business needed to go online, Peter became my sole—albeit part-time and unpaid—employee, dealing with the technical specs and requirements. After he died, I'd floundered to manage that area, Luddite that I am. Two nausea-filled days thinking I'd erased my entire database convinced me to admit defeat, and I began the search for a tech wizard. That had led me to Piper. And when my quest to fill my achingly empty hours resulted in more business than I could handle on my own, I added Maeve as office administrator/second-in-command and Indra as social coordinator.

They knew I was a widow. Knew that my husband had been killed in a hit-and-run. I trusted them implicitly when it came to Blynde Dating Agency. But we weren't *friends*. At first, I'd been too isolated by my grief and fury to make the effort. Now, it was too late. The window of opportunity had passed.

I wished I could call Lillian, the one person who knew me and would understand my distress. But she had left this morning for Vancouver. Her daughter was due any day and she intended to stay for a week or so after the birth, when it finally happened. She had enough on her plate without inflicting my drama on her. Besides, what could she do other than commiserate?

I scrubbed my hands over my cheeks. Enough wallowing. It was time to pull myself together and get some work done. I dragged to my feet, shed my coat, gloves, and hat, opened my door, and invited Maeve in, determined to salvage what I could of the business day.

A few hours later, I felt significantly better. Ticking tasks off my to-do list had always been therapeutic. But my stamina was flagging, and I decided against working any longer. No use pushing past the point of diminishing returns. I used the remote start so my car would be toasty and warm when I reached it.

Piper, then Maeve, then Indra, had called goodnight as they'd left. Six o'clock had come and gone. The office slept under a soft pall as I confirmed the front entrance was locked and set the alarm. I exited through the rear door, testing to make sure it was firmly secured.

Dusky blue twilight draped the alley. I walked to the parking lot at the side of the building, huddling deep into my scarf to avoid the bitter breeze whistling down the narrow lane. The days were noticeably longer than a month ago, but spring was double-digit weeks away. I could smell snow in the air.

A motion sensor flood light switched on abruptly. I flinched and then chuckled softly at my fright. Other than a dumpster in the far corner and my own vehicle, idling quietly with exhaust streaming from the tail pipe, the lot was empty.

The back of my neck prickled as I approached my car. I looked over my shoulder. Nothing. The sensation didn't ease, however, and I slid into my seat with a deep sigh of relief.

More eager than ever to get home, I backed out of my slot. As often seemed to happen when I was in a hurry, I hit every red light. I was drumming my fingers impatiently on the steering wheel at the fourth one in a row when a call from Carter popped up on my dash screen.

I'd added him to my Favourites so he could reach me even when my phone was in Do Not Disturb mode. I didn't want a repeat of this morning, when he'd been unable to get in touch. My heart leaped with hope. Was it possible Azalea had been found safe and sound?

I tapped accept. "Carter. Do you have news?"

"No."

The single syllable was soft and plaintive, and a surge of pity squeezed my heart. Today, I'd been reminded of my own tragedy. Yes, Peter's death had been sudden and final and, as of now, Azalea may yet appear, whole and healthy. That possible positive outcome didn't stop me from being able to empathize with Carter.

"I'm sorry to hear that." A fully loaded logging truck lumbered through the intersection as smaller vehicles darted past. "I spoke with Corporal Tam this afternoon."

"He wanted the name of the man Mom went out with that night." A faint hint of reproach tinted his words. "I had to tell him I didn't know, that he'd have to ask you."

I refused to feel bad for protecting Seth...er...my client. *Then* client. Whatever. "Well, the police are looking into it now. With all their resources, they're sure to find her soon." A tiny voice at the back of my head whispered they hadn't yet found Peter's killer. I ignored it.

"Maybe."

"Have faith, Carter. I know it's hard, but you have to believe she'll be found soon." I was exhausted and drained and, as much as I wanted to support Carter, I wanted home more. My solitary existence had begun to rub raw lately, but tonight, I craved it.

"I'm trying." He sounded as tired as I felt. "Ginnie? I don't want to be alone. Are you at home? Can I come by, just for a little while?"

The traffic light turned green, and the serpent of traffic eased forward. "Isn't there someone else you can go to? A friend or relative?"

"I don't have anyone. My girlfriend left me a few months ago. My dad's been gone for three years. My mom is all I have left."

"I'm sorry you feel that way," I said. "But are you sure that's true? What about cousins, aunts, and uncles?"

"There's no one in my extended family I'm close to." He sniffed. "I thought you'd understand. You're alone too. Your husband died. You don't have any kids."

I frowned as I pressed the accelerator to climb the twisting hill that led to my subdivision. "How do you know all that?"

He paused before answering. "I looked into you a little, before I suggested Mom join your agency. I read Peter's obituary online. I've been thinking about it a lot since she went missing. Being alone is something you and I have in common."

As much as I liked the young man, I felt a squiggle of unease knowing he'd googled me. I couldn't explain why I felt that way—his reason for doing so was perfectly acceptable—but I did. My yearning for the peace and solitude of my own home increased. "What about Coral or Belva? They're probably worried too. Maybe you could visit one of them."

"Coral likes to mother me, and I don't think I could handle that right now. Not with—" He broke off, but I had no trouble understanding the gist. "And Belva is out of town at a conference. Something to do with her accounting firm."

Accountant, not prison warden. Still, the career matched the persnickety woman I'd met. My accountant was a dry humourless man who communicated only through email. Being friends with him would never cross my mind. Apparently, Azalea felt differently.

Relying on years of experience keeping clients at arm's length without alienating them, I wrapped up the conversation on a positive note. "You're a strong independent person, Carter. I'm really sorry, but I can't invite you over tonight. We'll talk tomorrow, okay? And you can call me, anytime. I mean it."

By now, I was nearing my driveway. The car behind me slowed as I turned, its headlights washing over me as the garage door began to rise. "Carter? Are you there?"

"I'm here. Thanks for listening. I feel better now. Have a good night, Ginnie." He hung up.

I parked, closed the garage, and stepped into the refuge of my silent house. I needed a glass of wine. Maybe two.

Someone is in the house.

The thought appeared fully formed the instant my eyes opened.

I'd made myself a can of soup for supper. Yes, soup again, though I'd had it for lunch with Seth. It's the perfect food as far as I'm concerned. I also had two small glasses of wine. After half an hour of flipping through the offerings on Netflix, I'd given up, gone to bed, snuggled under my down comforter, and opened my e-reader.

It lay on my chest, the screen dim. I wasn't sure how long we'd both been asleep. I stared at the ceiling, groggy and only faintly alarmed. It wouldn't be the first time since Peter's death a dreaming sense of danger had woken me.

My lids were drifting shut when I heard the creak. I sat up, drowsiness banished by adrenaline.

Was that the door leading into the garage? It had certainly sounded like it. I'd been meaning to oil those hinges for weeks.

I knew I'd shut the garage's overhead door and secured the house's front door. But I never locked the access between the house and the garage. I'd gone through it to put an empty wine bottle in the recycling bin in the back yard. Had I locked the exterior door when I re-entered the garage? It was an ingrained habit, but I couldn't *remember* doing it.

I had heard nothing since the squeak of hinges. If someone was inside, they were being very, very quiet. Or had the muted screech been someone leaving, not entering?

The third possibility, of course, was that I was imagining things.

I disconnected my cell from its charging cable. It was just after midnight. Not as late as I'd thought. I brought up the phone keypad, squinting against the brightness of the screen.

Then I sat, listening with all my might. Through my open bedroom door, I could see nothing but the wall of the hallway opposite. The furnace kicked off and the silence deepened.

For two minutes, I kept my phone awake and ready. After five more minutes with no further sounds, I began to feel rather ridiculous. Obviously, no one else was in the house. The threat was all in my head. Still—

I'd never get back to sleep without a reconnaissance.

Sighing at my foolishness, I climbed out of bed and wrapped my robe around me. Shuffling in my fleecy slippers, I headed straight for the garage, turning lights on as I went.

I saw nothing out of the ordinary on my way there. When I opened the door, however, the squeak was exactly how I remembered it. And the outer door to the back yard was closed but unlocked.

I pressed my spine to the wall and flicked on the overhead light, head swinging from side to side like an agitated parrot. My car was parked in the centre of the space, surrounded on three sides by storage shelves, my snowblower and lawnmower, and the usual inventory any homeowner accumulates.

A weapon. I needed a weapon. I snatched up a can of WD-40 and wielded it unsteadily, my finger on the trigger.

Ever so slowly, I circled the car. Confirming no one was in the garage was not as reassuring as I'd hoped.

I twisted the deadbolt on the exterior door, hesitated, and then twisted it open again. If someone *was* in the house, I might need an escape route.

Methodically, I searched every room. No black-garbed intruder burst out of a shadowy corner. No crazed junkie attacked me with my own kitchen knife.

Once I'd covered every inch, including any cupboard or

closet big enough for an eight-year-old to hide in, I locked the garage door and collapsed onto my living room couch, taking slow, deep breaths, and waiting for my heart rate to settle.

I still lived in the house Peter and I had called our own for the thirteen years before his death. The fireplace had a raw edge wooden mantel on which rested our wedding portrait, framed snapshots from various trips, and a photo of each set of parents. The display was so familiar I'd stopped seeing it.

It caught my attention tonight, however.

Our wedding portrait was gone.

CHAPTER EIGHT

NEEDLESS TO SAY, I didn't get any sleep the rest of the night.

Constant patrols to double-triple-quadruple check the locks on all the doors and windows occupied most of my time. The rest was spent fretting and stewing and doubting my sanity. When was the last time I'd noticed the photo? *Really* noticed it? Had I put it away and forgotten I'd done so? On one hand, I hoped that was the reason, as that would mean there had been no burglar with a fetish for collecting wedding portraits running amok in my home. On the other, stowing something so precious away and not remembering was probably a sign of early-onset dementia.

I wasn't sure what would be worse.

A cold shower and hot coffee erased some of my exhaustion, but I was still a wreck when I went into the office, so early I beat even Maeve. I could have called in sick, I suppose, but I needed a break from the house. The missing photo had severely creeped me out. I was *certain* I hadn't moved it myself. But what on earth would a burglar want with it?

I was pretending to work when I heard the rear door open. My pulse sped up, even though I knew it would be Maeve. The cowering, fearful creature last night's experience had birthed was starting to piss me off.

I didn't flinch when a figure appeared in my doorway. Yay, progress. "Morning, Maeve!" I said cheerfully.

"What are you doing in already?" Her question was more bewildered than accusatory.

"Couldn't sleep." Not a lie.

"If I'd known you were here, I would have brought you a coffee too." She brandished a red takeout cup and then revealed a small yellow box with a lid folded into a handle. "But I've got Timbits."

"Sugar. Yes, please."

She approached my desk and offered the box. I depressed the tabs to open it, studied the doughnut holes packed inside, and chose one covered in powdery icing sugar.

"Take two." Maeve was always grave, but she regarded me with an expression even more serious than usual. "Make it three. You look like you could use the buzz. Are you feeling okay?"

"I'm fine." I popped the Timbit into my mouth. Sweetness flooded over my tongue, and I selected another. Chocolate, this time.

"There's not much happening today. You could go home early."

Mouth full of baked treats, I grunted an acknowledgment. Dating Sunday was almost three weeks ago, and we were finally getting through the influx of new clients. But Valentine's Day was coming up fast, which meant Hopeful Hearts. It was our biggest social event of the year and Indra was neck-deep in organizing it. I trusted her to do an excellent job. Still, I could never resist "sticking my nose in too often."

Her words, not mine.

Whether it was the sugar or the company, I spent the

next hour productive and peaceful. Indra and Piper both arrived before nine—usual for Indra, not so much for Piper—calling hellos as they passed my office but not coming in. I felt like a mother mallard with all her ducklings safe under her wing. We might not be friends, but we were a cohesive and clever team.

I wouldn't say I forgot about my nighttime adventure, but I certainly back-burnered it. When I wandered out of my office later that morning for a stretch and fresh cup of coffee, I was feeling pretty pleased with myself. Until Indra saw me.

She stood next to Maeve, a poster for Hopeful Hearts spread out on the desk in front of them. Today she was dressed in cool blues and stark whites and resembled a jolly snowman in her puffy sweater and crocheted bell skirt. When she looked up, her eyes widened. "Maeve was right. You do look dreadful." She clapped her hand against her mouth as if to prevent other non-compliments from spilling out.

"You should have seen her earlier," Maeve said. "At least she doesn't look like she's going to pass out anymore."

On the wall beside me hung a gallery of smiling couples. Years ago, one of my first matches had sent me a photo from their wedding and I'd proudly displayed it in my home office. Slowly the collection grew as other couples shared their happy moments. When I'd moved into this space, I'd continued the tradition.

I peered at the nearest photo. My ghostly image superimposed itself on the joyful shot of two blond women wearing white and kissing on a sandy golden beach. Even in the reflection, the bags under my eyes and wrinkles around

61

my mouth were clear.

I sighed. "I'm fine. Just tired. I told you I couldn't sleep."

"Why? I've never heard you mention having insomnia before," Maeve said. She and Indra regarded me, curious and concerned. They were sincerely worried about me. My heart warmed.

I hadn't intended to share my experience, but what would it hurt? Maybe they could come up with the explanation I hadn't.

Without revealing exactly how much I'd freaked out last night, I regaled the other women with my tale, even drawing Piper out of her office.

"Don't you have a security system?" She had badgered me into installing one for the office after a series of burglaries in the area last year.

"I've never seen a need." I waggled my hands dismissively. Behind me, the front door opened with a swoosh, and I lowered my voice. "Time to get back to work. I'm sure I only imagined a stranger in my house last night."

I turned to greet the newcomer. Seth Updike stood in the doorway, glaring.

"A stranger was in your house last night?" he demanded.

"No," I said. At the same time, a chorus of "Maybe," "She thinks so," and "I hope not" erupted from the other women.

"No," I repeated firmly, giving them my best stink-eye. "No one was in my house. I was hearing things, that's all."

Seth raised a skeptical eyebrow. "Did you see anyone? Was anything taken?"

I could answer the first question honestly but wasn't sure how to reply to the second. Piper jumped in before I could decide.

"She didn't see anyone and all that's missing is her wedding photo."

I threw her a daggered look. "I told you. I just can't remember where I put it." Wanting to prevent any further over-sharing, I asked Seth, "What can I do for you?" an instant before I remembered he was no longer a client. Crossing my fingers, I prayed he'd keep the conversation impersonal.

He didn't take me up on the opening I'd given him, thank goodness. "It has to do with what we talked about yesterday." His eyes flicked over my shoulder toward the other women.

I answered his unspoken question. "They know about Azalea."

"Oh. Good." He cleared his throat. "I spoke with the police yesterday. I thought I'd let you know how it went."

"That's not necessary." It wasn't, but that didn't mean I wasn't curious. Had he thought of anything to add to what he'd already told me?

"And I wanted to see you again."

Suddenly aware of three pairs of eyes following our exchange like spectators at a tennis match, I gestured to my office. "Why don't we talk in private?"

Ignoring a smothered giggle from Indra's direction, I waited for Seth to enter. Then I pointed a finger at each of my maddening employees. "Back. To. Work."

I shut the door on their grinning faces, circled Seth as widely as my small office allowed, and took my seat behind the desk.

He remained standing. I craned my neck to meet his eyes. "Sit down," I said irritably. "You're giving me a crick." The knot was already there from a night spent on my couch, but he didn't need to know that.

Dragging the visitor's chair nearer and resting his elbows on my desk, he studied me closely. "Tell me about last night."

I shifted in my seat, caught myself doing it, and stilled. "Tell me about your police interview."

"You first."

I didn't want to confess my idiocy, but I wanted to hear what he'd said to the cops more. My summary was even shorter on details than what I'd shared with the team, so it didn't take long.

"You don't have a security system." If he'd sounded even a smidge condescending, I would have shown him the door—immediately and with my foot. But he was matter of fact, thoughtful.

"I live in a good neighbourhood." Even so, I didn't want to spend another night like the last if I could help it. "I didn't think I needed one."

"There are some great do-it-yourself kits out there. The wireless ones are easy to install in an existing home, simple to set up and program."

I laughed. "I've never met a piece of technology I couldn't screw up, no matter how simple it supposedly is. I'll look into it, though. Maybe I can hire someone." I crossed my arms and swivelled my chair. "Your turn. What happened with the police?"

"I could do it for you." Apparently, he wasn't ready to change the subject.

"Install a security system?"

He jerked one shoulder in an offhand manner. "Sure. In fact, I've got one at the office gathering dust. A client ordered it and then changed his mind."

"How much?" He named a price that was suspiciously low. I narrowed my eyes. "No, really. How much? Include something for your time too."

"That's what we paid for it, I promise. You'd save me the effort of trying to get a refund from the distributor. As for my time..." He reached across the desk and traced my knuckles with one finger. "I can install it tomorrow afternoon. You can buy me dinner when it's done."

I still had reservations about letting Seth into my life. Letting him into my house would be a big step. The trouble was, I didn't trust myself to install a system correctly and hiring someone would take several days, if not weeks.

"I'll think about it." His confidence was addictive, but it wouldn't do to give in too easily. "When did the police call you?"

"They didn't. I went to them. As soon as you left the restaurant, I rescheduled a couple of work things and followed."

"I didn't see you there." Given my perturbed state when I left, I may have missed him. I could only hope he hadn't seen me.

"They put me in an interview room. I waited quite a while, but finally a Corporal Tam came."

He must have gone to Seth after he was done with me. "What did he ask?"

Seth leaned back and propped his right ankle on his

left knee. "Much the same questions you did. How did the date go. What did we talk about. When did I see her last. Had she said where she was going." His gaze dropped and he picked absently at the hem of his jeans. "He asked why I chose Blynde Dating Agency. I told him I liked the name." His gaze lifted. "And he asked if I'd known you or Azalea before this week."

Prince George wasn't that big a town and every so often I matched two clients who were acquainted with each other. I hadn't considered that with Seth and Azalea. "Had you? Met Azalea, I mean. I know you and I never did." I'm good at remembering names and faces. It comes in handy when running a dating agency.

And I would have remember meeting you *for sure*, a little voice inside me purred. I squelched it.

"No, I hadn't met her before," Seth said. "I'm not sure Tam believed me, though."

I knew what he meant. I didn't think the corporal had believed my answers to his questions into Peter's death, either. Remembering my own session with him still made me queasy.

Yesterday really hadn't been a good day.

"Did he tell you what his next steps might be?" I'd meant to ask him myself but had been too shattered at the end of my interview, wanting nothing more than to retreat.

"All he said was that inquiries were proceeding." He scrubbed a hand through his hair, leaving the short strands slightly dishevelled. "He mentioned one thing I wanted to ask you about, though. He said Azalea's son didn't know who his mother was having dinner with."

"I don't give out client information, even to family members. That's why I called you the first time. I'd promised Carter I would ask you about the date myself." I uncrossed my arms and sat upright in my oversized chair. "To be completely candid, though, I did have to tell the police. You understand I couldn't keep it from them. There's no client privilege in the dating game."

He waved that off. "Of course you had to. That's partly why I went as soon as I could. I knew they'd be calling once they talked to you, anyway." His brows drew together. "What I was wondering was why Carter didn't know. The way Azalea talked about him in the brief time we were together, I assumed she would have."

For a moment we sat in silence. I don't know what he was thinking about, but I was contemplating the relationship between mother and son. They had seemed so close. No wonder Carter was feeling adrift. I wished there was something I could do to comfort him.

Seth leaned an elbow on the arm of his chair and sighed. "If only I *did* know something that would help. I hope she turns up soon."

A thrill of fear prickled my cheeks. Azalea was really gone. She had disappeared. The police were investigating. This was *real*. It was *happening*.

Sweat sprang up between my breasts and on my neck. I struggled out of my cardigan as the hot flash enveloped me. The tiny handheld fan cached in a drawer called to me, but I would rather melt into a puddle before using it in front of Seth.

"About the security system." I had no reason to feel

threatened because Azalea had vanished, but the eerie sensation I'd experienced yesterday in the company parking lot and my inexplicably missing wedding portrait nagged at me. "Tomorrow afternoon, you said? I'll text my address. Do you like steak? If you're going to all this trouble for me, the least I can do is make you dinner."

CHAPTER NINE

AFTER ANOTHER MOSTLY sleepless night haunted by my imaginary intruder, I lost any remaining reservations about letting Seth install the security system. I hadn't been so restless and disturbed since the days following Peter's death. I needed to feel safe in my own home again.

My morning was occupied by a frenzy of cleaning. Since I was the only one who lived here, rarely had people over, and spent most of my waking hours at work, I tended to let things slide. Not that I was a slob. But I was certainly...relaxed...about my living quarters.

To keep myself company, I played Neil Diamond's Greatest Hits Volumes One and Two through the wireless speaker system Peter had installed in most of the rooms. Though he'd been an English teacher, technology had been one of the several other languages he spoke. He had patiently coached me until I was comfortable using it, though I still on occasion referred to his written step-by-step instructions.

The albums were on their third repeat when Seth arrived. I was in the living room replacing the books I'd removed in order to wipe down the shelves. Through the window I watched as his white pickup, *Updike Construction* in neat navy-blue font on the side of the box, pulled into the drive. I hurriedly slid in the last hardcover and turned off the music. The latter only took me two stabs.

He headed up the path, carrying a box about the size of a large roaster in gloved hands. I opened the door and Arctic air whooshed in. The sky was an icy blue, the sun a brilliant yellow, the snow a blinding white. A perfect—and perfectly chilly—winter's day.

"Hi." I stepped back so he could enter and shut the door, cutting off the cold. "Thanks for coming."

"No problem."

His head was uncovered and the sun streaming in the sidelight beside the door set the silver strands shimmering. Dark shades hid his eyes, though I had no trouble remembering the exact blue of his irises. His chin glittered with Saturday stubble, which I was irritated to realize I found mouth-wateringly sexy.

"Where can I put this?" He lifted the box.

I shook myself out of my stupor. "Right. Of course. Here, let me take it." Our fingers brushed as I almost snatched it away. It was much lighter than I'd expected. "You can put your coat in the closet. If you like."

Retreating into the living room, I waited as he tucked his gloves in his pockets, placed his parka neatly on a hanger, and slipped off his boots. He wore a long-sleeved grey Henley and well-fitting jeans that were worn but not decrepit.

I swallowed and commanded the teenage girl inside me to stop squealing. "I really appreciate this."

"I don't like the idea of you being here alone without protection." He took the box back.

With nothing for my hands to do, I felt even more twitchy. It had been a long time since a man had been in my house. Seth stood close but not too close. He was around average height but since I wasn't he was still several inches taller than me. The faint scent of sandalwood—one of my favourites—wafted toward me and I resisted the urge to inhale deeply.

I spun away, needing to put some space between us. "Would you like a drink? Coffee? Tea? Is it too early for beer?" I set a route to the kitchen. "Or do you want to get started right away? I thought we'd have dinner around six, but I don't know how long it will take you. Is that enough time? Or too much?"

A warm hand rested on my shoulder, halting my flight. "Ginnie."

I allowed him to turn me, embarrassment plugging my throat. I'd been acting like a putz but unable to prevent myself.

He held the box on his hip with one arm. The hand on my shoulder slid down my biceps and clasped my fingers. "Why so nervous?"

No beating around the bush with Seth. I bit my lip, my gaze fixed on the buttons of his shirt. "I spend my days designing relationships for other people. But I haven't dated since my husband died. Didn't plan on ever dating again."

"This is a date?"

Mortified, my eyes flew to his face. "Isn't it?" Oh my god, had I misread everything?

His startlingly blue eyes gleamed with amusement. "It could just be a friend doing a favour. I'd *rather* it was a date, but we don't need to call it that if you're not ready."

I relaxed a fraction. "We don't?"

He shook his head and adjusted his grasp so he could bring my hand to his mouth. The brush of his lips on my knuckles shivered through every cell in my body. "We don't. We just met. I don't want to rush you. Honest."

Heat licked my belly, and my fingers tightened on his. "If we're being honest..." I drew in a deep breath. "I like you. Probably more than I should. I just..."

"Need time. And I'm fine with that." He grinned, open and friendly, and released my hand. "All right, let's get started. It shouldn't take us too long."

"Us?" I wanted nothing to do with the thing until I absolutely had to.

"Us." He was determined. "Your house. Your alarm. We're doing this together."

It was going to be a long afternoon.

I'm not saying I enjoyed helping Seth set up the security system. But it didn't completely suck.

The least-suckiest parts might have had to do with Seth himself. He went about the task with a proficiency that pushed all my competence porn buttons. A glimpse of his abdomen as he stretched to grease the top hinge of the squeaky door that accessed the garage dried my mouth. And the way his nimble fingers handled his tools...

Ahem.

He hummed a low, tuneless melody as he worked. When I was in danger of succumbing to the urge to lay my head on his chest so I could feel it as well as hear it, I bailed, using the excuse of making dinner. I puttered around the kitchen prepping salad and potatoes and seasoning the steaks, viscerally aware of him moving about the house, testing alarm points and camera views while setting up the main panel. We'd installed it just inside the door to the garage, as that was my usual point of entry and exit.

I'd thought it would be weird to have a man other than Peter in the home we'd shared. Instead, I was reminded of the good times, when my husband and I had been a team, bouncing ideas off each other and working peaceably side by side.

A surge of grief gripped me. The argument we'd had the night he was killed hadn't been about something small and insignificant. It would have been a crossroads in our marriage, a life-changing event. I still wasn't sure we could have recovered from it. But that didn't stop me from wishing *every day* that my last words hadn't been the cruel and hateful accusations I'd flung at him as he'd stormed out the door.

"Okay. I think that's it." Seth entered the kitchen.

I blinked away brimming tears and smiled at him. "All done?"

He nodded. "Here's your phone. I've installed the app and you're good to go. I can walk you through the settings in case you have any questions."

I was bound to have questions—several dumb ones, I'm sure. "That's great. Thank you so much. How about we do that after dinner? Just put it on the credenza for now."

He frowned as he did as I asked. "You okay?"

Thank god for the onions I was slicing. I gestured at the cutting board. "They're potent. I'm going to mix them with green peppers and mushrooms and grill them with the steak."

His expression remained dubious, but he didn't prod further. "Sounds delicious. What can I do to help?"

"There's beer and white wine in the fridge, red on the counter by the coffeemaker. Help yourself. And if you don't mind pouring me some red that would be great." I directed him to where I kept the glasses.

"Any soft drinks?" He took down one tumbler and one wineglass.

"Yes. Sparkling water, cranberry juice, and a couple of cans of Diet Coke. I have ice cubes if you want them." I tidied up my prep area, stacking dirty dishes and utensils next to the sink.

He decanted the Malbec I'd requested into a glass and set it within reach. Then he extracted the cranberry juice and the bottle of water I'd fizzed up earlier today and placed them on the counter. Opening the bottom freezer, he searched for the ice.

I may have been distracted by the tight curve of his ass as he bent over.

After adding two cubes to the tumbler, he poured about an inch of cranberry juice and filled the rest with soda water. He saw me watching and quirked a wry grin. "No, I'm not an alcoholic. I might as well get that out of the way."

"There are lots of other reasons people don't drink." Though I had been speculating. Maybe my subconscious was looking for an excuse to sabotage my growing attraction.

"Yes. Mine is medical. I'm allergic to alcohol." He toasted me with his glass and took a sip of his brightly coloured concoction.

"I didn't know there was such a thing."

"It's not as common as peanuts, but it is definitely a thing." He leaned a hip against the counter. "I haven't had alcohol in more than thirty years. Not since the summer I was seventeen when I ended up in hospital after drinking half a bottle of beer I'd snuck from my dad."

"That sounds terrifying."

"It was. The ER doctor told me if I ever wanted to try it again to make sure I was sitting in a hospital waiting room." He grinned. "I've never bothered to take his suggestion."

Conversation came easily after that, interrupted only by trips to the barbeque to check the potatoes I was baking and, when it was time, to add the vegetables and steak. The clear skies of earlier in the day had been obscured by pewter clouds and a northern breeze was blowing, but my small deck was covered and relatively protected.

My kitchen was an open U-shape with the dining room on the side opposite the living room. We filled our plates, buffet-style, at the counter and took our seats.

"I haven't had a meal like this in a while." Seth closed his eyes as he savoured a tender morsel of steak.

I pulled my gaze away from the muscles flexing in his jaw and swallowed my own mouthful carefully. The tension stretching between us was as delicious as the meal. I needed a distraction.

"You have a daughter, right?" I blurted. I knew about her from the profile he'd filled out for the agency. We'd steered away from anything too personal earlier, but the subject of adult children was something I'd been thinking about a lot lately, given Carter and Azalea's situation.

"I do. Grace." His smile was unabashedly proud. "She's

in Edmonton right now, studying to be a dentist."

"That's great." I speared a mushroom. "You and her mother must be very pleased." I tried to sound casual but was pretty sure I failed. It was obvious I was fishing for details his profile hadn't provided.

His hands stilled. "I am. Her mother"—he resumed cutting his steak with slow, deliberate motions—"her mother hasn't been in the picture for a while."

The *No Trespassing* sign was big and bright. Not wanting to derail what had turned into an extremely pleasant evening, I took the hint and switched tracks to safer topics.

Afterward, Seth insisted on clearing up. He poured me another glass of wine and I sat at the table, watching. His motions were smooth and economical and unhesitating. This was a man who knew his way around a kitchen.

I wondered what else he knew his way around...

Maybe it was the wine that made me do it. Okay, it was definitely the wine. But as he rung out the dishcloth and hung it neatly over the gooseneck faucet, I sidled up to him and laid my hand on his back. He stilled for an instant before twisting slowly toward me, my palm sliding over his biceps to his chest.

"Thank you." Heat seeped through the cotton of his shirt, and I curled my fingers, bracing against him as I rose to my tiptoes. I still couldn't reach his lips, but he was quick on the uptake and leaned in.

Desire had been orbiting us all afternoon. The more comfortable I felt in his presence, the more my skin itched with need.

Our mouths met, clung, separated. He was so close my

vision blurred, so I shut my eyes. I pressed our lips together again. His hands gripped my hips, and I let my weight fall against him.

Like a spark reaching the fuse, the kiss exploded. I dug my fingers into his hair and speared my tongue into his mouth. He tasted tart and sweet and peppery. His grasp on my ass tightened when I nipped his lower lip. He groaned. I couldn't get close enough, wanted to wrap around him so tightly we melded into one.

A phone rang.

We sprang apart like virgins at a Catholic school dance and stared at each other. His cheekbones flushed scarlet and his blue eyes glittered. I panted, heart thundering, knees shaking.

The phone rang again.

"That's me." Seth picked it up from the windowsill above the sink where he'd laid it while doing the dishes.

I scrubbed my hands on my face, trying to regain some semblance of sanity. Before it could ring a third time, Seth answered.

Tinny, indistinct sounds leaked from the speaker. His face went blank, and he turned his back to me.

Not good news, then. Any vague hopes I'd had of picking up where we'd left off evaporated.

"I see," he said. "Yes. I'll come right away." He disconnected the call and slid the phone in his jeans pocket with a distracted air.

I stepped to his side and peered up at him. "Is everything all right?" Of course it wasn't all right. But what else could I say?

"That was Corporal Tam." Seth focused bleak eyes on mine. "Azalea's car has been found." I gasped and he must have heard my hope. He shook his head. "Just her car. There's no sign of her."

Disappointment crashed over me. "Where was it?"

"Parked on the street a few blocks away from Da Moreno's. Near a construction site."

I knew before he said the rest. Knew from the desolate expression blanching his face. Knew from the starkness in his voice. "Near *my* construction site."

CHAPTER TEN

WHEN CARTER CALLED Sunday afternoon asking to visit, I couldn't say no. The discovery of Azalea's car was a severe blow to even my determined optimism. It had to be worse for her son.

Also, I hadn't been able to get his words out of my mind. *You know what it's like. To have no one.* He was suffering, and I felt responsible. Logically, I knew this was bogus. Still, I was impelled to do what I could to ease his distress.

He huddled on my couch, clutching a mug of peppermint tea in both hands, his expression miserable. I sat in an upholstered chair opposite, my own tea untouched on the side table at my elbow.

"I tried to have hope, like you told me." His words were so soft I could barely hear them. "I wanted to believe it would all work out. Now..."

I still clung to hope, but even I couldn't deny the situation was ominous. He'd told me Azalea's purse and cellphone had also been found, abandoned along with her car. "I'm so sorry."

He looked young and defenceless, and my heart bled. If Peter and I had had children, seeing one of my own in pain might have killed me. And yet a tiny part of me wondered if I'd missed out. Could I act as surrogate parent to Carter, and perhaps give both of us some comfort? I struggled to find the right words—*any* words—that weren't naïvely Pollyanna-ish, hoping my presence offered some solace even if my silence didn't.

"I can't stop thinking about it." He raised his face to me, eyes desolate. "She's dead."

"Don't. Don't go there." He flinched at my sharp tone. I softened it. "It does no good, imagining worst case scenarios. You need to be strong."

"Were you strong? When he...Peter...died?"

I'd been a mess, but he didn't need to hear that. "You get through it. One day at a time."

"What was he like?"

I rarely spoke of Peter and didn't much want to talk about him now. But if it would serve to distract Carter, I could share a few details. "He was smart. I mean, really smart. Loved languages, whether English or Tagalog or computer. He was obsessive about running. He started going bald in his thirties and was self-conscious about it." I shrugged, not sure what else to say.

"Was he a good guy?"

"Yes." I thought for a moment. "For the most part." The part that had hurt me, that had devastated me, was nothing I would ever share with Carter, no matter how much I liked him.

For a few minutes we sat in silence, sipping our drinks.

"It's all my fault." The confession burst from him, aching with guilt.

"Of course it isn't," I soothed. "This has nothing to do with you."

"It is. It does." His lips trembled and he pinched them together. "I convinced Mom to sign up for your agency. I told her it was time to start dating again. D-dad has been gone for three years."

The stutter speared deep. If he lost Azalea too...and in this way...

"You wanted your mother to be happy. I'm sure this"—whatever *this* was—"has nothing to do with her dating."

"How can you say that? You, of all people?"

A flash of something bright and unsettling tore through the grief in his face. His tone was almost...scornful? "What do you mean?"

"I know about Seth Updike. I know he's the guy you set Mom up with. Which makes him the last person to see her. Now, her car and belongings were found at his construction site. What do you think I mean?"

My conversation with Seth the day after Azalea's disappearance echoed inside my head, just as it had last night after Tam's phone call.

"Where did you go after?"

"I drove by one of my worksites. It's near the restaurant and I wanted to check something."

I blinked the memory away.

Carter stared at me pleadingly, with no sign of the contempt I thought I'd seen earlier. "He has to have something to do with it. Doesn't he?"

"It's all circumstantial. There's no evidence against him."

"You can't *know* Updike isn't responsible, can you?"

"No. But I'll need proof before I'll believe it."

"Why?" All I heard now was a desperate hope for *something* to make sense in this tangled mystery.

Because I like him. Because I don't want to believe he is

being anything less than honest with me. Because I want to have wild monkey sex with him. These were not reasons I intended to say out loud. "Innocent until proven guilty, right?"

My attempt to lighten the mood backfired. Tea spilled as Carter slapped the mug on the low table between us before springing to his feet and striding about the room. "I can't stand it. The waiting, the uncertainty."

"You're desperate for answers. I can understand that." What would Azalea do in this situation? Would she hug him tight or give him space to let him deal with it on his own? "Nevertheless, you can't go around making random accusations."

"They're not random," he muttered as he paced. "He's connected. I know it."

It was pointless to argue further. I waited, sipping my tepid tea. It was several minutes before his steps slowed, his breathing eased, and his fists loosened.

"Sit down, Carter." I was quiet but firm.

He halted his perambulations. Without meeting my gaze, he returned to the couch.

"Have you talked to the police since they told you about finding your mother's car?"

He shook his head.

"Well, I've heard from Seth." He'd texted this morning and thank goodness he had. I'd been eaten up with worry and curiosity. Our exchange had been brief as he'd sounded tired—not sure how you sound tired in a text, but you know what I mean. "Her car was found *near* a project his company is working on, but not *on* the site. The project is only three blocks from Da Moreno's, the restaurant where he and Azalea had dinner. It's just a coincidence. That's all."

Carter slumped back against the cushions, all energy draining out of him. "I guess you're right. This proves she hasn't gone on a trip, though."

That was inescapable. Even if she'd flown somewhere, she'd never leave her car parked on some random street, let alone forget to take her purse and cellphone.

"Someone *has* to know something." I sat up straight and placed my empty mug on the side table. "Do you know if the police have talked with Coral and Belva yet?"

"Yes. Yesterday. Before..." Carter waved one hand in wordless explanation.

"What if I talked with them too? Maybe they'll tell me something they aren't comfortable sharing with you or the police." It was something proactive I could do. And it might offer Carter a little hope.

"You'd do that for me?" He perked up, pushing into a sitting position. For the first time since he'd walked in the door, he smiled.

"For you. For Azalea." And for Seth, though I kept that to myself. Besides, I'd always favoured action over reaction.

"That would be great." His thin face blazed with excitement. "I would really like that. What should we do first?"

The *we* gave me pause, but I could understand his need to have a role in finding his mother. Still, it would be best to manage his expectations. "It's good to have something to take our minds off our worries but remember we're not the experts here. Also, we both have businesses to run. Carousel deserves your attention too."

My cautionary words didn't dim his enthusiasm. "I know. But doing nothing about Mom, just waiting for news from the police...it's driving me crazy." His lips curved shyly. "I don't know what I'd do without you, Ginnie. I think I'd fall apart."

"Oh, I'm sure you'd be fine." I had to say it, but I didn't quite believe it. Carter was fragile, nervy, and a trifle immature. Maybe the combination should have irritated me, but I hadn't exactly met him under the best circumstances, and it was easy to cut him some slack. "We are all as strong as we need to be, when we need to be."

My words were prophetic. Though I didn't know that at the time.

Carter left shortly after, but not before I had him share Coral and Belva's personal numbers, along with a mini biography of each so I could plan my approaches.

"Coral is a professional volunteer." His expression was smooth and untroubled, except for a tightness in the corner of his mouth I wasn't sure how to read. "She and my mom have been friends forever. I used to call her Auntie Coral."

Belva, he revealed, was new to Azalea's circle. The family's long-established financial advisor had retired around the same time Warren Bickersley had died, so she'd needed to find a new one. "I call her Mom's accountant," Carter said, "but she does Mom's investments and stuff too."

I decided to approach Belva first, under the assumption she would have more free time on a Sunday afternoon than during the week.

"Yes?" Brisk and businesslike, even on her personal line.

"Belva Ginsberg? This is Regina Blynde. We met last Monday at Azalea Bickersley's house."

"Yes." Not a question. A statement of fact and not an encouraging one.

Right. This was going to be fun. "I know you've spoken with Carter and the police about Azalea's disappearance, but I hope you don't mind if I ask you a few questions as well."

"And if I do mind?"

I rarely dislike people on sight. Usually, I enjoy humans *because* of their foibles and quirks, not *despite* them. Belva, however, was testing my limits. I pulled on my professional persona and reminded myself I was doing this for Carter.

"I have no means to force you to answer," I said pleasantly. "I simply hoped you'd welcome a chance to help Azalea. I understand she's not just a friend but a client as well."

"Who told you that?"

I swallowed my first snarky response and kept my tone warm and even. "Carter. He's really worried about his mom."

"He worries if his mom gets a hangnail."

Taken aback by her snide comment, I wondered again why Azalea considered her a friend. "I know they're very close. And in these circumstances, he's entitled to be worried. Have you heard Azalea's car was found?"

"It was?"

She sounded sincerely surprised. I cautiously tugged on this moment of curiosity. "Yes. About three blocks from the restaurant where she was last seen. Her purse and phone were inside."

"But I thought..." She paused.

"What?" I prodded.

"I thought Azalea had gone on holiday without telling Carter. I know if I had a son as clingy as he is I'd need to get away once in a while." Azalea had never expressed resentment toward Carter in my presence, but Belva had known her longer. "I did wonder why she hadn't taken Coral with her, though."

"Coral? Why would she have taken Coral?"

A derisive huff puffed down the line. "She usually does when she goes on one of her madcap getaways. I have responsibilities. I can't just pack up and go when she asks. But Coral can. It never bothers her if she leaves one of her volunteer committees in the lurch because Azalea gifted her a swanky vacation."

Gifted her? I knew Azalea could afford it, but shelling out so friends could travel with you was well above my paygrade. "A holiday seems rather unlikely now, what with this discovery."

"Yes."

I waited several moments, but she added nothing further. "Can you think of any explanation for what's happened?" I prompted.

"Someone must have stolen her car."

"Maybe. But where is Azalea?"

"I don't know." Her tone was once again acerbic, yet anxiety teased at the edges. "The last time I saw Azalea was the evening you and I met. I have nothing more to add."

She disconnected before I could say another syllable. I

stared thoughtfully at my phone for a few moments, then went to put in a load of laundry and consider what tactics to use on Coral.

In the end, I had plenty of time to ponder my approach. Coral didn't answer her phone, so I left a voice mail explaining how I was trying to help Carter and asking her to call me back. Which she hadn't done by the time I arrived at work Monday morning.

I had just finished parking in the company lot and was climbing out when Indra's car careened in off the street. She pulled haphazardly into a slot and erupted from the driver's door before the engine quit ticking.

"Have you seen it?" She clutched my arm, pale and breathless.

A chill that had nothing to do with the winter wind slid down my spine. "Seen what?" All the Azalea-related worst-case scenarios I'd shoved to the darkest corner of my mind came surging into the light.

"The Facebook post. The one tagging the agency."

Not Azalea. Thank god. I let out a slow breath and refocused. "What Facebook post?"

"This one." She shoved her phone into my gloved hand.

An image of the Blynde Dating Agency logo with a huge red X through it glared up at me. Above it, I read:

*Have an account with Blynde Dating? Cancel it now or you might end up missing, just like...**see more***

Pulling off my right glove with my teeth, I tapped the screen with a trembling finger.

...Azalea Bickersley. Azalea's last known sighting was on a date arranged by Ginnie Blynde's agency almost a week ago. She thought she was meeting a potential love match. Instead, she disappeared. Don't risk it. Get out now.

The post had been made by a profile named Daters Beware. There were already several comments, and a new one popped up even as I stared in horror.

My first instinct had been right. Indra's devastating news *had* involved Azalea. Just not the way I'd dreaded.

CHAPTER ELEVEN

"WE HAVE TO DEAL with this right now." Indra snatched her phone from my hand and tugged me down the alley. "The account is brand new. This is their only post, but they're boosting it with ads, which is why it's getting traction. We need Piper. She might be able to trace who's behind it. I can make a complaint to Facebook, too, though I doubt it will do much good."

We spent the day doing damage control.

Maeve used the Blynde Dating profile to comment on the original post, but within a matter of minutes it had been deleted. Attempts to refute the claim with comments made by our personal profiles met with a similar fate.

Indra's complaint via Facebook support resulted in an automated reply. I still hoped we might get a response, but hours passed, and we'd heard nothing further. Piper met roadblocks at every turn when she attempted to track the profile. The account had no Friends, no About information, and the privacy settings were buttoned up tight. Maeve posted a clarification on our public-facing page and in our private group. Between the four of us, we responded to every comment there. That seemed to stem the panic somewhat.

Our website traffic held steady which, at first, I took as a good sign. Until I realized that new signups were below average and unsubscribe rates higher than normal.

Of the three membership interviews I had scheduled that day, one cancelled and one gave no hint she'd heard anything. The last mentioned the Facebook post but she seemed undisturbed by the allegations, laughing them off as social media melodrama.

At the end of our meeting, I shepherded her to the front door. It opened as we reached it, and in came Coral Loughty. With all the fires currently burning, the call she hadn't returned and the promise I'd made Carter had vanished from my mind.

"Hello, Ginnie." Coral's hands fluttered restlessly. "I did get your message yesterday, but I wanted to discuss it with Carter first. I hope it's okay I just dropped in."

"No problem. Thanks for coming." Given today's circumstances, the sooner Azalea's disappearance was cleared up, the better all around. "Why don't you go into my office, and I'll be right there." I pointed her to the open doorway.

My client watched her leave with bright attention. "Is she a member too? I wouldn't mind being matched with her."

"No, she's not a member. But don't worry, I already have a few women in mind. You won't be disappointed."

She had a few more things to say, and I couldn't help fidgeting, knowing Coral was waiting. I also couldn't afford to alienate a client, especially not today, so I let her run down at her own pace.

Finally, I ushered her out and turned to Maeve. "The woman in my office is Coral Loughty, a friend of Azalea's. If she's not gone in fifteen minutes, interrupt us so I have an excuse to end our conversation." As much as I wanted to interview Coral, I had the feeling she might stick like a barnacle and an escape plan was simply good sense.

Maeve nodded and drew her lips together. "Will do."

Coral was standing at my desk, her back to the door, when I entered. She turned quickly and a piece of paper drifted to the surface, as if she'd dropped it. I didn't say anything. She was welcome to snoop. I never left confidential documents where random visitors could see them.

"You talked to Carter, you said?" I gestured her to a chair. "Did he tell you about Azalea's car?"

"Isn't it just awful?" She sank into the seat, her fuchsia parka sliding sibilantly on the vinyl. A slouchy toque in matching shades covered her curls. "The poor boy sounded shattered. Has there been any more news?" Despite her concerned expression, her tone held a hint of ghoulish delight.

"Not that I'm aware of." Seth hadn't communicated with me since our brief text conversation yesterday. I pushed aside a buzz of anxiety over his silence. "Thanks again for coming to see me. I appreciate your willingness to help."

"About that." She smoothed a palm over the dark blue denim covering her knee and plucked off an invisible piece of fluff. "As Azalea's best friend, I feel responsible for Carter. She will expect me to look out for him while she's gone. I wouldn't want him to get his hopes up for no reason. What do you think you can do that the police can't?"

"I won't know until I try." If she wasn't here to assist my amateur efforts, why had she come? I pressed on. "You're not the only one who feels an obligation toward Carter. Azalea is my client. I like her as a person. And I like Carter too. I want to do whatever I can."

"Very noble."

She didn't roll her eyes, but I sensed she wanted to. It was time to turn the tables. I wasn't going to let her insult me in my own office. "Does Carter have the same reservations about my involvement?"

Her tone fell flat. "No. He seems excited about it. That's what bothers me."

"I don't see how my asking and you answering a few questions can hurt."

The urge to contradict me quivered across her face before her expression smoothed out. "Fine. I suppose you can't make things worse." She crossed her arms over her chest.

I'd take what I could get. "When did you last talk with Azalea?"

"Tuesday evening. I'd forgotten she was out and called her to chat. She answered—she always answers my calls—but said she had to go because she was on her way to meet the love of her life."

The over-the-top enthusiasm sounded like Azalea, even though, according to Seth, she'd taken his rejection graciously. "Do you have any thoughts on her car being found with her purse and cell phone inside?"

Coral's shoulders slumped and sincerity replaced the sullenness in her voice. "It makes everything so much worse, doesn't it? I mean, I was concerned before, but not *worried*, you know." Unlike Belva, she didn't have to be pressed now I'd gotten her started. "I really thought she'd just gone on a little trip. I did wonder why she hadn't invited me along, because she usually did."

I couldn't see how this confirmation of Belva's statement affected Azalea's disappearance, but I followed up anyway. "I heard that she was very generous with her friends. That she often paid for you to travel with her."

Coral's eyes filled with tears. "Yes. She was wonderful that way."

My desk phone buzzed, and I answered.

"Your fifteen minutes are up," Maeve said in my ear.

"Thanks for letting me know. I'll deal with it right away." I hung up and turned to Coral. "I'm sorry, I must get back to work. If I think of any other questions, can I call you?"

"I suppose." Her agreement was begrudging, but I'd take it. She left in a flash of fuchsia.

Dispiritedly, I reflected on our chat. I had learned nothing of importance. Nothing I recognized as important, anyway.

This amateur sleuthing gig wasn't going to be easy.

At five o'clock, the team sprawled in attitudes of exhaustion on the couch and visitor's chair in my office. I rubbed my temple, caught Maeve looking at me with raised eyebrows, and dropped my hand.

"We'll get through this." I hoped my cheerfulness didn't sound as forced as it felt. "I'm not sure what we did to piss off whoever is behind Daters Beware, but it's not the first bad review we've been given." The minute I said it, I felt terrible. "Not that Azalea's disappearance is anything to joke about."

Indra flapped a limp hand, Piper shoved her glasses up her nose, and Maeve offered an uncomfortable smile.

"You've been troopers today. Every one of you. Thanks for the hard work."

"When we find out who's behind this, I'm going to give them a piece of my mind," Maeve said fiercely. "If they had a problem with us, then just say so. Don't use that poor woman like this."

It was possible whoever it was thought they were providing a public service by warning people away, but I understood where Maeve was coming from.

"They're cowardly too. Hiding behind an anonymous account. Pah." Piper was taking her failure to break through the profile's barriers personally.

But it was Indra who surprised me the most. Ever the peacemaker, I expected her to say something soothing. Instead, her contribution was vituperative. "They don't care who they hurt. It's like when someone vandalizes a building. They get their jollies from spoiling things for others." Her eyes narrowed. "Well, I for one am not going to let them ruin what we have here. This is the best job I've had, and I'm not letting some anonymous little slime destroy it."

"You said it, sister." Piper held out her fist and Indra bumped it. Maeve nodded with such vigour her bun wobbled.

The back of my throat burned. For the first time since hiring these women, I felt like we were more than employer/ employees. Less like individuals who worked *near* each other and more like colleagues who worked *with* each other.

Almost like friends.

I clung to the thought. Maybe there was something positive I could salvage from this crappy, crappy day.

SUSPECT ATTRACTION

Seeking a distraction from the chaos of the last week, I spent Monday evening learning my new security system. Understandably, Seth had left in a rush on Saturday without giving me the orientation he'd promised, and since then, my fear of a second intruder—if I'd even had a first one—had been buried as new anxieties replaced old.

I carefully reviewed settings, chose notifications, and familiarized myself with how to use the damn thing. I needed to get over this aversion to new technology. Lord knew what advances would be made before I turned eighty. I didn't want to be left behind.

I went to bed smugly satisfied I had done everything exactly right and certain I'd have my first undisturbed sleep in several nights. Instead, I lay awake, replaying—not for the first time—my conversation with Coral.

I couldn't shake the feeling I'd misunderstood some of the undercurrents of our little chat. Coral's relationships with Azalea and Carter seemed nuanced and complicated. I just wasn't sure how it mattered. If it did.

An alert rang out and my phone screen lit up. I groaned. That would teach me to be overconfident. Dollars to doughnuts the neighbour's cat had set off one of the exterior cameras, though I'd adjusted the sensitivity several times.

Muttering under my breath, I picked up my phone and peered at it.

Carter stood on my front step. As I watched, he pressed the doorbell, and my phone chimed once more.

My first thought was pride. Maybe I hadn't screwed the

technology up.

Close on its heels, though, was panic. Why on earth was Carter disturbing me so late at night?

After disabling the alarm—yay, me, for remembering how—I wrapped my robe about me and raced to the front door, my heart pounding in my chest.

I flung it open, but before I could say more than "Carter, what's going—" he barged past, his boots leaving wet snowy tracks on my hardwood floor.

"She's been kidnapped!" His arms flailed wildly, out of control. "My mom's been kidnapped!"

I stared, stupefaction silencing my tongue.

Carter grabbed his skull as if to keep it from bursting. "I got a phone call. It was my mom. She said she was sorry, begged me to give them what they wanted. I didn't know what she was talking about. I asked her if she was okay, if she could tell me where she was, but the kidnapper came on. His voice was robotic, distorted. He said if I wanted my mom back, I had to give him one million dollars. What do I do? What do I do?"

My reply was immediate, even as I grappled to accept his horrifying revelation. "We have to call the police."

"No!" He leaped forward and seized me above the elbows.

His wiry build belied his strength. I was going to have bruises tomorrow. "That hurts, Carter! Let me go."

He held me fast. "We can't call the police. He threatened to do things to Mom if I told them. Unspeakable things." His dark brown eyes bore into mine.

My brain spun as I tried to make sense of it all. "Are you

sure it was her?" I asked stupidly.

"Of course I'm sure." He gave me a little shake. "I can't handle this alone. I'll go insane. You have to help me, Ginnie. Please, please, help me."

If it weren't for the throbbing in my biceps where Carter's fingers banded my flesh, I would have thought I was dreaming. The world had an oddly muffled, underwater quality.

His hands tightened, this time using me for support as his knees buckled. I broke through the surface of my shock. "You need to sit down." I slid a shoulder under his arm and guided him toward the couch. He dropped into it, limbs flaccid.

"I'm going to get you a glass of water. When I come back, we'll figure out what to do."

My own knees wobbled as I made my way to the kitchen. This couldn't be happening. Azalea was rich, but kidnappings didn't happen in my town. They just didn't.

I took down a glass, retrieved the pitcher of water from the fridge, and filled it. Carter slumped on the couch, head back, eyes closed. Despite his plea, I was tempted to sneak to my room, where I'd left my phone beside my bed, and call 911.

If I did that and he was right and the kidnapper harmed Azalea, I would never forgive myself.

I returned to the living room. One bare foot landed in the puddle of melting snow collecting around Carter's booted feet and I shivered. "Here." I nudged his knee with the glass. "Drink this."

He took it absently and swallowed it down in long gulps,

finishing it before I was settled in the chair opposite. I curled my feet onto the seat and pulled a lap blanket over my knees, wishing I'd made myself a hot drink.

"Okay," I said. "Start at the beginning. Tell me everything."

CHAPTER TWELVE

"I ALMOST DIDN'T answer." Carter discarded the glass and huddled into his parka, though the room was warm enough. "It was an unknown number. But then I thought, what if it's Mom, calling from someone else's phone since she didn't have hers."

He stared past me as he spoke, as if reading a script off the wall. "She said *Carter, my love* and I was so happy. But then she started crying and saying I was to do whatever I was told and the kidnapper took the phone away from her."

"His voice was disguised?"

He nodded. "One of those voice-changer things, I think. I had one when I was a kid, as a toy. It made him sound like an alien, all mechanical and scratchy." He shuddered, his eyes closing briefly. "I don't want to tell you the things he said he'd do if I called the police. They make me sick."

I didn't want to hear them. "You don't have to. But you know he said them to frighten you. He doesn't really intend to do them." I hid my crossed fingers in a fold of the blanket, warding off the lie. It was definitely possible the abductor would follow through on his threats, at least to some degree. But if I pointed that out, Carter would never let me call the RCMP.

I took another tack.

"You said he asked for a million dollars. Can you get that much money?" Despite their wealth, I doubted Carter or Azalea had such a sum lying around within easy reach. Their funds would be tied up in assets and trust funds and other secure banking things I didn't know or understand.

"No. I tried to tell him that, but he just kept saying I had to get it if I wanted Mom back." He dropped his head into his hands. "He's going to call again at midnight. He says I better have it figured out by then or he'll…" A sob choked off his words.

It felt like hours since Carter had arrived, but the clock on the living room wall declared it wasn't even eleven yet. "What time was the first call?"

"I don't know. I was watching TV. I haven't slept well since Mom went missing. After he hung up, I just sat there for a while. I couldn't believe it was real. Then I thought of you and came here."

I wished he'd gone to the police instead. "But it was this evening? Not earlier in the day?"

He lifted his head, eye sockets red from pressing them with the heels of his hands, and sniffed. "Yes, this evening. Maybe about an hour ago? I can check my phone, but why does it matter?" He rubbed his knuckles under his runny nose.

I uncurled from my chair, retrieved a box of tissue from the kitchen counter, and handed it to him, my thoughts revolving rapidly.

"Why didn't he call during banking hours?" I returned to my seat. "It's not like you can get a million dollars from an automated teller."

Carter cleared his sinuses and blinked. "I don't understand."

I didn't blame him for his befuddlement. I barely knew

Azalea, and this development had thrown me for a very large loop. He had to be scared out of his mind, never conducive to clear thinking.

"It must be a tactic," I said. "He wants you frightened, panicking. Calling when it is impossible to meet his demands puts extra pressure on you, makes you desperate." Another thought struck me. "Do you think someone might be watching your house? Maybe he called so late because it is an unusual time for visitors. If you had alerted the police, even if they came in unmarked vehicles and not in uniform, they'd be easy to spot."

He stared at me, and I realized my mistake, several beats too late. *Oh, shit.*

"We don't know he's spying on you. That was just me thinking out loud." Note to self—don't do that again. "Even if he is, he won't hurt your mom because you came here. I could be anyone. Your accountant or your banker. He wants the money. That's all that matters to him in the end." Please, please, *please* let me be right.

Carter sucked in a long, gasping breath, and then another, before he was able to reply. "Do you think so?"

I nodded. I *had* to think so. The alternative was not to be borne.

We both knew Carter was going nowhere until the kidnapper called again. He removed his boots, apologizing vaguely for the mess he'd made of the living room floor, and unzipped his parka, though he kept it on. Occasionally, shivers wracked his thin frame.

For the most part, we sat in silence, sipping the small, medicinal shots of Drambuie I'd poured, Carter shuddering with every taste of the powerful liquor. I refrained from repeating my suggestion we call the police. That could wait for now.

The more I thought about it, the more certain I was the abductor wasn't expecting to get the million dollars he'd asked for. I'd done my fair share of negotiations, though never with someone's physical safety on the line. The first large ask was to make a second, smaller demand more palatable. That's what we'd hear during the next phone call. I hoped.

As the seconds ticked down to twelve o'clock, Carter shrank into himself. He placed his phone on the table in front of him and tucked his hands into his armpits, rocking gently, releasing from his tight, tense ball to compulsively tap the screen whenever it dimmed.

I'd floated the idea of recording the conversation. He'd agreed only when I promised not to take it to the RCMP. I accepted his decree, though I fully intended to get him to change his mind as soon as possible. Trying to handle this on our own only put Azalea in more danger. We needed professional help, no matter what the kidnapper threatened.

Case in point. Neither of us knew how to record an incoming call. Our solution was to have Carter put his phone on speaker and use the voice memo app on my phone to save it. I prayed I wouldn't screw it up.

Midnight came. Silence.

Two minutes after. My heart pounded so hard it made me dizzy.

Three minutes. He was toying with Carter. I couldn't comprehend the cruelty behind such behaviour.

At twelve-oh-three and fifty-seven seconds, the phone rang.

Carter snatched it up, swiped to connect, and tapped the speaker icon. "Hello? Mom? It's Carter. Mom? Talk to me."

I started the recording and held my phone beside Carter's. Both our hands trembled.

Though he had told me the kidnapper was using a voice changer, I still jolted when the harsh, distorted syllables erupted from the speaker. "Do you have the money?"

"I'm sorry. I told you before. I don't have that much. Please don't hurt my mom."

"Your mother has it. Go to her accountant. Get it from her."

Carter's expression was agonized. "Belva won't give it to me without a rea—"

He was cut off by that terrifyingly calm, robotic voice. "Tell her whatever you need to. Just get the money."

"But a million doll—"

"I will take half. Five hundred thousand. It must be cash. I will call again in thirty-six hours."

"I want to talk to my mom. Can I talk to her? I need to know she's safe."

The abductor continued without acknowledging Carter's plea. "Thirty-six hours. Wednesday at noon. Your mother is a beautiful woman. You want her to stay that way, don't you?"

The connection cut off.

Carter sprang to his feet and rushed to the door. "I've

103

got to talk with Belva. I've got to get the money now." He thrust one foot toward his boot and missed, wobbling, off balance, too distraught to think straight.

"It's after midnight." I slipped in front of him, my back to the door, preventing him from opening it. "She won't be able to do anything. The people we should be calling are the police. They'll know what needs to be done, can start making it happen."

"No!" His eyes wheeled in his head like a terrified horse. "No police."

The kidnapper had given us a short reprieve. I'd try again in the morning. Speaking of which...

"If you won't go to the police, there's nothing we can do until the banks open. Until then, I don't think you should be alone. Why don't you stay here for the night?"

He froze midway through his second attempt to get his boot on, one foot in the air. "Can I?"

"Of course. What you're going through is terrible. I want to help all I can."

"Thank you." He slumped against the wall, parka gaping open, his socked feet only adding to his vulnerable appearance. "Thank you so much."

"Okay, then. Let's get some rest so we can do what needs to be done tomorrow with a clear head." I wanted to hug him tight and tell him everything would be all right, but I wasn't sure it would. I made do with a pat on the shoulder and fresh towels.

At six, after an extremely restless night, I gave up and tiptoed to the kitchen to brew a pot of coffee. I was standing next to the counter, yawning, when Carter appeared. I doubted he'd gotten any more sleep than I had. His curly hair was pressed flat at the back and his clothes were rumpled, so he must have lain down at least, but his face was haggard and dark circles bagged under his eyes.

"I'm sorry, did I wake you?" I asked.

He shook his head. "I'll have a cup of that when it's ready, please."

I poured two mugs, and we went to the living room, he on the couch and I in my chair. I was already beginning to think of them as our 'usual' spots.

I'd hoped a night's rest, such as it was, would make him more amenable to the idea of telling Corporal Tam, but only got as far as "Carter, I really think—" before he held up his hand and stopped me.

"No, Ginnie. Don't ask again. I'm not calling the cops. Not yet."

It was the first hint he'd given that he was softening to the idea. I pressed my lips together and bit back any further nagging.

"What are you going to tell Belva?" I asked.

"The truth. I have to. She'll never give me the money otherwise. I'll call her soon and ask if I can see her at home, before she goes to work. It will be more private there."

I nodded. "What about Carousel? Will you open today?"

"Probably. I'll go crazy just sitting around at home."

I nodded again. "Will you be okay on your own?"

His smile was tired but sincere. "I'll have to be, won't

I? You can't stay with me twenty-four/seven. Don't think I don't appreciate all you've done already, though." He drained his cup and stood. "I should go home so I can clean up before meeting Belva. My story is crazy enough. I don't need to look the part."

His attempt at humour, weak as it was, was encouraging. Maybe common sense would triumph over panic. He had to bring in the authorities. We couldn't deliver the money without official backup. That was just stupid. I followed him to the front door.

He pulled on his boots and coat and then hovered awkwardly for a moment. "Can I hug you?"

"I'm so glad you asked." I stepped in and wrapped my arms around him. "I've been wanting to do this since last night."

He squeezed me back. He was a few inches taller, his torso slim under his puffy coat. I couldn't remember the last time I'd hugged anyone. Lillian, when she'd told me she was going to be a grandmother, probably. Months and months ago.

Wow. I used to be quite touchy-feely. I hadn't noticed the change before now. I hugged him tighter.

"Thank you," he whispered to the crown of my head. "Thank you."

"Let me know how it goes with Belva, won't you? Or if anything else...happens."

He released me and opened the door. It was still dark outside, the snow blue in the shadows.

"Good luck." I waved goodbye, shut out the cold, and offered a short silent prayer for Azalea's safety before starting my own preparations for the day.

It might be hard to believe, but I forgot about abductions and ransoms and threats for short swathes of time during that long day. Blynde Dating was under attack, and I needed to focus what little energy I had after another sleepless night on bolstering our defences.

Clients alerted us to a second nasty Facebook post from Daters Beware though we were unable to see it for ourselves. Unsubscribes were out-pacing new signups, and every few minutes Maeve was fielding another anxious phone call from a member wondering if the accusations were true.

The camaraderie I'd sensed yesterday was still active between the other women, but I felt distant and disconnected. The urge to share Carter's news was strong and keeping it from them felt like a betrayal. But my promise not to tell the police encompassed everyone, and I would honour it. For now.

I *hated* keeping secrets. Two years of hiding the truth about Peter's last hours had worn my stamina for such behaviour thin.

CHAPTER THIRTEEN

WHEN SETH'S NAME lit up my phone screen in the early afternoon, my heart leaped to my throat before plummeting to my toes. Wanting to tell my team was an insistent urge. Wanting to tell Seth was a fierce compulsion. I wanted his take on this development, to hear his thoughts, discuss his ideas. Maybe he could devise a game plan that would convince Carter to go to the police, since I'd struck out.

It didn't matter. It wasn't my call. My mother wasn't in danger. She was with my father, safely sipping Mai Tais while on a six-week cruise from the Pacific to the Caribbean via the tip of South America.

I swivelled my office chair sideways and propped my feet on a half-opened desk drawer. "Hello, Seth. How are you?"

"I've spent far too much time with the police, repeating *I don't know* over and over again. But other than that, I'm fine." He sounded exhausted. Sleepless nights were going around. "How about you?"

"I'm okay." My reply was honest, though I had to clamp down on a multitude of other—and more honest—answers. I had so many questions to ask, so many theories to discuss, but I couldn't add to his burden. "Guess what? I figured out the security system all by myself."

"Well done. I knew you could conquer it." The teasing note in his voice was there only for an instant. "I'm sorry I had to leave so abruptly Saturday."

"Not your fault." That evening felt like years ago.

After that scintillating exchange, we were silent for a long time. Everything I wanted to say dammed my throat.

When he finally spoke next, he sounded more like the Seth I was getting to know. "What are you up to tonight? I'd like to see you again. Maybe this time we won't be interrupted."

Heat flushed—not flashed—through me as I recalled exactly what we'd been doing when Tam had shattered the mood. I wanted to be with Seth, but— "I don't know if that's a good idea." How could I spend a pleasant, potentially passionate, evening with him, knowing what Azalea was going through?

"I see," he said, all traces of amusement absent. "Things are different now. Well, I won't keep—"

"Wait. Don't hang up." He didn't reply but neither did the connection drop. I hurried to clarify my comment. "I want to see you. I do. It's just...I'm not sure tonight is the best night."

"That's all right. I understand." He couldn't understand, not really. He didn't have all the facts.

I was so tempted to blurt everything out. Spending hours with him would only make that temptation stronger. "I'm dealing with a few disasters right now. I doubt I'll be good company."

"Yeah? Which one of us spent the best part of their weekend talking to the RCMP?" Thank goodness his tone was wry, not bitter.

"Right. You're right." I didn't want to sit at home alone, biting my nails, waiting to hear from Carter. Damn it, I could enjoy Seth's company without breaking my promise. "You know what? Why don't we be miserable together?"

"There's no one I'd rather be miserable with than you." Amusement once again sparkled in his voice.

My toes curled. Who knew it could be arousing to make a man laugh? "Seven o'clock. My place. See you then."

I shouldn't have given in to impulse and invited Seth over. And not just because of Azalea's situation. I should have stayed late at the office. Ordinary administrative tasks were falling by the wayside as I dealt with the Facebook attacks, and I had a lot of catching up to do.

By the end of the day, though, I was glad I had. My brain was muddled from lack of sleep and the information on my computer screen danced before my eyes. Staying later would only result in work that would have to be redone.

He arrived at the dot of seven, carrying a colourful mixed bouquet, shielded from the cold in clear cellophane.

"Flowers?" Master of the obvious, that's me. When was the last time someone had brought me flowers?

Peter's funeral didn't count.

"I thought you might need cheering up." He handed them to me and began to shed his outerwear. "Grace, my daughter, knew I signed up for your agency. A couple of hours ago she forwarded a nasty Facebook post to me. I brilliantly deduced that was one of the things you are dealing with. I can't imagine it's been good for business."

I grimaced. "Not exactly. But we'll get through it." I had to remind myself the agency's troubles were nothing compared to Azalea's with a frequency that made me feel guilty. "Does she know you went on a date with Azalea?"

Seth shook his head as he hung his coat in the closet. "No, thank god."

"Are you going to tell her?"

"I suppose I'll have to if Azalea doesn't turn up soon."

Or news of her abduction leaks out. I ground my teeth together to stop myself from divulging the details to him then and there.

"Things are a real mess, aren't they?" I cradled the bouquet and the wrapping crinkled. "Thank you for these. They're beautiful. Come with me while I put them in water."

In the kitchen, I laid the flowers on the counter and slipped the scissors out of the knife block. "Can you get a vase down for me? They're over the fridge."

He opened the cupboard. "Any one in particular?"

"The blue one should be good. Just put it in the sink for now." I slit the cellophane and disentangled a bright pink Gerbera daisy from the bunch. "Help yourself to a drink. The fridge is full of cold ones, or we can make tea or coffee, if you'd rather."

He opened the fridge and twisted to look at me. "You stocked up."

I'd made a quick stop at the grocery store on my way home to get a selection of soft drinks and juices. "I wanted you to have options other than cranberry cocktail and diet cola."

"Thank you." An odd expression crossed his face but was gone before I could analyze it. "What about you? Wine again?"

"I'll have something when I'm done here. But don't wait for me."

He selected a can of ginger ale, remembered where the glasses were, poured it over ice, and took a seat at the table. As I snipped stems and arranged blooms, we slipped into easy conversation, just as we had on Saturday.

A hot flash surged through me. I dropped a flower and the scissors and shrugged out of my cardigan, tossing it onto the back of the chair beside Seth.

His hand gripped my wrist. "What's that?" He stared at the ring of bruises around my biceps, revealed by my sleeveless tank.

I'd forgotten all about them. "It's nothing." Carter hadn't meant to hurt me. I wasn't going to rat him out.

Seth inspected my other arm with a grim expression. "Those look like fingerprints."

"It was an accident. I'm fine."

His hand trailed from my wrist to my shoulder. Goosebumps rippled on my skin. Leaning forward, he planted soft, closed-mouth kisses on each purple mark. My breath caught as his head brushed the side of my breast.

"All better?" His eyes glittered. He knew what his touch had done to me.

"All better," I replied on a sigh.

The doorbell rang and my phone, lying on the counter beside me, lit with a notification. The spell between us broke.

I pointed at the device proudly. "See? I set that up all by myself."

The wrinkles around Seth's eyes deepened and again I felt that odd thrill at making him smile. I debated ignoring whoever was at the door to continue what he'd started. Then I checked the screen.

Carter stood on the front step.

I stared at the phone, then at Seth, and then back at the phone.

Shit.

"Are you going to answer it?" Seth's eyebrows quirked. "Or is it an unwelcome guest?"

"I don't suppose you'd consider hiding in the closet for a little while, would you?"

His eyebrows rose higher. "You mean *I'm* the unwelcome guest?"

The doorbell rang again.

"Look," I said. "I don't have time to explain. Carter Bickersley is at the door. He will not be pleased to meet you. If you want to avoid a confrontation, the spare room is down the hall. But I have to let him in."

I strode to the front door. Seth's footsteps followed. So much for hiding. Not that I'd expected him to, but it would have made the next several minutes less fraught.

I opened the door and Carter started talking. "I did it. I told Belva. She didn't believe me at first, but I played the recording you made yesterday and then she did. She says she'll have the money ready by ten tomorrow. That gives us two hours befo—"

He stepped past me into the foyer, saw Seth, and froze.

I tried to bluff it out. "This is a friend of mine. He was just going." It was possible Carter was surprised only because I had a guest, not because of who that guest was. He knew Seth's name, but what were the odds he knew him by sight?

"Seth Updike." Carter's pale face flushed with angry red. "What are you doing here?"

Good, evidently. Damn internet. It was too easy to track people down.

Seth's eyes narrowed, but he said mildly enough, "Ginnie invited me over. What are *you* doing here?"

Carter pressed his lips together and flashed me a silent angry plea.

"I'm helping him with something," I said to Seth and then swung my gaze to Carter. "And Seth is just visiting. It has nothing to do with our...project."

The atmosphere eased. Maybe we'd make it out unscathed.

And then Seth asked, "What recording? And what money?"

"None of your damn business." Carter glared at Seth before directing his attention to me. "Make him leave, Ginnie. We need to talk."

I stood with my back to Seth so I couldn't see his expression. His silence, however, had a pretty clear *screw you* vibe. Not in an *I'm the man and I know what's best* way. In an *I'm here for Ginnie and I'll do what* she *wants* way.

Don't ask me how I knew this. I just did. And that made my decision easy.

"We should tell him, Carter."

"No!" Desperation replaced anger. "Too many people know already. I told you last night what will happen to my mom if the police find out."

Behind me, Seth inhaled sharply. He'd put two and two together.

"Who have you told other than Belva?" I asked.

"Coral. I told Coral. She kept asking me how I was, how I was holding up, did I need her to stay with me for a while. I told her I'd spent the night here yesterday. The rest of it slipped out when I tried to explain."

I gripped his forearm. "Take off your coat and boots and come sit down. You're right. We do need to talk. But Seth is staying."

Reluctantly, and throwing frustrated glances in Seth's direction the entire time, he took a seat on the couch.

Seth carried an ottoman from the corner and placed it beside my chair. I saw his gaze flick to the bruises on my arm, to Carter, and back again. "He was here last night?"

"Yes. He was very upset. I couldn't let him go home on his own."

His expression grew thoughtful, but he didn't question me further, for which I was thankful. He focused on Carter, speaking calmly with only a faint hint of tension underlining his tone. "I want to make sure I'm not jumping to conclusions. You mentioned money. Has Azalea been...kidnapped?"

The hesitation before his last word revealed both disbelief and acceptance. I knew the feeling.

Carter remained mute, so I answered. "Yes. Carter received a ransom call yesterday."

"Shit." Seth barely breathed the word.

"Exactly. Carter spent the day arranging payment." I looked at him and he jerked his chin in an unhappy nod. "The kidnapper will call tomorrow at noon with further instructions."

"And you haven't told the police."

Carter broke his black silence. "No! He threatened to hurt my mom if I did. We can't tell them."

"You have to. They have resources we don't." Seth's tone brooked no opposition. I prayed he'd have better luck than me. "Do you want to get your mom back or not? Think of what's best for *her*. You know you should tell the RCMP. I get that you're scared and worried and can't believe this is happening. But they are your best hope. *Azalea's* best hope."

"After I pay the ransom." Carter bent but didn't break. "Once Mom is safe. Then we'll go to the cops together."

"You're assuming the kidnapper is telling the truth." Seth was implacable. "What if he doesn't release Azalea once he has the money? What if he takes it and demands more?"

I should have thought of that argument yesterday. It seemed so obvious now. Carter's lips tightened and the lines around his mouth deepened as the implications sank in.

"Call the police," Seth said. "For your mom's sake. I didn't know her well, but what I did know I liked. She deserves every chance she can get."

"Ginnie?" Carter's eyes widened, beseeching me.

"Call Corporal Tam. I know it's scary. But you have to. Call him now and have him come here."

Slowly, he stretched out a leg and extracted his phone from his hip pocket. "Are you sure about this?"

I nodded. "I am."

He dialled.

CHAPTER FOURTEEN

AN HOUR LATER, three more people were seated in my living room.

Tam brought two other officers with him. All were dressed in plain clothes yet exuded the indefinable aura of *cop*. Each had arrived in a different vehicle, clogging my driveway and taking up space on the curb. I wondered if my neighbours would notice. In the last couple of years, only Lillian and delivery drivers had come to my door.

Uncertain of the protocol of having police in my home, I fell back on habit and offered beverages. "Carter, did you want a little brandy again? You look so pale."

He shook his head. "I think I'll just have water."

I turned to Seth. "How about you? Brandy? Whiskey?" The moment the words were out of my mouth I shook my head. "Sorry. I'm a little discombobulated. I forgot about your allergy."

"It's all good. Let me help you." He took my hand in a warm grip, and we moved to the kitchen.

The female officer, dark-skinned with cropped black hair and an impassive expression, accepted tea. The male officer, freckle-skinned with stringy red hair and an impassive expression, declined all offerings.

Tam drank Coke from the can, though I'd provided a glass. I did my best to act normally—was there a normal in this situation?—but couldn't help remembering his parting shot after our interview. Had he looked further into Peter's death? Did I want him to?

We had more pressing concerns than a two-year-old hit-and-run to discuss.

To give Tam credit, he wasted no time berating Carter for the delay. In my presence at least. Who knew what he said to his colleagues in private.

"All right then." He squeezed and released the thin aluminum absently, making a soft popping noise. "I've called in the special unit that deals with these situations."

The other officers nodded. Tam had introduced them but hadn't defined their roles, so I didn't know if they were the unit or were simply approving his procedure.

"They've got all sorts of fancy-schmancy doodads and gizmos for tracing the ransom money. We'll need access to the cash as soon as possible, so once we're done here, we'll get you to take us to this Belva Ginsberg, see if we can speed things up."

Carter's nod wobbled.

"There's other stuff they'll want to do to your phone, trackers and recorders and whatnots." I didn't know if he was dumbing things down for us civilians or if he really didn't know what technology was available. It didn't matter which was the truth, I suppose, since the special unit was in charge of that.

"If we're not ready by noon, when the kidnapper said he'd call"—Carter gave a tiny squeak and Tam waved a soothing hand—"if we're not ready, our negotiator will handle it."

"I promised I wouldn't call you in," Carter moaned.

"Kidnappers expect the police to be involved," Freckles

said. His voice was unexpectedly deep for his reedy frame. "They consider that part of the process. Our presence won't put your mother in any additional danger."

Tam shifted his bulk on the dining room chair Seth had carried in for him. The wood creaked but held. "We'll know more after tomorrow's phone call but be prepared for a lengthy undertaking. We could be talking days, not hours, once our negotiator is involved."

Carter paled and licked his lips. "But the kidnapper will do the exchange, right? He'll give my mom back?" Seth's warning had grown deep roots.

"Try not to worry." The female officer spoke for the first time. "Everyone wants your mom back safe and sound. We'll do whatever we need to achieve that result."

This appeared to appease Carter, though I noticed she'd skirted a direct answer. I met Seth's eyes, and he gave a tiny nod. He'd noticed too.

Shortly after, the three officers swept Carter away, leaving a ringing silence behind.

I stood at the front window and watched all four vehicles leave—Tam in the lead, then Carter, then the two other officers. Seth placed his hands on my shoulders. I tensed at the unexpected touch, then relaxed.

"We did the right thing." His thumbs pressed into the tight muscles at the back of my neck, and I released a sigh of pleasure. "Convincing him to call the police."

"I know. It's just not a guarantee that this will end happily. I can't imagine how scared Azalea must be right now."

He didn't reply. His massage continued as I stared out

the window at the snow-covered street, wishing I could lean into his strength, shore up my confidence with his.

After the revelations that had led to Peter's death, I'd built walls to protect myself from that depth of pain ever again. Seth was wearing away those defences.

His hands slowed and rested lightly on my upper arms. "It's getting late. I should go."

The inflection on his second statement gave me an opening. The question was—did I want to take it?

Squaring my shoulders, I turned to face him. "You don't have to." I slid my arms around his waist and laid my cheek on his chest. My heart tripped anxiously. "I don't want you to. Not yet."

"Ginnie." Seth breathed my name so quietly I almost didn't hear it.

Exactly one week ago, he had said goodbye to Azalea and she'd driven away from him and into a kidnapper's clutches. Less than a week ago, I'd fiercely rejected even the suggestion I allow him into my life.

How had my barriers fallen so quickly? When had I changed my mind? Why did his embrace feel so *right*?

His hand swept up and down, fingertips tracing the valley of my spine. The other gripped my hip and urged me closer. I burrowed in and lifted my chin.

For long aching seconds, we stared at each other. His nostrils flared and my pulse hitched before kicking into a gallop. His sandalwood scent seduced me, softened my bones, heated my blood. I flattened my hands on his back, the planes of muscles firm under my palms, and touched the tip of my tongue to my upper lip.

Glittering blue eyes asked a silent question. I nodded and opened my mouth in invitation.

The hand on my hip drifted higher, past the swell of my breast, over my collarbone. I shuddered at the trail of embers sizzling under my skin. His fingers tilted my chin as his thumb glided over my lower lip. My tongue darted out to taste him and his eyes went from dark azure to fresh denim.

When his mouth finally lowered to mine, a sense of inevitability weakened my knees. This was what I'd wanted since Saturday's volatile kiss. Hell, it was what I'd wanted since my first sight of him at the agency office that fateful Monday.

With a light grip on my ponytail, he held me in place as his tongue explored my mouth with panty-melting confidence. Desire spiralled from my core, hotter than any hot flash and certainly more welcome. His hand cupped my rear and tugged me closer as his mouth plundered mine. I pressed against him, slipping my jean-clad leg between his, seeking relief for my swelling breasts and tight nipples.

Something else was swelling. I rubbed against him with a purr of approval.

What had started as a search for comfort kindled into something more as years of pent-up desire and days of frustrated worry erupted. I slipped my hands under his shirt, shuddering as my palms met the warm flesh of his abdomen. His muscles rippled at my touch, and he groaned into my mouth.

Headlights washed against my closed eyelids. I opened them. We were framed by a wide window in a well-lit living room, as easy to see as if we were on a movie screen. I broke the kiss and dragged him into the corner, where built-in bookshelves formed a cozy nook.

He pulled me close, but it was too late. Carter's devastated face stole my focus, and I was once again consumed by images of Azalea, frightened and alone.

I clasped Seth's wandering hand and took a tiny step back without completely breaking our connection. "Wait. Just a minute." The synapses in my brain fired in bewildering patterns. I struggled to explain myself. "I want you. Badly. But tonight?"

"What do you mean?" The lobes of his ears were red, his gaze darkly intense.

I wanted to sit down, but Seth had moved the round tufted ottoman that usually resided in this corner. I shifted from foot to foot. "You'll think I'm crazy. It just feels, I don't know, disrespectful. To Azalea. I feel guilty, being with you while she's in danger."

His gaze dropped away from mine for a brief instance. "So much has happened in the last week."

"Yes, exactly. It's overwhelming." I reached for his free hand and clutched both tightly. "I want you. I do. But I may have taken too big a step tonight, asking you to stay."

His thumbs bumped over the tendons on the back of my hands as he studied my face. "I want you to be sure, Ginnie. Absolutely sure before we go any further."

I nodded. A small, shadowed silence gathered between us.

He set his shoulders, and a pained chuckle vibrated his chest. "I guess I really am going this time."

I was still tempted to ask him to stay. *So* tempted. It had been years since I'd been with a man, and his embraces and kisses had watered a part of me I'd thought withered and sere.

Lillian would totally say "I told you so" if she knew what I was thinking.

"It's for the best," I said reluctantly. "Maybe tomorrow, once Azalea is safe..."

"I can wait." He kissed my forehead. "Goodnight, Ginnie. Sleep well."

I did. But only after taking myself in hand and finishing what we'd started.

I'd hoped Carter might call with an update before I left for work on Wednesday morning, but I heard nothing. Maybe he was still upset Seth and I had convinced him to call the police. Maybe the police were restricting his phone access in order to keep the line clear for the kidnapper. Maybe there was nothing to tell.

All the maybes were killing me.

The uncertainty certainly killed my productivity. I wasted a lot of time staring at the screen, wondering what was going on, wishing Seth was around so we could wonder together. My team still didn't know about the abduction and Tam had been very clear about keeping the lid on regarding the ransom demand.

"Political kidnappers seek the notoriety, want their exploits broadcast to the world," he'd said. "But the ones in it for money generally want to keep it on the down-low. This is revenue generation, plain and simple. Publicity can screw with their return on investment."

I didn't think my accountant would consider kidnapping a viable business model.

There hadn't been a third Facebook post, so I didn't even have that to keep my mind off Azalea. The furor seemed to be dying down. We were still behind our weekly averages for new signups but unsubscribes seemed to have peaked and were now holding steady.

The radio silence continued all day. My fingers itched to call Carter, but I didn't. Who knew what he and the police were dealing with? I didn't want to mess anything up by calling at exactly the wrong time.

I did talk with Seth at around two-thirty. He sounded as frustrated as I felt about the lack of information. Even so, it was good to hear his voice and have a chance to unburden myself to someone in the know.

The afternoon dragged on. Lillian was still out of town, waiting for the birth of her grandchild, but I fully intended to take the stairs to the second floor and attend dance class tonight without her. I badly needed to burn off some of this nervous energy.

Just after four-thirty, Indra arrived in my office to catch me up on the plans for our Hopeful Hearts event. I don't think I hid my distraction very well, though, as she shot me several puzzled glances during our forty-five-minute meeting.

When my cell rang, an unknown local number appearing on the screen, I snatched it up. "Sorry, Indra, I've got to take this."

Hoping against hope it was Carter calling from a

different device and not a stupid spam call, I answered. "Hello?"

The eerie droid-like voice scraped an icy chill down my spine. "Bring the ransom to Paddlewheel Park in one hour. Come alone. If I see any cops, she's dead."

CHAPTER FIFTEEN

IT WAS SO FAR from what I was expecting I said the most brainless thing ever.

"I'm sorry. What?"

The computerized voice continued. "Leave the money inside the gazebo under the picnic table. One hour, starting now."

"I don't have it. I'm not—" Protests were pointless. The connection had been broken.

Indra stared. "What's going on, Ginnie? You look like you're about to faint."

My cheeks prickled and a wave of light-headedness swamped me. Sucking in a deep breath, I let it out slowly. "No. I'm not going to faint. But I have to go."

Mind racing, I scrolled through my recent call list, looking for the date of my lunch with Seth, when I'd been summoned to the detachment. I hit the redial button, pushed back from my desk, and staggered to my feet.

Indra rose too. "Ginnie! Tell me what's going on."

"I don't have time to explain." Snagging my coat from the rack, I struggled to don it while holding the phone to my ear.

"Ginnie!" Indra followed me out. Maeve looked our way with a startled expression, but I ignored her, too, and headed for the rear door.

"Corporal Tam."

I never thought I'd be happy to hear that gruff, growly voice. "It's Regina Blynde. The kidnapper called me. I have one hour to bring the ransom."

Behind me, Indra squeaked, "Kidnapper?" Anything else she might have said was cut off by the slamming of the heavy metal door.

Tam blurted an obscenity. "So much for negotiating. Did he mention the drop?"

"Paddlewheel Park."

"Hold on."

I sprinted down the shadowy alley, thankful for the sturdy ankle boots I'd chosen to wear that morning. The fingers holding my phone were icy, but I'd abandoned my gloves in my office.

As I slid into the driver's seat, Tam came back on the line. "You know the gas station at 20th and Queensway?"

"Yes."

"We'll meet you there. Drive carefully and don't rush. The last thing we need is for you to have an accident on the way."

I tossed my phone onto the passenger seat, put the car in reverse, and hit the gas. It leapt backward like a startled whitetail, and I stomped on the brake, rear bumper inches from the metal dumpster.

Apparently, his advice was warranted. I drew in several deep breaths, slowing my rabbiting heart rate. Then I exited the lot and made my way sedately to the gas station, where two marked police cars were parked nose-to-tail, exhaust streaming from their tailpipes.

When I pulled up, a uniformed officer stepped out from each. The one nearest me approached and I rolled down my window. He leaned in, one hand on the roof of my car, the other resting casually on his holstered firearm. "Regina Blynde?"

I nodded.

"The response team will be here soon. How are you doing?"

I answered on automatic pilot. "I'm fine. How are you?"

"I am well." His voice held a hint of a South-Asian accent. Dark eyes smiled kindly from under thick brows. I must have looked as frazzled as I felt, for he added, "Everything will be fine. Trust the team. They'll walk you through it."

His colleague said something I didn't catch.

He tapped the roof of my car. "Excuse me for a moment." He straightened and stepped away from my window, which I immediately rolled up. Despite the warmth blasting from my heater, I was shivering.

This was crazy. Why had the kidnapper called me? How had he even *known* about me, let alone had access to my phone number? I mean, a lot of people knew it, but they were all clients, friends, or family. Come to think of it, how had he gotten *Carter's* number?

Was it possible the kidnapper was someone he or I knew?

I didn't have time to reflect further as a squadron of cars, both marked and unmarked, converged on the gas station.

Five hundred thousand dollars in small bills made a hefty package.

I gripped the handles of the black duffle bag—cliché,

much?—that Tam had given me and struggled to lift the strap onto my shoulder. Staggering slightly, I lugged it toward the white-framed gazebo, trying to look composed, not petrified. The path was icy and slick and shrouded by the dark. I navigated it carefully.

I'd had a lot of advice and information thrown at me in the frantic minutes before I'd left the gas station, but it boiled down to one directive.

Stay calm.

Tam was only one of many people mobilized by my call. I recognized the dark-haired woman and Freckles from last night, but the person in charge was a grim woman with short salt and pepper hair and the posture of a soldier. If anyone told me her name, I didn't remember it. "We don't want to spook him," she'd said. "Get in, leave the bag—unless you receive further instructions—and get out."

The 'further instructions' addendum made me extremely uneasy. I wanted to get everything over with, but expert consensus was this wouldn't be the final drop site. "It's too open, too isolated," Grim Woman said. "Too easy for us to spot whoever comes to retrieve it."

While officers fussed around making last minute preparations, Tam briefed me on the day's events. Or lack of them. The reason Carter hadn't given me an update was because noon had come and gone with no contact from the kidnapper. If I read between the lines correctly, officials had been scrambling to come up with another game plan when I'd called.

What this deviation from the kidnapper's schedule might mean for Azalea I didn't want to contemplate.

Paddlewheel Park, a small meadow clinging to the edge of the Fraser River, was quilted in crusty snow. Towering cottonwoods gripped the bank with their deep roots, the silty water mottled by chunks of ice. Swiftly moving floes blinked in and out of the light spilling from nearby houses.

On this blustery January evening, I was the only visitor. The gazebo stood stark and silent, silhouetted against the sandy cliffs on the far side of the wide river. I increased my pace, the duffle banging against the back of my legs.

Though I'd been told to expect it, I startled when my phone rang. I took the last few steps into the gazebo, dropped the bag onto the bench seat of a picnic table, and answered, heart in my throat.

"Yes?" My eyes strained to see into the shadowy corners of the hexagonal shelter.

"Go to the university. At the first parking lot, stop directly under a streetlamp, as far away from any other vehicles as possible. Wait for further instructions." The call disconnected.

I hoisted the bag, growing heavier by the minute, and jog-walked back to my car. "Did you get that? I'm to go to the university next."

"Copy that." The voice in my left ear was amazingly crisp and clean. I clung to the fact I wasn't as alone as I felt. Unmarked police vehicles were discreetly stationed at various locations near the park, including a communications van crammed with high tech gear.

The Prince George campus of the University of Northern British Columbia had only one entrance, if you discounted a gravel back road that also led to a wilderness hiking area. I assumed this bottleneck would make it easier for the kidnapper to see if I was being followed. Grim Woman had been confident my escort would be invisible. I wasn't sure what help they would be if they stayed too far away, but what did I know?

A ring road encircled the university's block of buildings. I took the first right into a huge parking lot. Six or seven vehicles, dusted with the light snow that had fallen several hours earlier, were parked here and there. I headed away from them, toward the copse of trees separating the campus from a nearby athletic complex, pulled up next to one of the towering light poles, and left my engine running.

Tam's rallying point had provided several benefits, including the chance to top up my tank. At least I could keep warm while I waited without worrying about running out of gas. As much as I hoped this evening would end soon, I wasn't the one in control. I couldn't risk missing a rendezvous because I'd had to fill up.

The kidnapper made me wait this time. Maybe he didn't know I'd arrived. Maybe it was all part of his plot. Whatever. The minutes crawled by.

My ear bud was on a private channel, just me and my contact in the communications van. I couldn't hear any chatter between other members of the squad, and I'd been warned to speak only when necessary. Something about the kidnapper possibly monitoring signals. I hadn't really understood what I'd been told. So, all I did was sit, picking a hangnail bloody and craning my neck every five seconds to make sure no one was approaching from behind.

I didn't jump when the phone rang this time. I was too

relieved he'd finally called.

"Your next destination is Exhibition Park. There is a yellow dumpster near Kin Two, next to the stables. Hide the bag behind it and drive away."

My fingers tingled. This was it. I knew it. "What about Azalea? Where will she—"

I was talking to empty air.

I confirmed my unseen protectors knew where I was going next. It was only a five-minute drive. Traffic grew heavier as I neared the drop site, and my pulse spiked.

Exhibition Park included a six-thousand seat hockey arena, three smaller ice rinks labelled Kin One, Two, and Three, an outdoor ice oval, various barns and buildings used by 4-H clubs, and the parking necessary to accommodate all these activities. A large reader board at one entrance declared the Prince George Canyon Cats were playing a home game, which explained the congestion.

Something was going on at the Kin arenas, as well. A section of the parking lot was roped off and food trucks attracted crowds of bundled up customers. The whole place was lit up like Christmas. I bumped over cables snaking under protective coverings as I struggled to find a parking spot, creeping along while avoiding pre-teen girls toting large equipment bags, accompanied by their attendant families. A charter bus pulled up in front of the doors leading to Kin One and disgorged a horde of players.

My black duffle bag wouldn't look conspicuous in this atmosphere. As long as no one saw me stashing it behind the dumpster, I would get away with a clean drop.

There was no missing the bright yellow bin the

kidnapper had mentioned. I passed it more than once before I finally found an open space near the ice oval. A lone skater glided in easy strides around the frozen surface, leaning forward from the hips, one arm swinging, long blades shining sharp and bright.

Sweat beaded my upper lip as a hot flash engulfed me. Perfect. Just what I needed. I opened the door, stood, and unzipped my coat, welcoming the bite of freezing air and huffing with relief.

"Are you all right?" the voice in my ear asked calmly.

"Yes. I'm heading to the dumpster now." I retrieved the duffle, which now felt like it weighed a million pounds, from the rear seat.

The scent of horse manure greeted me as I approached the stables. I'd always found it a rather pleasant smell and, perhaps oddly in the circumstances, it soothed me.

The bin was surrounded on three sides by battered wood fencing. I scanned the area. The only moving vehicle was heading the opposite direction and no pedestrians were looking my way. I ducked into the enclosure and sidled between the bin and the fence. Cold emanated from the metal container. Some of the garbage inside hadn't had time to freeze. The odour of stale grease and pungent refuse made my nose wrinkle.

At the rear of the bin, several slats were missing in the fencing, and the vinyl siding of the barn was less than an arm's length away. I tucked the duffle into a protected corner, hidden from any casual passersby, and then sidled my way back to the front.

When I stepped onto the roadway, I garnered a curious

glance from a small boy trailing behind two adults and an older girl toting the ubiquitous equipment bag. My hot flash had receded, and I zipped up my coat as I strode back to my car.

"I did it," I said, once inside. "It's in place."

"Well done," my earbud replied. "Please return to the detachment as previously instructed."

I reached for the key to turn the ignition and realized my hands were trembling. Tucking them under my thighs, I leaned my forehead against the steering wheel and focused on breathing.

"Is everything okay?" my ghost asked.

"Just need a minute," I said shortly.

When would the abductor come for his money? He wouldn't risk leaving it where it was too long. I assumed he was counting on the confusion and busyness of the area to shield him, but that couldn't be expected to last for more than a couple of hours.

The police had to be watching the dumpster by now. What would they do? Would they grab the kidnapper if they had the chance or follow him to his lair?

But the more important question was...

When would Azalea be released?

CHAPTER SIXTEEN

I DIDN'T SEE CARTER at the debrief session. It appeared I was still on a need-to-know basis. The police wouldn't even tell me where he was, though I was assured he was being kept informed and was well-looked after.

"What do we do now?" I asked Grim Woman. Tam referred to her as Sergeant Mehta, though I still didn't remember being introduced.

"We wait. We have eyes on the drop site and will continue to monitor your phone. We'll know the moment anything happens."

Yeah, the 'monitoring my phone' had come as a shock. I'd allowed it to be taken from me at the gas station rendezvous—I mean, what choice did I have?—and it had been returned with the warning that they were now able to review all my communications. As well, all my privacy and Do Not Disturb settings had been deactivated, ensuring the kidnapper could reach me at anytime.

I guess I wouldn't be sexting with Seth in the near future. Haha.

It was well after ten o'clock by this time. Mehta offered me an escort home. I demurred, desperately needing some normalcy in my life. She and Tam shared a glance.

"I think we'll send someone anyway," Mehta said. "Just as a formality."

I was too tired to protest further.

In the parking lot, I let my car warm up as I debated

doing what I really wanted to do but wasn't sure I should. My escort, an extremely youthful-looking officer in a marked vehicle, waited for me to reverse out of the slot.

Screw it. Ignoring the electronic supervision, I sent Seth a message.

Are you still awake?

The dots danced immediately. *Yes. Have you heard anything?*

It was too complicated to put in a text. I bit my lip, thought, and then typed *Can you come to my place?*

On my way.

I headed home, trailed by my babysitter.

When I drew within sight of my house, Seth's pickup was already idling at the curb. Tears prickled the back of my nose. I sniffed them back, scolding myself for my weakness. I was exhausted, that was all. Having someone waiting for me at the house that had felt so empty for so long was no reason to cry.

I punched the garage door opener, rolled past his truck, turned into my driveway, and pulled into the garage. He followed me up the drive and my police escort took his spot at the curb.

Seth and the young officer met me next to his pickup.

"Is everything okay?" Sharp lines slashed between Seth's brows. "What's going on?"

"Do you know this man, ma'am?" my escort asked at the same time.

I smiled at her. "Yes. He's a friend." Then to Seth,

"Everything's fine. I'll explain this"—I waggled my gloved fingers at the officer—"soon."

The officer gave Seth a searching look, as if committing his description to memory. "Have a good night, ma'am." She strode back to her car. Seth and I went in through the garage and I disarmed my security. By the time we had discarded our outerwear and were in the kitchen, the police vehicle was gone.

"Well, at least she's not camping on my doorstep until morning." I sagged against the counter and rubbed the heels of my hands into my eye sockets.

"Put me out of my misery, Ginnie. Tell me what's happened. Have they...found...Azalea?"

His hesitation told me exactly what he was thinking. "No. Not yet. But we're hopeful. The ransom's been delivered. Now all we can do is wait."

"We? I get the feeling there's more to your story."

"A lot more. You see, the kidnapper called me."

Seth stared. "You? Why you?"

I shrugged. "I don't know. I got the call about quarter after five this afternoon."

Without taking his eyes off me, Seth opened the cupboard where I kept my glasses, took down a tumbler and a wineglass, and reached for the bottle of Malbec sitting on the counter. "This sounds like it's going to take a while. Go sit down. I'll bring us drinks."

Alcohol might have smoothed the raggedest of my edges, but red wine did not agree with me this late at night. I asked for tea instead and Seth puttered about with familiar ease, setting the kettle to boil and exchanging the glassware for mugs and tea bags.

I took a seat on the couch so I could have a view of the man in my kitchen. Not that I expected him to vanish or steal the non-existent silver. I just wanted visual confirmation I wasn't alone.

"Do you have any lemon?" he asked, head buried in the fridge.

I huffed out a soft chuckle. "Middle crisper drawer. Right in front of your face."

"Got it."

Were all men fridge blind? Peter had never been able to find anything in plain sight, either. It was a nostalgic, cozy thought, without the usual stab of pain.

Seth handed one mug to me and settled beside me with another, close enough I could feel his warmth but not quite touching. "Okay. Tell me all."

By the end of my tale, my tea was finished, and I was slouched with my back to the arm of the couch, my legs draped over Seth's knees. The position was natural, easy, and I never wanted to move again.

"You've had quite the night." He plucked my mug from my limp hands and placed it beside his on the coffee table.

"Understatement of the year." I slumped sideways, resting my head on the back cushion. "I should be wound up, worried about Azalea, wondering when we might hear something. But I'm too tired." I gave up and closed my eyes.

"It's the stress." Warm hands encircled my socked foot and began to rub.

My bones melted. "You'll put me to sleep doing that."

"Then I'll carry you to bed."

Those words said in Seth's rich tenor sparked scenes on the back of my closed eyelids. Sexy, erotic scenes.

If anything could break through my exhaustion...

"Stay the night." I kept my eyes shut, afraid I'd lose my courage if I could see him. "I don't want to be alone."

Echoes of Carter's plea reverberated at the back of my mind. He hadn't been far from my thoughts all day, but in this moment, I was selfishly glad the police were responsible for him.

A raspy fingertip traced a line of fire from my forehead, down the bridge of my nose, to my lips. "Ginnie."

I opened my eyes.

Face shadowed, expression intent, blue eyes molten, Seth studied me. "What are you asking? Do you just want company...or something more?"

"More." I cupped his scruffy jaw with my palm. Somewhere during this long fraught day, I'd lost all my inhibitions when it came to Seth. I sat up and nipped his earlobe. "And this time I won't change my mind. I want you. *All* of you."

He groaned. "You're upset. You're tired. I should go." At odds with his words, one hand slid from my foot to my waist and under my blouse. The other wound behind my back and cupped my nape under my ponytail, urging me closer.

I nuzzled his throat, inhaling his sandalwood scent. He lifted his chin to give me better access. "No, you shouldn't. You really, really shouldn't."

"You're not thinking straight."

Exasperated, I pulled away. "I'm trying to seduce you here. Do you want to have sex or not?"

"Oh, god, *yes*." Muscles flexed in his cheeks as his jaw worked. "Please don't regret it later."

"I won't." I had no idea where Daring Ginnie had come from, but I liked her. Two years of guilt and self-recrimination had made me a faded version of myself. It was time to reclaim the woman I'd been. "Wait. Are you trying to warn me you're no good in bed?"

That snapped him out of his gentlemanly funk. He glared. "What a low blow."

I stroked his chest, humming low in my throat. "Well, if that's what you like..."

It took half a second for my innuendo to register. When it did, he shoved my legs off his knees, surged to his feet, and grabbed my hand. "Bedroom's this way, I take it." He tugged me down the hall.

"Yes." Liquid heat flooded my belly. I was going to do this. *We* were going to do this.

I hadn't bothered to make my bed that morning and not all the dirty laundry had made it into the basket. Maybe I should have apologized for the untidy state, but I didn't. He wasn't here to judge my housekeeping skills.

Seth yanked me into his arms and kissed me. His lips were firm and smooth and his tongue demanded entrance. I opened my mouth and his taste filled me, tart and tangy and tempting.

"Not good in bed." He muttered the words against my neck. "I'll show you."

I giggled breathlessly. "That's the plan."

"Brat."

His mouth claimed mine, a delicious assault that

softened into a provocative exchange of give and take, offering and accepting. My fingers stroked up his abdomen to his chest, wiry hair tickling my palms. His T-shirt lifted with my movements, and he broke the kiss long enough to jerk it over his head and discard it onto the floor. I had a quick glimpse of silvery strands scattered on his pecs and arrowing down to his waist before his hands on my breasts made me gasp and close my eyes.

"Sensitive?" He gentled his touch.

"Yes. Don't stop."

His fingers deftly unbuttoned my blouse and pushed it aside. "Pretty," he breathed. He cupped my breasts again, thumbs brushing my aching nipples.

I didn't think he was talking about my lingerie. Since I hadn't exactly planned on having sex tonight, I was wearing one of my everyday bras, plain and sturdy. I dropped my head back and arched my spine, inviting more caresses.

"Kneel," he commanded. "On the bed."

Giddy with lust, I did as he asked, the deep mattress soft but supportive. His hair brushed my chin as he lowered his head. Moist, open-mouthed kisses branded my skin from collarbone to collarbone.

I needed that mouth on my breasts. Now. Reaching behind, I unhooked my bra and wriggled. One sleeve of my blouse caught on my wrist, and I tugged to remove it. The bra was trickier, but I managed to escape it with most of my dignity intact.

Seth was no slouch. He took up my wordless invitation immediately. My pulse pounded like thunder as he licked and sucked, drawing my nipples into ever tighter points with lips and teeth and fingers.

Desire gushed from my core, and I didn't hold back my shriek. Panting, I gripped his skull, pulled him away from my chest, and kissed him with thanksgiving and joy.

"Did you just..." He regarded me hungrily.

I nodded. "Don't worry, I'm not done with you yet." My hands flew to the waistband of his jeans. His erection bulged behind the thick denim, and I flattened my palm against it. He groaned, eyes darkening.

I slipped open the button and unzipped the fly. His sigh held equal parts relief and anticipation as I slid my hand inside his briefs and clasped him.

Was there anything as wondrous as a man's firm cock? Hard as iron, smooth as silk, hot as flame. I exhaled, ensuring my breath wafted over the tip, and he jerked, thrusting forward. His fingers tangled in my hair, wrapping the long strands in his fist in a way that was both controlled and controlling. Wetness bloomed at my centre once more.

I played with him, stroking and exploring, noting the differences between him and Peter. Nothing shocking. Just enough to remind me this was not my husband. Acknowledging these contrasts only made me hotter.

I'd been faithful throughout my marriage, but I'd been the only one. Maybe whatever this was with Seth was a long-delayed rebellion. An illicit thrill rippled through me.

Without releasing him, I straightened up on my soon-to-be aching knees so our mouths could meet again. He was a delightful kisser. I wondered what else his mouth was capable of.

Even as our lips and tongues danced in unpracticed

choreography, Seth's hands found the snap on my slacks, unfastened it, and slid around to grasp my ass. Impatient, I shoved his jeans out of my way. "Let's get naked."

He didn't need to be told twice. Our remaining clothes vanished, and we lay on the bed, skin to skin. I moaned as my breasts pressed flat on his chest and the bar of his cock burned against my belly.

"If you don't have condoms, we should maybe—"

I leaped off the bed. "Don't go anywhere." In the en suite, I unearthed an open box of condoms from what had been Peter's side of the vanity. I wasn't even sure why I'd saved it but was thrilled I had in this moment. I returned to the bedroom, waving it triumphantly over my head. "Voilà."

Seth's smile was devilish. "Well, then, hand one over."

I waited in feverish suspense as he sheathed himself and then fell to my back and opened my arms. "Please. Now."

He positioned himself between my legs. "I want you to know, whatever happens, I really, really like you, Ginnie."

I curled my calves behind his thighs and lifted my ass. "I really, really like you too. Now gimme."

He laughed, notched himself at my entrance, and thrust.

"Ooooh." I shifted a little, adjusting to his fit. "There. Yes."

He propped an elbow on each side of my head and rocked. It didn't take us long to find a rhythm. Golden light streaked through my veins, sparking and exploding. I was enveloped in his scent, sheltered by his body. Feeling him inside me reignited the fire doused by Peter's betrayal.

The pressure built, tingling at the base of my spine and in my hips. I shouted, legs straightening, as the orgasm overtook me. Seth kept up his pace. I clung to him with weak limbs and whispered encouraging words in his ear until he stiffened, groaned, and collapsed on top of me.

CHAPTER SEVENTEEN

CHESTS HEAVING, WE lay pressed together for a moment. At least, I thought it was only a moment.

"Ginnie." Seth's breath tickled my ear, and I jerked. "You fell asleep."

"Sorry." I yawned and stretched.

He reached between us to secure the condom and sat back on his heels. "Give me a minute. And try to stay awake a little longer. We need to talk." He headed for the en suite.

I retrieved the comforter from the floor and covered myself. As the afterglow faded, awkward thoughts corkscrewed through my brain. Was I that out of practice? Had he not taken as much pleasure as I had? Maybe I'd been too forward, too pushy. But I had always been vocal about what I liked when it came to sex. I couldn't change that. Wouldn't want to.

He reappeared. I watched him with longing as he walked naked across the floor. Was this the last time I'd see him like this? He sat on the edge of the mattress near my feet, and I drew up my knees, hugging them, my bare arms on top of the puffy bed cover.

"I'm glad you convinced me to stay." His sideways smile looked oddly shy for a currently nude man who had recently rocked my world.

Relief made my stomach flip-flop. "You are?"

"I don't like the idea of you being alone, not until Azalea is home." He found my foot under the covers and patted it, his hand warm and solid. "You're tangled up in this now and who knows what the kidnapper might do next."

My happiness dimmed. I would have rather heard he'd had the best sex of his life and never wanted to leave my bed again. Still, I could appreciate the caring behind his words. "I'm glad you stayed too."

"Would it be okay if..." He trailed off. Again, I was struck by the contrast between his unashamed nakedness and the diffidence of his speech. This was a man of many layers.

When he didn't finish the sentence, I did for him, hoping I was guessing right. "If you stayed the night?"

He nodded.

I threw back the comforter and sidled to the middle of the bed. "I would like nothing better."

I dropped into sleep like a rock down a well and woke just as abruptly.

Seth was shaking my shoulder. "Ginnie. Your phone is ringing."

The trill echoed down the hallway from the living room. I must have left it there last night, too intent on getting him into my bed.

Rolling off the mattress, I staggered toward the sound, pausing only to grab my robe from the hook on the bedroom door. The house was cold and dark. I had no idea how long I'd been asleep.

My phone rang again. Leaving it uncharged and unattended had been a terrible mistake. What if the battery had died? What if Seth hadn't heard it ringing? How long did I have before the caller disconnected?

I snatched it off the coffee table. An unknown number. "Hello? Hello?"

A pause, a click, and then—

"This is the fraud department of the Bank of Montreal. There has been a security breach of your credit card. Please press—"

I ended the call with a vicious tap. Some days I really miss phones that can be slammed down in disgust without risking their destruction.

Seth spoke from behind me. "Who was it?"

I turned. He had a towel wrapped around his waist and his arms crossed as if trying to conserve body heat. "Spam. A freaking spam call." I pinched the bridge of my nose.

His shoulders lowered. "I thought..."

"Yeah, me too. But no." I glared at my phone as if it was the device's fault. Which I guess it kind of was.

"Not knowing is hard. Waiting is harder." A tiny shiver rippled through him.

"It's not even six." My furnace was scheduled to keep the house cooler at night. "Let's go back to bed."

This time I brought my phone with me and plugged it into the charger on my nightstand. I lay on my side and Seth curled around me. His skin was chilly but warmed quickly.

"Try to get more rest." He cuddled me against his chest.

Peter hadn't been a snuggler, and I'd been sleeping alone for so long I thought the position might make me fidget. Instead, I fell into a deep enough doze that, when my phone rang again, I thought it was part of a dream.

Propping myself up on one arm, I stretched out the other

and flipped the phone over so I could see the screen. Six-thirty exactly. Behind me, Seth shifted, too, one hand coming to rest on my hip.

It was another unknown number. I accepted the call and tapped the speaker icon, bracing for more disappointment. "Hello?"

My brain snapped fully awake when the familiar robotic voice said, "1111 First Avenue. Let the cops know. 1111 First Avenue." The line disconnected.

"That's him." I shot out of bed, Seth scrambling out after me. "I'll call my RCMP contact, make sure they heard it too. And it wouldn't hurt to pray that this isn't a wild goose chase. Let's go."

As Seth and I neared the address, we were overtaken by several police cars in full emergency mode, lights flashing, sirens blaring. Obviously, the time to keep covert had passed.

I gripped the shoulder strap of my seatbelt with a sweaty hand. Seth was driving, an offer I'd accepted with relief. "I wonder if the ransom was picked up. Is that why he called, do you think?"

"I don't know." He turned right onto First Avenue. A block ahead, the road was cluttered with emergency vehicles in all shapes and sizes, including two ambulances. They'd called in the cavalry this morning.

He found a space at the curb, and we jogged the final metres. Several uniformed officers milled about on the sidewalk in front of a multi-story warehouse with a massive unloading dock and the words "Self Storage" painted in giant letters on its facade.

One officer blocked us with a raised hand. "A police incident is in progress in this area. You need to leave right now."

"I'm Regina Blynde." I inhaled deeply, breathless from nerves more than the quick pace. "Sergeant Mehta requested my presence."

His expression flared with recognition. "Yes, I was given your name. But only yours." He narrowed a questioning glare at Seth.

"This is Seth Updike. Corporal Tam will vouch for him." I didn't want to leave Seth behind, but I would if I had to.

Luckily, the name-dropping worked. "Wait a moment. An officer will escort you."

We followed the woman he summoned up the flight of steps that ran along the wall inside the loading dock. On the landing, she opened a battered grey metal door, and I heard voices coming from a doorway a few metres ahead. Seth at my heels, I followed her to a stuffy overheated office.

The room was crammed with bodies in steel-blue winter jackets, wide brown utility belts with holsters, and heavy black boots. At the far side, a middle-aged woman with frizzy blond hair in a navy parka with the stuffing erupting from a tear in the sleeve stood between Mehta and Tam.

"I don't know what you're talking about." The blonde's voice was tarry with cigarette smoke. "There are no people living in my units."

"She's a captive, not a resident." Mehta had obviously said this before, based on the testiness of her tone.

Tam noticed us. His gaze encompassed Seth, but his

expression didn't change. He nodded at our escort, who nodded back and departed. Without preamble, Tam said, "Anything more?"

I shook my head. "No."

"Right then." Mehta faced her team. "You have your assignments. Bolt cutters will be handed out by the tactical unit."

"Bolt cutters?" the woman squawked. "You can't just—"

"We can and we will." Mehta waved her off like swatting a mosquito. "A hostage is on this property. Every second counts."

I flattened against the wall to avoid being swept out with the tide of officers. Seth took refuge in the hallway and reappeared as soon as the last uniform vanished.

"What can we do?" I asked. Azalea was somewhere in this building. I couldn't sit meekly by.

Mehta didn't see it that way. "Stay here with Mrs. Murphy. Keep your phone handy. Let us know at once if you hear anything." She strode out the door.

Tam was no more sympathetic. "An officer will be here in a minute. No one leave this room." Then he was gone too.

"Goddamn it!" I clenched my fists and glared at Seth. "I hate this."

"I can't believe they're cutting the locks." Mrs. Murphy's jowls jiggled with indignation as she paced behind her desk. "I won't be responsible for replacing them. I won't."

We ignored her. Seth rubbed my arm consolingly. "It'll be over soon."

"I hope so." The thought wasn't as comforting as it should be. Recovering Azalea wasn't the end. No matter how kindly she'd been treated—and there was no guarantee of that at all—she'd still be traumatized. Her life would never be the same.

My phone buzzed with an incoming text. I dug it out of my parka pocket, expecting an acknowledgment of the hurried message I'd sent Maeve telling her not to worry if I wasn't in at my usual time.

On the lock screen notification, I read *Unit 272.*

"I know where she is!" I grabbed Seth's wrist and yanked him out of the office, leaving Mrs. Murphy behind, wide-eyed and gape-mouthed.

From the police presence we'd witnessed, I'd expected to find the place crawling with officers. Instead, we raced down the hall without catching sight of one blue uniform.

"Where is everyone?" I crashed through a door marked "Stairs" and pounded up a flight. My breath puffed out, misty in the unheated stairwell. Seth's footsteps echoed in time with mine.

An exit marked with a large numeral two led into a long hallway with more corridors branching off it and lined with grey metal roll-up doors. At the far end, two officers armed with heavy-duty bolt cutters lowered one shut with a clang.

"She's in 272!" I shouted. Fluorescent tube lighting buzzed as the four of us sprinted toward each other in a terrible parody of a romantic reunion. Cold air rasped in and out of my lungs.

The four of us met at an intersection and turned down the passage marked *260 to 280.*

I looked left. *263...265...* The wrong side. I looked right. *268...270...272.* "Here!"

"Please stand back." The male officer placed the jaws of the cutter around the shackle and squeezed. It snicked through the shiny metal like a knife through cheese.

His partner, who had been communicating via her shoulder radio even as she ran, produced a small bag from a pocket. With gloved hands, he removed the lock, placed it inside the bag, and bent to raise the door. It clattered and creaked upward, revealing a dark, cold interior.

At first, I thought the space was empty. A sense of failure swept over me. My shoulders sagged at the setback.

The two officers entered the small narrow room. A light went on, automatically triggered by their movements. They knelt next to a long lumpy bundle tucked into the angle of the floor and the back wall, less than three metres away.

Oh, no. No.

The female officer worked on latex gloves as she and her partner spoke quietly to each other. Using her thumb and finger, she carefully eased up the fabric covering one end of the bundle.

No. No.

Faded blue eyes bulging out of swollen sockets. Mottled, blotchy skin transforming the face into a livid mask. Tangled blond curls crusty with rust brown filth.

My stomach heaved and I clamped my lips together.

We'd found Azalea. But it was too late. Much, much too late.

CHAPTER EIGHTEEN

THE MALE OFFICER LEFT his partner and ushered us, without ceremony but scrupulously polite, back to the office. It felt wrong, as if I were deserting Azalea when she needed me most, but he made it clear we had no choice.

On our way down the stairs, we met Mehta, Tam, and several others on their way up. They moved with a stoic deliberation that nevertheless revealed their disappointment. They, too, had hoped to find Azalea alive. This was not the outcome any of us wanted.

Oh, god. Carter. His premonition had been right. Azalea was dead.

In the office, Mrs. Murphy had squashed her fleshy hips between the arms of her desk chair. She was accompanied by a middle-aged officer whose delayed arrival had allowed us to be on hand when Azalea's body was found. He gave our escort a shamefaced glance. I wondered absently if he'd be disciplined for the error.

"Will someone please tell me what's going on?" Mrs. Murphy demanded.

Neither of the officers answered. Seth met my eye and shook his head in a minuscule movement. Fine by me. The authorities could deal with her.

He offered me the dented folding metal chair that was the only seat other than the one Mrs. Murphy occupied. I didn't bother putting up a bold face. I wanted to sit, so I did. He leaned against the wall beside me. The officer took a watchful stance near the door, locking the stable after the horses had bolted.

The minutes crawled by. Mrs. Murphy's complaints and queries quieted. When Mehta and Tam finally appeared, the four of us were entombed in an uncomfortable silence.

"You two." Mehta jerked her chin at Seth and me. "Come along." We followed her into the hall. Mrs. Murphy's querulous voice, once more raised in irritated refrain, was cut off when Tam closed the door after us.

Mehta stopped a couple of metres down the hall. "Walk me through what happened after I left the office."

Our story didn't take long. There wasn't much to tell.

Seth stood at my elbow, emanating calm, wordless support. Mehta asked him if he had anything to add. When he shook his head in the negative, she didn't push for more. I had the feeling most of her attention was elsewhere.

"All right." She rolled her shoulders as if dislodging a heavy weight. "We'll continue to monitor your phone. If anything happens that you think we should know about, use the number we gave you."

"How long will you be listening in on my calls?"

"As long as necessary."

Yeah, that wasn't exactly a useful answer. But I'd do more than submit to an invasion of privacy if it meant finding Azalea's killer.

I finally recognized the tension that had been coiling in my belly since catching sight of her body. Fury. White hot fury. I was no expert, but I wasn't an idiot, either. Azalea hadn't looked newly dead. She'd been killed days ago, I was sure of it. The kidnapper—make that murderer—had been toying with us all this time.

"What about the ransom?" I asked. "Did anyone come for it?"

Mehta hesitated, her expression impossible to read. "We still had a team watching when you called this morning."

So, no, then. All the anxieties, all the preparations, all the efforts. For nothing.

"You're free to go," Mehta said. "Later today we will release a media bulletin. While this was a kidnapping scenario, we embargoed all details, but we can't delay any longer. Until that time, stay off social media and don't speak to any reporters. They will get the scent soon enough and won't hesitate to show up at your home or business. Redirect all questions to us."

I nodded. Murder certainly wasn't unknown in our town, but to have a member of one of our upper echelon families, especially one so community-minded and respected, kidnapped and killed? There would be no keeping the lid on this. It was going to go national.

"Let me know if I can do anything more to help," I said.

"Of course."

Something in her tone made my shoulder blades draw together. I was hit by a belated realization.

I was a suspect. Mehta put on a good show, so good I hadn't even thought of the possibility until now. But the sharp intelligence in her dark eyes as they flicked from Seth to me and back again warned me not to take her at face value.

Outside, all emergency vehicles other than police units had departed, taking with them any sense of urgency. Now there was no chance of finding Azalea alive, speed was no longer of the essence. The focus had switched from recovery mode to investigative process.

I could only hope they'd be more successful in this case than they had been in Peter's.

In Seth's truck, I leaned back against the head rest and closed my eyes.

"You okay?" Seth took my hand, his fingers warm and reassuring.

"Better than Azalea," I replied bitterly. His grip tightened then relaxed. I opened my eyes. "Sorry. That was an awful thing to say. I just can't quite believe it yet. She was so vibrant, so energetic. I feel like I knew her so much longer than I did."

"I know what you mean." He pressed my hand again and then reached for the ignition. "Where do you want to go? Home? Work?"

The dashboard clock revealed it wasn't yet nine o'clock. The day had been decades long already. "Work. I need to tell my team before it all goes public. They deserve to know what happened first."

We made a detour to pick up doughnuts and coffee. I ordered an extra-large double-double instead of my usual medium black.

Seth asked to borrow my office so he could make some calls. "I need to get a few things covered, for this morning at least. We'll see how it goes after that."

I understood his reluctance to tempt Murphy's Law. I

was waiting for the other shoe to drop too. This was the calm before the storm.

I was so drained I could only think in clichés.

He found a parking spot on the street in front of the agency. We had bought sugar and caffeine for everyone, so our hands were full as we shouldered through the front door.

Maeve, Indra, and Piper stood in a solid line on the near side of the reception desk. They wore identically grim expressions. Even Indra, who rarely looked anything but chipper and enthusiastic. The other two could do irritated with the best of them.

"What is going on?" Indra scowled. I didn't know she could. "You answer the phone, go as pale as death, and scarper out of here without a word of explanation, muttering something about a *kidnapper*."

"I asked the police to call." At the gas station yesterday, before I left for the first ransom rendezvous, I'd badgered Tam into having an underling contact the agency and tell them whatever was appropriate. I knew they'd be wondering what the hell had happened.

"Yes. So helpful." Piper's sarcasm was unexpectedly comforting. That, at least, hadn't changed. She wiggled her fingers in air quotes and spoke in a nasally voice. "Ms. Blynde is helping us with our inquiries. Please do not attempt to contact her until otherwise notified."

To be honest, I hadn't really expected them to worry. Not as much as it seemed they had.

Maeve rounded off the attack. "And then nothing until a casual text at six-thirty this morning, as if it were an ordinary day. You have some explaining to do, Ginnie."

I heard Ricky Ricardo in my head and stifled a hysterical giggle.

"I'll let you deal with this." Seth placed his cardboard tray on a free corner of the desk and plucked his coffee from the holder. With one hand, he opened the box I carried, selecting a Boston Cream from the assortment. When he bent to kiss me, I raised my mouth to his without conscious thought. "I'll be as quick as I can."

He vanished into my office and shut the door.

Once again, my team greeted me with identical expressions. This time, open-mouthed shock. I sighed.

"This could take a while," I said. "Let's use Indra's office. Maeve, can you put the sign up?"

They trooped in behind me and we all found seats in Indra's cozy space. She had painted the walls a soothing green and her visitor's chairs were plump and comfortable.

"Enough stalling," Piper demanded. "Spill."

My report on the kidnapping and murder distracted my team from Seth's public display of affection, thank goodness. I had no idea what I would have said if they'd asked me to explain *that*.

"The poor woman." Indra sniffed and dabbed her eyes with a crumpled tissue.

"Her son must be devastated." Maeve's dislike of Carter had softened after learning the tragic news.

Thinking about Carter and what he must be going through made the back of my nose burn. He didn't deserve this. Azalea didn't deserve this. It was heartbreaking all round, and I wasn't sure he'd be able to handle it. My chest ached with pity.

The doughnuts were eaten, the coffee drunk, and Seth had joined us. Back throbbing, I shifted in my chair, seeking to relieve tense muscles. He reached out and rubbed my nape. I offered him an exhausted smile.

"Any idea how long she's been dead?" Piper, the analytical one, had asked incisive questions throughout my recital.

"I would guess days. But Carter spoke with his mom during the first ransom call so she must have been alive Monday night."

"This is crazy." Her knee bounced with nervous energy. "I can't believe it. I mean, I believe it, but I can't *believe* it."

I knew exactly what she meant. I'd seen Azalea's discarded corpse, and I still couldn't shake the feeling of unreality.

But it had happened. It was real. I desperately wished it wasn't, for so many reasons.

Maeve nodded her head slowly, her bun undisturbed. "Sometimes the world is a terrible place."

"Whoever did this needs to be punished. Needs to go to prison for years and years." The vindictive light in Indra's eyes contrasted sharply with her round, cheerful cheeks. "Hopefully the police catch him soon."

I'd trusted them to find Peter's killer and they'd gotten nowhere. "What if they don't? Sometimes the bad guy gets away."

Seth's grip on the back of my neck tightened for a moment before he resumed his soothing motion. "We'll have to trust that won't happen this time."

I couldn't get an image out of my mind—Carter huddled on my couch, bereft and broken, blaming himself for his mother's disappearance, fearing she was dead. Now that fear had come true. Who could he turn to? Who could help him get through this?

I couldn't replace his mother. But I'd never been good at sitting back and trusting others to solve my problems. I needed to *fix* this.

I pointed at Piper. "You're the internet wizard. Do you think you can find some time today to build a full portfolio on Azalea?"

Maeve spoke before Piper had a chance to reply. "Why?" She peered at me with suspicion.

Not quite ready to put my fledgling idea into words, I hedged my answer. "I told Carter I'd help. That I'd do what I could to find out what happened to his mother."

"But that was before...this morning." Indra's red-rimmed eyes widened. "You can't mean you'll go on with it."

I lifted my chin. "Yes, I do." I jumped from my seat and paced. Five steps one way, five steps back. Piper tucked her ankles under her chair to avoid being trampled. "The police will do whatever it is they do. Look for DNA, search for fingerprints, follow any technological trail. But that doesn't mean I can't ask questions too."

"Ginnie." Seth's patient tone raised my hackles. "You don't want to compromise the investigation by—"

"What's to compromise?" I stopped pacing and planted my hands on my hips. "Like it or not, I'm a part of this. The killer called *me*. *I* was the one who delivered the ransom."

I thought of something else. Not as important as Azalea's death, not as personal as Peter's unsolved case, but still something to take into account. "My business was attacked when Azalea went missing, remember? Can you imagine what it'll be like when her *murder* becomes public?"

My team sat silent as they absorbed that hard truth. Seth appeared unconvinced. I shoved aside his disapproval.

"I'm in." Piper rose and went to the door. "You looking for anything specific?"

My frustration at their initial lack of enthusiasm cooled. At least one of them was on board. "Review the background check we already did, make sure nothing jumps out in hindsight. Then follow the procedure for when someone hires us to look into a person they met outside the agency. You might keep an eye open for the names Belva Ginsberg and Coral Loughty." They were the only people I knew associated with Azalea. It was a logical place to start.

CHAPTER NINETEEN

PIPER NODDED, OPENED her mouth as if to say something, changed her mind, and vanished. The click of her office door closing punctuated the quiet she left behind.

I could feel Seth looking at me but avoided his gaze and directed my words to Maeve and Indra. "I know this skirts the line of what we do here. Fact-checking clients is one thing. Investigating a murder is something else entirely."

"I want to help, but I wouldn't know where to start." Indra spread her hands helplessly. "Piper, I get. She's scary when it comes to ferreting out information. But what can I do?"

"Azalea had to have been targeted. No halfway intelligent kidnapper would snatch a random woman off the street and expect her family to have enough money to pay a ransom. So how did he choose her?"

"She went to lots of charity galas and community events." Indra tapped her bottom lip with a neatly manicured fingernail. "I could take a look at what was hosted over the last few months, call up the organizers, find out if Azalea attended, if anyone showed any particular interest in her."

"Excellent. Do that."

"If you think of anything for me," Maeve said, resigned, "let me know. Until then, I'll keep the ship afloat. We still have a business to run."

I wondered if I was the only one to hear her unspoken *for now*. "I appreciate that." The survival of Blynde Dating

Agency was minor compared to murder. Yet I had a duty to my team and my clients to keep it afloat.

I stood in front of Seth. The lines around his eyes and mouth cut deeper than usual and his shoulders hunched forward. "Don't attempt to talk me out of this. I'm doing it."

"You need to think about it. Really think." He brushed one finger down my cheek, and I resisted the urge to lean into his touch. "This man has killed one woman already. What's to stop him from killing...again?"

You, he'd been about to say. I shivered.

"I won't do anything dangerous. I promise." I was just going to ask a few questions. It was probably a waste of time, but it was all I could do, and I had to do *something*.

For Azalea and her son. For my business. And for my own piece of mind.

"I need to see Carter." I headed for the door. "Can you take me home so I can get my car?"

Seth was silent as he drove, and I let him be. I might prefer to have his approval of my plan, but I didn't need it, and I certainly wasn't going to nag him into it.

He pulled into my driveway. I unbuckled my seatbelt while the wheels were still rolling.

"Wait." He put the truck in Park. "I've been thinking."

I didn't like the sound of that. I said with forced jocularity, "I could hear gears grinding but wasn't sure if it was your truck or you."

He drummed his fingers on the steering wheel. "You're determined to do this, aren't you?"

163

I studied his profile. A muscle in his jaw clenched rhythmically. "Yes."

"I don't like the idea of you putting yourself in the path of a killer." The twitching muscle sped up. "It could be dangerous."

"We vet people all the time. This won't be any riskier than that." I wasn't quite that naïve, but I wasn't going to let nebulous fear derail my intentions, either. "The minute I find out something important—*if* I find out something important—I'll tell the police."

"I would hope so." He slid me a sideways glance then returned to staring out the windshield. "I trust you not to do anything dumb. I can't help worrying, though. We've only known each other a short time, but I wouldn't want anything to happen to you."

My annoyance eased. "Nothing will. I promise." I hoped it was one I could keep.

"There's one other thing I'd like to know." He squared his shoulders and twisted to face me.

Now what? "Yes?"

"I get the feeling this is...personal. As if you have a deeper reason for going the extra mile than keeping your business operating or avenging a client or helping Carter."

It was a little troubling he could see through me like that, but there was no point in denying it. "I suppose I do."

"Care to share?" He focused on me, blue eyes patient and intent.

I hesitated. His tone was noncommittal. I could say no, and he wouldn't push. But if I did, it would be drawing a line in the sand. It would be a pivotal moment between us.

Maybe I could explain without baring my soul completely.

"You know I'm a widow. My husband's name was Peter." My fingers tangled together tightly. I hated talking about this.

He nodded.

"Just over two years ago, he went for a run after dinner, like he did almost every day." Well, not quite. We usually didn't have a marriage-defining argument before he left. "He was struck down by a vehicle and killed. The police never found who did it."

"That's terrible." He reached over and worked his fingers between mine. "It must be awful, not knowing the truth. Not having anyone to blame."

"Yes. I felt—still feel—that I should have done more. That I should have been able to help discover what happened. I don't want to feel that way two years from now about Azalea. I want to do all I can to resolve this."

"I can understand that, I guess." He squeezed my hand. "Just be careful, okay?"

"I will. I'm going to talk to people. Nothing more."

"All right." He searched my face and let out a long breath. "I have to go. There are a couple of work things I need to handle."

I leaned in and pressed my lips against his. His free hand cupped the back of my head. My tongue teased his mouth open, and I fanned the spark between us until it flared bright and sweet before pulling reluctantly away.

"Are we good?" I felt relieved and guilty in equal measures. Relieved that he had accepted my explanation.

Guilty that I hadn't told him the whole story. I wasn't ready to confess that Peter and I had been arguing about his infidelity. That I'd told him I would never forgive him, had shouted hateful, terrible things. Had basically chased him out the door and told him never to come back.

Which he hadn't.

Seth lifted my hand to his mouth and bussed my knuckles. "We're good. Call me later?"

"I will."

I waved him off and entered my house, smiling as I dealt with the security system he'd installed. His concern for my safety was sweet but unnecessary. I was a big girl. I could take care of myself.

The peace and quiet inside enfolded me and I took several deep inhalations as I headed to the en suite. I desperately needed a shower. Discovering Azalea's body had left a stain on my skin I had to wash away.

The hot water rinsed off my exhaustion as well. Invigorated and determined, dressed in clean clothes, hair loose down my back, I scrolled to Carter's number.

Mehta had warned me the police were still monitoring my calls. Even if they did consider me a suspect—I couldn't quite wrap my mind around that, but it was certainly a possibility—there would be nothing overtly suspicious about calling Carter to offer my condolences.

He answered on the third ring. My throat closed up at his tentative hello. What on earth did I say to a son whose mother had been found murdered?

Get it together, Blynde. Just be honest. "Carter. I am so sorry. I don't know what to say."

"Thank you."

I wasn't sure what I'd expected, but it wasn't the calm vacancy I heard. Had he been given a sedative? "I'd like to come see you."

"Belva and Coral are with me." The lack of emotion in his voice was disturbing, whatever it's cause.

"It's good that you're not alone. Would it be okay if I came over too?"

"Coral thought we should go to Mom's house. I can't bear to be there. I'm at my apartment."

"I understand." My anxiety over how Carter was handling Azalea's death intensified the longer I talked to him. "Please. Can I come over now?"

"I'd like that." The words were welcoming but the tone remained flat.

"What's your address?" He answered in the same monotone. I hung up and hurried to my car.

I debated my course of action as I drove. Belva and Coral had been on my list, but I'd wanted to speak with them separately, not in concert, and certainly not in Carter's presence.

I'd just have to see how things went.

Carter lived on the top floor of an upscale four-storey condominium complex. A brusque female voice answered my call and buzzed me through the entrance. I rode the elevator up, hands pressed into my pockets.

I should have brought something with me. Food or flowers. A sympathy card at the very least. I'd been on the receiving end of such gifts after Peter died. At the time, all I'd wanted was to be left alone and only belatedly appreciated the thought behind the offerings.

It wasn't like me to forget such social niceties. Maybe recent events had left me more muddleheaded than I believed.

The elevator opened into a small square lobby with two glossy black doors. The one on my left had a charcoal and cream winter-themed wreath hanging on it. The one on my right was bare.

The door with the wreath opened and Belva stood in the entrance. "You're here," she said flatly.

Pleased to see you too. "Hello. I am sorry for your loss."

She rolled one shoulder in passive acknowledgment. I wondered again at the incongruity of this dry, severe woman's friendship with someone like Azalea, whose presence filled a room with light. *Had* filled.

Reminding myself appearances were often deceiving, I stepped into the apartment, a model of modern architecture and decor. Huge floor to ceiling windows looked east, though the view of the city was partially blocked by a stand of tall pines and spruce bordering acres of soccer fields on the other side of the road. The furniture was white with clean lines and minimal upholstery. Artwork, mostly large undecipherable blotches and blobs, provided dramatic pops of ruby, sapphire, and amethyst.

Azalea had once hinted that Carousel, Carter's flower shop, was more of a pastime than a profession. Was it profitable enough to cover even half of the condo's expenses? I suspected family money was subsidizing both.

Speaking of flowers...almost every flat surface was laden with an elegant arrangement in hues that complemented the artwork. I was relieved I hadn't picked up a bouquet from the grocery store. Talk about carrying coal to Newcastle.

Two small sofas and two low armchairs were gathered around a knee-high glass-topped table in the middle of the spacious living room. Carter sat at the end of one of the sofas, Coral in one of the matching armchairs. She greeted me with a jerky nod, her eyes noticeably swollen and red, her face pale.

I lowered to the cushion beside Carter. It was hard and unyielding. "I am so sorry about your mother. How are you holding up?" Though I kept my tone low and soft, the apartment was so quiet my words rippled through it like pebbles tossed into a pond.

"I don't know." He turned his head toward me, his expression disconcertingly blank. "I feel kind of fuzzy."

"The doctor gave him a pill." Behind the sofa, Belva loomed like a bird of prey. Her head jutted forward at a belligerent angle, chin cocked, shoulders hunched. She was dressed all in black. It might have been in deference to Azalea, but I had the feeling it was her customary wardrobe choice.

"He didn't want to take it, but we insisted." Coral toyed with the string at the neck of her navy-blue sweatshirt. This subdued shade was a definite contrast to the vibrant tints I'd seen her wear the other times we'd met. "The poor boy's so distraught."

"You were there when they found her." Carter turned toward me. His head wobbled, as if his neck was struggling to hold it up. "You saw her. Was she...did she..." He gave a short sobbing gasp and buried his face in his hands.

CHAPTER TWENTY

NO WAY IN HELL would I give him a description of the scene, if that's what he was asking. "Yes, I was there. Have the police given you any information?"

"They told me about the storage unit." Carter lifted his head, his earlier wiped-clean expression now cracked and shattered. "I begged them for more, but they won't say anything else. They must know more. Why won't they tell me?" Carter tucked his hands into his armpits and huddled into himself.

"You're cold. Let me get you a sweater." Coral jumped out of her seat and hurried out of sight. Carter watched her go with empty eyes.

"They're not telling me anything, either," I said. "What happened after you left my house with the police on Tuesday night?"

"He's in no condition to be answering questions." Belva gripped the back of the couch with bony fingers and glared at me. "Especially nosy, inquisitive questions that you have no right to ask."

Carter appeared to be fighting through his fog. "I don't mind. Ginnie's my friend. She's helping me."

I resisted the urge to squirm. I had done little to earn this commendation. "You don't have to. Not if it will upset you."

"It won't. What's the worst that can happen now?" His lips bent in a tragic smile, inviting me to share in the terrible irony. "What do you want to know?"

"Where did you go when you left my place with Tam

and the others?"

"To the police station. They asked me all sorts of questions. Did I know anyone who was angry with my mom. Was I aware of anything suspicious happening in the last few weeks." He fell silent.

I waited for more. When it wasn't forthcoming, I gave him a gentle nudge. "And had you? Seen anything odd, I mean?"

"No, of course not." A spark of pride brightened his voice. "Everybody loved Mom. You couldn't stay angry at her. Not for long. And everything had been normal as far as I knew."

"How long were you at the police station?"

"Until about midnight. They let me come home then. A couple of officers stayed with me. Early yesterday morning more officers came. They set up some sort of communications centre over there." He waved a hand toward a long dark wood table surrounded by tall-backed chairs near the window. "They took it away today after"—he choked, and tears thickened his voice—"after they told me she'd been found."

Coral reappeared with a pale blue cashmere cardigan. "Here you go." She draped it over Carter. He appeared not to notice.

Belva patted his shoulder in an awkward show of comfort. "Maybe you should rest. You don't need to do this." She shot me a venomous look. The hairs on the nape of my neck stood up. Were the few questions I'd asked enough to engender such hostility? Or was I missing something?

"It's okay." Carter picked up the glass of water sitting on

the table in front of him, sipped it, and then took another sip before continuing. "When the kidnapper didn't call at noon, even more police came. I got the feeling they didn't know what to do next."

I could commiserate. I didn't know what to do next either. "Did you have company the whole time?" I hated to think of him going through the agony of waiting alone.

"Yes. Mostly they talked among themselves and ignored me. I didn't mind. I tried to watch TV in my bedroom. It was just white noise. All I could think about was my mom."

"I don't know why you didn't call me. I had no idea what was going on or I would have come to take care of you." Coral might have been trying to sound sympathetic, but peevishness leaked through.

Maybe she heard it herself, because she sniffed and wiped invisible tears from her cheeks. "I'm sorry. I'm just so upset. Azalea was my best friend. I can't believe she's gone."

Belva was still glaring at me like I'd kicked her puppy, but Coral seemed eager to talk. "When did you find out?"

"I called Carter a few hours ago to see if he'd heard anything. He told me then. I was devastated but insisted on coming over immediately. I knew he would need me."

An odd sense of satisfaction lurked behind the concerned smile she gave him. Before I could address that, Belva spoke.

"I think it's time you went. After all, you barely knew Azalea."

I couldn't stand her hovering over me like an attack dog any longer, so I rose, circled the table, and sat on the opposite sofa. "She wasn't just a client to me. I liked her. And I like

Carter. I'm here to support him."

Belva's thin cheeks flushed. "What good have you been so far? Azalea disappeared after a date you arranged. You were the person the kidnapper called to deliver the ransom. You were there when her b-body was found." The tiny stutter was the first sign of distress I'd seen in her.

"You're right. Now explain how I have benefitted from any of it. Because that's what you're implying, isn't it?"

Her jaw jutted. "I don't know how. But the police will find out."

"That's enough, Belva." Carter rubbed his eyes with the heels of his hands. "You're just looking for someone to blame. We all are. But it's not Ginnie."

Her lips pressed together. The lines of strain creasing her mouth made her look older, even more severe.

Pity flared and I asked my next question quietly, stamping down the rancor her accusation had ignited. "Earlier this week, you told me the last time you saw Azalea was the Monday evening you and I first met. You didn't have any contact with her after that?"

Belva's eyelids fluttered. "I spoke to her the next day. Tuesday," she conceded sullenly. "She asked me to look into one of her investments."

"Was that something she often did?" Azalea hadn't been a micro-manager when it came to dating, but who knew what she was like with her personal finances?

"Not often, but it wasn't unheard of." Belva's reply was sharp and irritated. I was losing her.

"Was there something special about this particular request? Did she seem worried or anxious at all?"

"No."

I wondered if the kidnapper had tried to extort Azalea before taking the drastic step of abduction. "Did she ever ask for large sums without explanation?"

But Belva wasn't willing to cooperate any longer. "You have no business snooping about Azalea's private affairs."

"Yes, Ginnie, that's not cool," Coral echoed. "You're not the police."

She inflected the pronoun, and I wondered if Tam had asked the same questions. Was I following a trail already trampled by the authorities?

Carter sat silent, paying us no attention. His gaze was abstract, staring at nothing. I stood up. "If there's anything you need, Carter, please let me know." To the women I said, "I'll see myself out."

Despite this, Belva followed me to the door. She even waited to make sure I got on the elevator. I wasn't sure what she thought I would do if not escorted—hide in a spare room perhaps? For what reason?

My phone buzzed with a text as I stepped into the main floor lobby.

Help, Maeve wrote. *We are besieged.*

She wasn't exaggerating. Despite the signs stating our parking lot was for employees and clients of nearby businesses only, it was jammed with marked media vehicles. I found a space on a cross street and hustled toward the office.

At the corner, I stopped. The sidewalk in front of our agency was boiling with reporters in tidy but warm wool coats, camera operators wearing parkas emblazoned with station logos, and the eclectic crowd of onlookers such a scrum invariably attracted. I eased out of view and headed for the alley. No one had staked out the rear entrance. I trotted unmolested through the frozen slush and slipped inside.

In the reception area, Maeve and Indra chatted quietly. The throng was visible through the wide window to the right of the front door, but no one was attempting to enter.

"When did they show up?" I unwound my scarf and stood beside Indra, facing the window. At the moment, no one outside was paying us any attention, though it still felt like being on the wrong side of an aquarium.

"The first arrived about half an hour ago." Maeve pointed at a lanky bald man and short blond woman. "A television reporter and his camera operator. They were standing at my desk before I realized who they were."

"Did you speak with them?"

"If you don't count 'please leave,' then no. You said not to."

"The police said not to," I corrected absently. "We're just following instructions. How did you get them to go?"

"I refused to answer his questions, and he finally gave up. He was mainly interested in talking to you. As soon as they were out, I locked the door."

"I wonder how long they'll stay." The crowd didn't seem to be thinning. As I watched, another vehicle pulled up, stopped long enough to eject a heavily made-up woman wielding a selfie-stick, and then drove away.

"It's already been too long," Maeve said grimly. "I had

two no-shows for the applicant interviews you asked me to handle. Both of them used that horde as an excuse."

"I recognize one of the reporters from a station in Vancouver," Indra said. "I don't know how they got here so fast. The media release only went out about an hour ago."

"I imagine they have other sources. Maybe they found out about the abduction and were already on their way up." I navigated to the web browser on my phone and searched *Azalea Bickersley*. I needed to read that release. "Where's Piper?"

Maeve snorted. "She said we were thinking too loud and went home to work shortly after you left. She's missing the show."

I scrolled through my search results until I found a PDF of what the RCMP had released. A quick scan revealed it was skimpy on details and hadn't mentioned Blynde Dating at all. Mehta had warned me we'd be targeted, but I hadn't really believed her. How had they linked us to the murder so fast?

Oh. Right.

"Damn Facebook posts."

Indra and Maeve looked at me, eyebrows raised.

"That must be why they're here," I explained. "They found the Facebook posts warning people away from us after Azalea went missing."

If we ignored them, they'd go away sooner or later. But sooner was definitely preferable.

"They want to talk to me, right?" Maeve nodded. "Did they give any hint they knew I was involved with delivering the ransom or finding Azalea's body?"

She shook her head. "No. They asked for the owner, mentioning you by name. That's all."

I sucked in a deep breath and wrapped my scarf around my neck again. "I'm going out there. Maybe I can get them to leave."

"But we're not supposed to talk to them." Indra wrung her hands.

"I won't say anything about the investigation. But I have to try. We can't have them scaring away any more clients."

I unlocked the front door and stepped onto the sidewalk. All heads swung my way. Questions rained down as bodies jostled for position, hands extending cellphones and cameras.

I remained silent. The tip of my nose tingled with cold. Slowly the cacophony quieted.

"I have a short statement to make." Gah. I probably should have prepared something before leaving the sanctuary of the office. Too late now.

More questions peppered the chilly air. It gave me time to sort out my thoughts. Once they realized I wasn't going to answer, they quieted again.

"I have been asked by the RCMP to direct all inquiries to them, so I will not be commenting on their investigation. I will say that what happened to Azalea Bickersley is a tragedy and Blynde Dating Agency will be providing the police all possible assistance."

A hail of questions followed. Out of the deluge, one stood out. "Have they asked to access your client list?"

Oh, god. I hadn't even thought of that. "You'll have to ask them."

I repeated that mantra several more times. Into a sudden lull, a new question dropped.

"Do you have any comment on the arrest of Seth Updike?"

My breath discharged in a puff of condensation. "What?"

The reporter, a man with curly salt-and-pepper hair and a wide nose, waggled his phone at me. "I just received word that a man named Seth Updike has been taken in for questioning. Do you know who he is? What connection does he have with Azalea?"

"You'll have to speak with the RCMP about that," I repeated mechanically. I cleared my throat and opened the door enough to squeeze through. "Please leave. I have nothing more to say." I stepped inside and shot the bolt.

"How did it go?" Indra asked.

"Seth's been arrested." The words fell clumsily from my numb lips. "One of the reporters asked me about it."

She clapped a hand to her mouth. Maeve's lips pressed so tight they disappeared.

"No." Indra shook her head. "I don't believe it. Maybe the reporter was yanking your chain, trying to get you to reveal something."

"Why would he think I cared? No one knows about me and Seth."

Except my team. And whoever Seth might have told. Maybe it wasn't as close a secret as I thought.

"Look."

Maeve pointed out the window and I turned my head.

The sidewalk was empty. They were hunting fresher prey.

CHAPTER TWENTY-ONE

I IMMEDIATELY CALLED Seth. There was a chance the reporter had been misinformed. Or lying. My call went unanswered, and the chance grew slimmer.

I left a message. The police were welcome to listen to it. I wasn't going to abandon Seth and didn't care who knew.

The afternoon wore on. In between fielding phone inquiries from persistent members of the media, we soothed panicked clients—to no avail, mostly. Our database was losing entries as fast as residents of a medieval village succumbing to the Black Plague.

I itched to call Seth again, but knew it was pointless. He would get in touch when he could.

If he could.

I wasn't going to think about that.

When my phone rang and Lillian's name appeared on my screen, I stared at it blankly. Then my mental gears shifted with a jolting clunk into friend mode. "Hey, there. Are you a grandma yet?"

"This morning at 11:37." She sounded dazed but happy. "A boy. Seven pounds, eight ounces. They haven't decided on a name yet."

"Congratulations! How's the new momma doing?"

"Awesome. It was a long labour..." She went into details, and I did my best to respond appropriately. It wasn't easy. My attention kept drifting to Seth and Azalea.

Lillian wound down. "I'm sticking around for a few

more days, help them get settled. I should be back in time for dance class next week." In the background I heard a muffled but unmistakable hospital public address announcement. "Speaking of which...did you ever call that hottie you told me about?"

A giggle escaped. Then a full-blown laugh. I might have been a little hysterical. I was so tired of holding it together. "Yeah. About that." I choked back more snickers. "Are you in a hurry?"

"Everyone's napping right now. I have some time. What's up?"

"You can't tell anyone, Lillian. Promise me."

"Now you're scaring me. Of course I promise."

It took me several minutes, and I don't know how coherent my story was, but I felt lighter for having told it.

"Oh, my god," Lillian said. "You had sex with a murderer."

"Seth's not a murderer," I replied sharply.

"Isn't that what they all say? 'He was such a nice, quiet neighbour. Who knew he had a woman shackled to the wall in the basement?'"

"Stop it." This wasn't the reaction I'd expected. I regretted telling her.

"I'm sorry. I shouldn't be teasing you." Her tone sobered. "Still. You only met the man last week. What do you really know about him?"

"I read his profile when he signed up for the agency. I know his favourite colour and what kind of books he likes to read. I know what type of woman he's looking for. I know he has a daughter, likes outdoor activities, owns a construction company." So much and yet so little.

"None of which rules out criminal tendencies. What about the important stuff? Who's the mother of his daughter? Was he married before? Could he be married now? Is his company solvent or failing?"

Sweat sprang up on my palms. Seth's application had indicated his last long-term relationship had ended more than a decade ago, but he wouldn't be the first person to lie on the form. And during the long conversations we'd had, he'd been reticent to speak of his past. It had seemed perfectly innocent at the time. After all, I hadn't told him everything, either.

But now it took on a sinister cast.

"I want to trust him, Lillian." She would hear the entreaty in my voice. She knew me too well not to. "He's the first man I've felt close to since I found out Peter cheated on me." I would cling stubbornly to that trust until proven otherwise. Despite my misgivings, despite Lillian's suspicions, I knew Seth was a good guy. Knew it in my bones.

A sigh billowed into my ear. "I feel responsible. If I hadn't encouraged you to go out with him..."

"I'd still be tangled up in this because of Azalea. She was a client, remember."

"It's a lot to handle. Are you doing okay? Really okay? This is me you're talking to."

"I'm fine."

"Do you want me to come home? I can catch a flight tomorrow."

There. There was the Lillian I knew. My emotions settled with the offer. "No, of course not. Stay, enjoy that new grandbaby."

"Call me if you need me. I mean it. Anytime. We'll probably be up all hours with the little one, anyway."

I disconnected and laid my phone on my desk. As much as I hated it, Lillian's concerns were warranted. How well did I really know Seth? Had I let sexual attraction dull my survival instincts?

No. I couldn't be that stupid. My imagination was running amok, that's all. I needed to see him. Needed to talk with him. But until then, I had a business to save.

I'd hoped to hear from Piper before the end of the day, but she remained incommunicado. That was her modus operandi—locking herself away until her task was complete—and I'd learned there was no point in nagging her. She'd let me know when she had something worth sharing.

Indra had compiled a list of charity and society functions during the last six months. In between her usual duties, she was calling organizers, asking whether Azalea had attended, and if so, had anything caught their attention.

"The trouble I'm having," she told me, "is that many of these events are run by volunteer committee. And committee members swap out more often than Taylor Swift makes costume changes during a concert."

"Please keep at it." I didn't have high hopes for this strategy, but Azalea's social life was one of the only avenues we had the resources to investigate. "Now, though, it's time to go home. It's been a crazy day, and who knows what tomorrow will bring."

I shooed Indra into the front office and repeated my directive to Maeve. She squinted at me, her usually stern expression softened with concern. "What about you? To be blunt, you look terrible."

I felt terrible too. Drained and frustrated and worried, all tangled in a ball of insecurity and sorrow. "Soon. I have a couple of things to wrap up. Then I'll go straight home. I promise."

They went, Indra looking over her shoulder with an anxious yet sweetly suspicious expression. I kept my word, however, and left once I had finished reviewing the increasingly depressing website stats. At least our Facebook hater hadn't posted anything today.

At home, I poured a large glass of wine and set a pot of water on to boil. Today called for comfort carbs and lots of them. Macaroni and cheese would fit the bill nicely.

In the living room, I collapsed into my chair. My gaze wandered to the mantel, catching on the empty space where my wedding portrait used to be. I'd forgotten that mystery in the strife of the last couple days. It seemed rather petty to worry about it now.

It did remind me about my security system, though. I wasn't yet in the habit of arming it every time I came home and realized I had forgotten this evening. Too lazy to walk to the main panel, I used the app to activate it and felt more of my tension ease.

Not that I expected the killer to show up on my doorstep. And if he did, *he* was the one who should be scared. I had a bitter, angry bone to pick with him.

SUSPECT ATTRACTION

Half an hour or so later, as I scraped the last of my macaroni from the bowl, my phone rang. My heart thudded, a heavy, uncomfortable thump of remembered terror, before expanding with relief. Seth.

In my eagerness, it took two tries to swipe the screen correctly. "It's me," I said, managing to sound both breathless and idiotic. "Are you okay? What's going on? Where are you?"

"I'm at home. I'm okay. They let me go." He sounded empty of all emotion, listless, exhausted.

"So, it's true? You were arrested?"

"No, not arrested. Interviewed, though. Interrogated. I was there for six hours."

"Why? You'd already told them everything,"

"I'm still the last person known to have seen Azalea alive."

I heard swallowing. Another man would probably be shooting back scotch after such a harrowing day. With his alcohol allergy, that release was denied Seth, and I wondered what he turned to.

He continued bleakly. "I kept expecting them to demand to search my house, my truck, my office. But all they asked was if they could examine my phone."

"Did you let them?" My hand clenched into a fist.

"If I didn't, it would look suspicious. Since I have nothing to hide, it was a waste of their time." Irritation burned through his despair.

Eager to accept his annoyance as evidence of innocence, my muscles relaxed. "I'm so sorry you had to go through all that." I was apologizing an awful lot lately. Even for a

Canadian.

"Not your fault." More swallowing, and then he drew in a breath. "How's the sleuthing going? The cops squandered a day on me. I hope you made more progress."

I hated to disappoint him. "Not really. I visited Carter to offer my condolences. Coral and Belva were there."

"Do I know who they are?"

I had a vague recollection of Carter mentioning them the night he and Seth were at my house, but I doubted we'd given Seth any particulars. "Coral Loughty is Azalea's best friend. They've known each other for decades. Belva Ginsberg is a more recent friend and also Azalea's accountant-slash-financial advisor. I asked a few questions, but didn't have the heart to push too hard. Carter had been given a sedative and was pretty loopy."

For a moment we were both quiet. "You're really okay?" I asked again. I'd be a mess if the circumstances had been reversed. "It must have been terrifying."

"It wasn't pleasant. But in some ways, it was simple. All I had to do was tell them the truth. Over and over and over again."

"Do you want company?" I wanted to comfort him but was seeking my own reassurance as well. "It's okay if you say no. Maybe you'd rather be alone or talk with your daughter. It's too bad she lives so far away."

"I miss her every day. I won't be calling her, though. I haven't told her what's going on and she's smart. She might hear something in my voice." He whispered the next words. "I hope she never finds out about all this."

He didn't need me to point out the obvious—that if the

murderer wasn't caught soon, it would be better to come clean before she discovered his involvement via the media. "So, about that company?"

"Yes," he said. "I want company. But only you, Ginnie. All I need is you."

For some reason I'd expected Seth to live in an ultra-modern house in one of the brand-new subdivisions south-west of downtown. He was a contractor after all, and I'd assumed his home would be a showcase.

Instead, he lived on a small acreage just outside the city limits in a long, low rancher that had to be fifty years old. Not that it wasn't well-kept. Even in the winter twilight, I could see the board fences lining the long, recently plowed drive were freshly painted, the house had modern siding and windows, and the many outbuildings were tended and tidy. It exuded an air of simple, unpretentious coziness.

I had fallen in love before I reached the wide-open parking space near the attached double garage.

He must have been watching for me, as I didn't have time to knock before the door opened. "You found it all right, then." He ushered me in.

"No problem at all." The houses were scattered and isolated in this rural area, but his instructions had been easy to follow.

He hung my coat in the closet, waited until I'd toed off my boots, and then enfolded me into a hug. The embrace told me more about his desperate state of mind than any words. I held on tight and let him draw what strength he could from my presence.

"Thanks for coming." He pressed a kiss to the top of my head before releasing me.

"You're welcome." I laid a palm on his chest and felt the heat of his body seep through the thin cotton of his shirt. His blue eyes glittered into mine. "I'm glad to be here."

He stepped back and I got my first good look at the interior of Seth's home.

As much as I'd loved the outside, the inside took my breath away.

"Wow." My mouth dropped open. "Seth. This is gorgeous. Did you do it yourself?"

"My design and my crew, yes. Would you like a tour?"

"Very much."

I'd come in the front door, which opened into a spacious foyer. A sunken living room to my right boasted a fieldstone fireplace. It was perfectly complemented by the contemporary hardwood flooring, squishy leather seating, and wide bay window. Ahead of me, a kitchen any chef would kill to call their own boasted acres of ebony cupboards, quartz counters, pendant lighting, a natural gas stove and double-wide refrigerator.

Seth explained the renovation as we moved from the main living area to the hallway, pointing out where he'd knocked down walls and repurposed spaces.

The main bath was an oasis of seafoam green hues, glistening tile, and gleaming fixtures. "I could live in here," I said.

"Wait until you see the en suite." His grin sparkled as brightly as the LED lighting and his eyes had lost their haunted expression.

Pleased he'd shrugged off the day's trauma, I grinned back. "What's in here?" I reached for the handle of a closed door.

"Nothing." He stepped forward abruptly and pressed his back against the panel. "That was Grace's bedroom when she lived here. It's become a bit of a catchall. I'd be embarrassed for you to see it."

"It can't be that bad." I reached forward again, chuckling.

He snagged my hand, brought it to his mouth, and brushed his lips tantalizingly across my knuckles. "Wouldn't you rather check out *my* bedroom?"

Bubbles fizzed up my arm and settled low in my belly. "Now there's an idea."

CHAPTER TWENTY-TWO

HE LED ME TO the master suite, a peaceful sanctuary of dark wood furniture and navy-blue paint. And he was right—the attached bathroom did put the main one to shame. Jacuzzi tub, huge glass-walled shower, heated floor. "I change my mind," I said. "I want to live here."

"It's nice, isn't it."

"Understatement of the year." I gave it one last longing glance before turning back to the bedroom.

Throughout the tour, Lillian's warnings niggled at the back of my mind. But no matter how hard I looked, I saw no evidence of a woman in Seth's life. The few photos on display showed Grace—Seth had proudly pointed her out—at various ages, some with her father, most solo shots. No cosmetics cluttered either bathroom counter, no jewellery lay discarded on the dresser. The house was neat, but not obsessively so, and all the belongings I did see could easily be ascribed to Seth.

I'd known I had nothing to worry about. Regardless, it was a relief to be certain.

I paused at the foot of the bed, the smooth counterpane and plump pillows simply begging to be messed up.

"Well." I tugged his belt loops to draw him nearer. "Thanks for the tour."

"You're welcome." His hands settled on my hips, warm and firm. I leaned in, my breasts brushing his torso. "Thanks for taking my mind off everything."

"My pleasure." Sparks of attraction skittered over my skin. His eyes darkened as I danced my fingertips up his chest and over his full lips. "I wonder what we should do now?"

He nipped with gentle teeth. I slipped my thumb into his mouth. His tongue swirled the tip with erotic slowness before releasing it. "Have something in mind?"

My core liquefied, igniting with heat. I stretched up and nibbled his neck. "You bet I do."

Our first time together had been playful, exploratory. This time we went up in flames, reckless and desperate.

Maybe it was the stresses we were under. Maybe it was an impetuous celebration of life.

Whatever it was, we both felt it. Our actions were frantic, wild. In moments our clothes were strewn about the room, the bed covers tossed back, and we fell onto the sheets in a tangle of arms and legs, mouths and hands.

Plumping my breasts together, he tasted them, switching from one to the other, bringing me to the edge then drawing me back, again and again. I pulled his hair and muttered increasingly incoherent commands, which he ignored.

He slid lower, between my legs, and licked, long and languorous strokes, with a final little flick that hit me just right. One...two...three. I exploded, a maelstrom of stars rocketing behind my closed eyes, my shriek echoing in the empty house.

I lay there, dazed and panting. He reached into the nightstand and extracted a condom. "Thank god," I said drunkenly. "Were you a Boy Scout?"

His grin was wicked, his cheekbones fiery red. He

propped my hips up on a pillow, tugging me this way and that. I didn't have the strength to protest. Not that I wanted to. His assertiveness rekindled my lust, and I let him arrange me exactly where he wanted me.

He placed my feet flat on the mattress and swept his hands up my shins, down my thighs. His cock, swollen and ready, bobbed against his abdomen. He sat on his heels, thumbs holding me open, dipping inside, and seemed content to toy with me.

Well, I wasn't content. I lifted my hips. "Fill me, Seth. Please fill me."

"Not yet." He continued to play with me, tickling and teasing, until I was writhing once more.

"Now," I begged. "Now, oh god, now, please."

Bracing himself with his hands near my shoulders, he knelt over me and slowly, tormentingly, filled me.

I wrapped my arms and legs around him and clung as he rode us both into oblivion.

I woke up lying on my side, one arm tingling from compressed nerves. Weak moonlight streamed in the tall narrow windows that flanked the head of the bed, glossing everything in silver.

Seth's hand rested on my hip, heavy and warm. Long, slow breaths wafted against my nape.

I needed to pee.

Moving slowly, I slid out from under his arm. My hair tugged and I had an awkward moment, half on and half off the mattress, before I extricated the long strands from beneath his shoulder. I found my blouse on the floor, shrugged it on against the chill of the house, and made my yawning way to the main bath.

I could have used the en suite, I suppose, but in my sleep-addled state I figured I was a guest in Seth's house and, as such, should use the guest facilities.

I hadn't meant to stay over. But all the disruptive nights I'd spent the last week or so had caught up with me, and I'd fallen asleep while Seth was disposing of the condom. He had woken me up long enough to invite me to stay, and I'd been too cozy and peaceful to refuse the offer.

I had no idea what time it was. Once I'd relieved myself and washed up, I peeked into the kitchen and checked the clock on the stove. Five forty-seven. I needed to go home before I went to work. Now I was up, I might as well stay up.

Tiptoeing down the hall, I decided I would get dressed before waking Seth to let him know I was leaving. I passed the closed door to Grace's old room and hesitated, grinning through another yawn as I recalled his pained expression when I'd asked to look inside. Given the neatness of the rest of his home, I doubted it was as much of a disaster as he'd implied.

Then a thought struck me. A nasty, suspicious thought that Seth didn't deserve.

I had no right to do what I did next. I like to think if I hadn't been half-asleep, I would never have done it. But that is just making excuses.

I opened the door.

And ruined everything.

The room was small. A single bed with a white headboard and a bare mattress rested under the window and a white dresser stood against the wall on my right. Several cardboard boxes were piled in one corner and six or so large plastic containers in another.

The innocent view calmed the worst of my qualms. It was ridiculous to suspect Seth was hiding something other than a messy room. A wave of tenderness swept over me. He was obviously more house proud than me if he felt it necessary to hide this neat clutter.

I didn't bother turning on the light as I drifted a couple of steps further in. Flattened boxes leaned against one wall. A black felt marker and packing tape dispenser lay on the dresser next to a stack of frames.

I picked up the top frame, tilting it so the moonlight revealed its contents, the colours muted in the dimness of the room.

A woman with long dark hair, dark eyes, and dusky skin smiled up at me. She sat in a Muskoka chair on a dock, a lake lined with cabins in the background, and held a wineglass high as if toasting the photographer.

The next photo showed the same woman, though several years younger, holding a baby. In the next, another version hugged a teenage girl—Grace, I realized after a few seconds—their cheeks pressed together. Seth's daughter wore a flat graduation cap and a black gown and bore a strong resemblance to the unknown woman.

I laid the three photos down with careful precision and

noted with odd detachment that my hands were trembling. My breath sawed in and out of my lungs as if my throat was made of jagged crystal.

I reached for the light switch and blinked when brightness flooded the room.

Two photos remained.

In one of these, a very young Seth smiled proudly, his black tuxedo stiff with newness. The woman clung to his arm, her shiny black hair covered by a gauzy veil, a sweeping white wedding dress draping from her breasts to the floor. She gazed up at him adoringly.

In the other, Seth, looking much as he did today, and the woman sat on a white sand beach, palm trees in the background. His arm stretched forward in the unmistakable selfie pose. Her head rested on his shoulder and their matching smiles glowed.

I set the frames on the dresser, propping them up against the wall. The couple from the past and the couple from the present stared back at me, expressions frozen in time.

Every doubt, every reservation, every misgiving I'd ever had about Seth came rushing back.

He was a liar. Just as Peter had been a liar.

And I was an idiot.

Seth's sleep roughened voice called from the bedroom. "Ginnie?"

I didn't move. Couldn't. I simply waited. A minute or two later, footsteps thudded softly. A swiftly indrawn breath declared Seth had seen the light falling into the hall. The footsteps quickened.

A swirl of air told me he'd entered the room, but I didn't

look up. He said nothing.

I brushed the image of the bride with one finger, the glass cool and smooth. "Who is she, Seth?" My voice was firm and composed, I was pleased to note.

He paused, only an instant, but it felt like forever. And in that pause all my unspoken hopes for the future shattered like ice on a shallow pond.

"I shouldn't have hidden them." He sounded resigned. But not guilty. Not ashamed. "I should have told you about her."

Wrath coiled in my gut. How could he not feel remorse? He'd sat in my office the day we'd met and told me his last relationship had ended a decade ago. The beach photo betrayed that falsehood. "Who is she?" I repeated through clenched teeth.

"Priya Jatt," he said quietly. "My wife."

I was not shocked by his admission.

"You're married." My hands clenched into fists, and I crossed my arms, curling into the stabbing pain lancing my stomach. A cool draft reminded me I wore nothing but an unbuttoned blouse that barely reached my hips. I started for the door, head averted so he wouldn't see the devastation I knew was plastered on my face. "I need to get dressed."

He let me pass without comment and followed me to the bedroom. I was excruciatingly aware of my ass hanging in full view. My misery morphed into fury. Humiliation did that to a woman.

"I *was* married." Seth spoke softly. "She passed away."

I paused the search for my clothes but kept my head down. I could see his legs out of the corner of my eye. He'd put on sweatpants at some point. How dare he have the presence of mind to get dressed?

"And of *course* I believe you. You've been completely forthright up until now. Well, that makes it all better." My sarcasm was saccharine sweet.

"It's the truth. She's been gone two years and one month. Almost exactly."

"Fine. She's dead." He sucked in a breath. I felt a pinch of regret for my bluntness but steamrollered on. "Why the big secret? Why not just tell me? I told you how my husband died. That might have been a good time. Pretty easy to segue into the topic then." I sat on the bed and thrust one foot into my panties with a violent shove.

"I know."

I caught a toe in the second leg-hole and wriggled it free. "I assume she's Grace's mother. Or is there another woman you're not telling me about?"

"Ginnie—"

"No. You don't get to sound hurt. I'm the one who was lied to." I suppressed the nagging voice that reminded me I hadn't been completely honest with him, either.

"Do you recognize the name? Priya Jatt?"

"No." I frowned. "Should I?"

"She was a writer. Novels. Literary fiction. Her debut won the Giller Prize."

"I don't read much literary stuff." My slacks were half under the bed. I snatched them out, pulled them on, and felt a burst of relief. This was not a conversation to have naked.

"I thought you might recognize it anyway. For a different reason."

"Why should I?" My bra was on the floor behind Seth. The heel of his bare foot was on the strap. I decided I didn't need it and buttoned my blouse.

"Because I think she had an affair with your husband."

CHAPTER TWENTY-THREE

MY BRAIN JAMMED like the wheel of a grocery cart on a discarded grape.

Mouth gaping, I looked at him straight on for the first time since I'd found the photos. He was naked from the waist up, hair rumpled, expression bleak. The shame slashing across his features was proof he'd lied again.

He didn't just *think*. He *knew*.

My mind kicked into gear, the jolt an almost physical sensation. I managed to stutter, "W-what? What do you mean?"

"I could be wrong. She never told me. I'm just guessing."

He didn't believe his own words. He knew he was right. I waited for more, shock holding my tongue.

"That's partly why I didn't say anything before." He winced. "And that sounds like I lied to protect you, but that's not the whole truth. I almost told you Wednesday, after we had sex the first time, but I chickened out. I was a coward."

We need to talk. He had been thinking about our dead spouses, not our budding relationship. Conflicting emotions snarled like a loose ball of yarn in my belly. I swallowed down nausea. "Tell me. Tell me everything."

He jerked his thumb over his bare shoulder. "I'll be back in a minute. Will you wait? Please wait."

I nodded. He didn't have to worry I would flee. My legs didn't have the strength to stand.

He disappeared down the hall. I sat, trying to knit all I'd

learned in the last minutes into a recognizable shape.

He returned with a manila envelope. "I found this about a month ago." He handed it to me and then lowered himself to the mattress an arm's length away, moving slowly. Like an old man. Or a bomb disposal specialist.

I lifted the flap and drew out several sheets of paper. A newspaper clipping fluttered to the floor and I bent to retrieve it.

A photo of Peter slapped me, propelling my already spinning head into a faster whirl. My heart pounded as if I'd run up several flights of stairs. It was the write-up following his hit-and-run accident.

Prince George no longer had a daily newspaper with home delivery. One issue was published weekly. If you wanted a copy you had to search for a neighbourhood box and get it yourself. Whoever had clipped this story had thought it important enough to go to all that trouble.

Other sheets were computer printouts of a later online story, his obituary, and an ad for Blynde Dating Agency. I laid them on my lap and pressed my hands onto them, paper crinkling under the force. "What is all this?"

"I found them when I was packing away Priya's things." His mouth quirked in a strained smile. "I'd been putting off doing that for far too long. It seemed so...final."

I knew what he meant. I still had boxes of Peter's belongings. I would never open them, never need anything from them, but I couldn't bear to get rid of them, either.

"At first I thought maybe they were an idea for a new book," Seth said. "But then I noticed the date and things started to fall into place."

They were starting to fall into place for me too. He'd said his wife had died two years and one month ago. That was about six weeks after Peter had confessed he'd been having an affair. After I had screamed at him, demanding a divorce.

After he'd died.

"Priya experienced depression and anxiety. She dealt with it through yoga and meditation and therapy until Grace was born. Postpartum, though, she had real difficulties, which required medication. That was one of the reasons we decided not to have more children."

"What does that have to do with Peter?"

"In the months before your husband was killed"—he gestured at the newspaper clipping laying face up on my lap—"Priya's behaviour changed. She grew distant and irritable and spent a lot of time away from home. I was concerned, of course, but every once in a while she needed to adjust her coping strategies, and I thought this was just one of those times. I should have paid more attention, I know I should have, but instead I gave her the space I thought she needed.

"In the weeks after Peter's death, things got worse. Not that I connected the two at the time, of course. In a complete reversal, she no longer left the house. Her moods became even more erratic. She said she was taking her meds, and the number of pills in the bottle kept going down. Yes, I checked."

He slid me a shamefaced glance, as if expecting me to berate him. I didn't. I would have done the same thing.

When I said nothing, he went on. "Challenging her made things worse, and she'd always managed before, so I kept my distance, stopped nagging. I trusted her. Trusted she'd find her way back to me." His voice broke. He squeezed the bridge of his nose and then wiped his eyes.

My arms ached to embrace him, to offer what comfort I could. But I wasn't ready to forgive his subterfuge.

"Grace came home from university for the Christmas holidays and Priya brightened up. She seemed settled and stable again." He gazed blindly into the past, grief bowing his spine. "It was her idea that Grace and I go skiing on New Year's Day."

I wanted to stop him. Wanted to press my hand to his mouth and prevent him from saying what I knew was coming. But I didn't.

"We were gone about ten hours." He squared his shoulders and met my eyes. "She must have taken all the pills she'd been hiding the minute we left."

I'd been spared seeing Peter until after he'd been tended by the Coroners Service. I couldn't imagine what Grace and Seth had gone through. We sat in silence for long minutes before he spoke again.

"Did you know? That your husband was having an affair?" His question was tentative. *Yes* meant his lies had been unnecessary. *No* meant he had demolished my memories of a happy marriage.

"Yes." I stared at my clasped hands but didn't see them. I was watching Peter, his brown eyes narrowed in resentment, as he jerked on his reflective vest, tied his runners with vicious yanks, and slammed out the door. "I told you he went running the night he died. I didn't tell you we argued before he left. We argued, because he had just told me."

"I see."

"He blurted it out after dinner. As we were clearing the table." My shoulders slumped. I untwisted my fingers and picked up the pages in my lap, matching the top left corners of each sheet as if that would unlock the way to healing. "He didn't tell me her name. I wouldn't have forgotten it."

"No. I don't imagine you would."

"You know the worst thing?" I wanted to take the words back as soon as I'd said them. They were the doorway to my deepest humiliation. "Never mind. Forget I said that."

"What can be worse than having a spouse betray you?" Seth's own pain reverberated, deep and clear. He understood that much. Maybe he *could* understand the rest.

"It wasn't the first time." I closed my eyes and breathed through the mortification. "He'd cheated before, in the early years of our marriage. And I took him back. I keep wondering how many times he played me for a fool, between the first and the last. I never had the chance to ask."

"He was the fool, for cheating on you."

"That night, he apologized, said he was going to break it off. That he'd made a mistake, that he loved me and hoped we could work through it. I didn't care. Didn't want him as a consolation prize. I called him horrible names, said terrible things, lashed out with everything I had. I was bleeding inside. I wanted him to bleed too. When he left the house, I shouted at him to never come back."

My words lay between us like shards of glass. There it was. I'd wanted to punish Peter, and my wish had been granted.

"You can't possibly blame yourself for his death. It was a

dreadful coincidence. It's not your fault." Seth's hand lifted before dropping back to his thigh. "Just as Priya's suicide isn't mine."

"Doesn't make it any easier to accept, does it?"

"No."

Once again, silence dropped over us like a pall.

"I should go." I rose, holding back a groan. My body felt battered and bruised. And not in the good way that excellent sex caused.

"For what it's worth, I'm sorry I wasn't truthful." Seth stood with me. The sky had lightened as we'd talked but the room was still sombre with shadows. They hollowed out his eyes, dyed the silver stubble on his chin to charcoal. "I should have told you, as soon as...well, as soon as."

"Yes." I moved toward the hall.

"Will I see you again?"

I paused, one hand on the door jamb, and spoke over my shoulder. "I need to think, Seth. Give me a couple of days, okay?"

He didn't come with me to the front door.

I drove home on autopilot. Showered, dressed, and went to the office.

What else was there to do? I couldn't sit around moping all day. Mostly because that was all I wanted to do.

Neither Maeve nor Indra seemed to notice anything odd with my behaviour. Or if they did, they must have ascribed it to Azalea's death. After all, no one would dream I'd just learned that Seth's wife and Peter had had an affair. That

Priya had ended her own life while swamped with grief for my husband.

As the shock waned, I thought of several questions I should have asked. Top of the list was *Did you sign up for Blynde Dating because I was Peter's wife?*

He'd known who I was before he filled in an application—the advertisement included with the news articles and Peter's obituary was proof of that. Had he honestly been looking for a companion as he'd said at our first meeting, or had he applied in order to spy on the wife of the man his own wife had slept with?

Was that the *real* reason he'd told Azalea he was attracted to me? Because joining the agency had been a ruse all along?

Had *anything* in our relationship been authentic and true?

These uncomfortable queries stung like August hail, and work provided little solace. We were still leaking clients in a steady drizzle and new applications were at an all-time low. At least the reporters weren't pestering us today.

Just after the office opened, a police officer arrived and took statements from all of us, including Piper who had again appeared uncharacteristically on the dot of eight-thirty.

Which of us had had contact with Azalea? Did we know her other than through the agency? Where had we been the Tuesday evening she disappeared? What about Monday, when the first ransom calls came? The authorities knew my movements from Wednesday evening until Azalea's body had been found, as I'd filled in any blanks for Mehta that morning, but the others gave their information. None of us had alibis for every minute. The officer didn't seem too concerned. She was just crossing T's and dotting I's as far as I could tell.

After that excitement, I went back to staring uselessly at my computer screen until Maeve's calm measured footsteps approached my office. Shaking off my lethargy, I greeted her with a smile that I hoped didn't look as tired as I felt.

"I finally had a chance to look at the most recent security report." She halted beside my desk.

"I've told you not to bother with that unless there's a reason." The report was generated by our alarm system and provided a list of which fobs were used to gain access to the office and when the alarm itself was turned on or off. Reviewing it always felt like a make-work project to me, as we'd had no issues since it had been installed.

"Kidnapping, ransom, and murder aren't reasons enough?" she said tartly.

I didn't take offense. The disruptions were hard on her—she liked more than her hair to be neat and tidy at all times. "You're right," I said placatingly. "Is everything status quo?"

"No. I think we've got a glitch." She frowned. "The logs show the back door was accessed three times within a three-minute span on Wednesday night, around eleven o'clock. The alarm wasn't deactivated and it never alerted, either. It's like someone repeatedly opened the door but closed it before the alarm went off."

"Definitely sounds like a glitch." I sighed. Have I mentioned I hated technology? "I'll make a call, get someone to look into it." Probably next week, when I had more energy. It wasn't going to the top of my to-do list. Not that I would tell her that.

She nodded, pleased I had promised to take action. "Indra and I are doing takeout from Abani's for lunch. I'll get you something too."

"That's okay. I'm not hungry."

"I'll get it, and you'll eat it." Her gaze was narrow, her tone brooking no defiance.

"Yes, Maeve," I answered meekly.

CHAPTER TWENTY-FOUR

AS I WAS DESULTORILY picking at the sandwich Maeve had brought, I heard Piper arrive. A minute later, she strode through my door, tablet in hand, and dropped into the chair on the other side of my desk.

"Okay, this is what I've got." No hello, no how-are-yous. Her frames today were a mottled purple that matched the streak in her hair. "Do you want a full recap or just the interesting stuff?"

I'd been so caught up in Seth's revelations that I was a little slow on the uptake. Then I caught her drift. "Just the interesting stuff."

"Carter was born five months after Azalea married Warren Bickersley. By all accounts the marriage was a happy one. Carter is their only child. Warren died from a rare blood disorder three years ago this coming May. After he was diagnosed, he donated a crap ton of cash to the Canadian Cancer Society. There were several news articles about it."

I waited for more.

She spread her hands. "That's it. That's the interesting stuff. No scandals, no lawsuits, no family drama. Not that I could find, and I'm damn good at snooping."

"Nothing that hints at why she might have been kidnapped?"

"Other than the fact she's wealthy? Maybe the wealthiest person in the city? Nope." She referred to her tablet, swiping the screen upward. "She's listed on the board of several charities. She or members of her extended family own or are invested in half the businesses and industries in town. Including Carter's flower shop, by the way."

"He doesn't own Carousel?"

"Nope. He's managed it since it opened about a year and a half ago, but his name's not on any papers associated with it."

That fit in with what Azalea had told me herself, about the shop being a diversion more than a necessity for Carter. I didn't see how the confirmation changed anything.

"Well, thanks for trying."

"Oh, I'm not done yet." Piper sounded determined. And a determined Piper was not to be trifled with. "I have a few other ideas. I'll let you know." She strode out of the room.

I googled Warren Bickersley as I chawed my way through the rest of my sandwich. Articles about the donation were easy to find. One included a photo of a blond man with blue eyes, a head taller than his also blond, also blue-eyed wife. His obituary had been front page news and provided additional photos as well as many details of his life and career.

I studied everything thoroughly, a stray thought tickling the back of my mind.

Then I picked up my phone and called Carter.

Carousel was in a neighbourhood of older homes that were gradually being converted into offices and retail spaces as downtown expanded. A smallish two-storey building with a single dormer perched over the tiny enclosed front porch, its cheerful blue siding and yellow trim glowed even on this blah February day. As I walked up the snow-edged path, I caught a glimpse of a large shed, decorated in the same hues, in the back yard and accessible from the alley.

Inside, nothing remained of the original rooms. The main floor had been gutted, leaving an open area flooded with natural light yet somehow cold and clinical. Kitschy trinkets, candles, and other home decor items did little to soften the white on white on white—ceiling, walls, floor—colour scheme. The air held a chill I assumed was necessary to keep the displayed flowers fresh.

On a long, glossy, also white table near the back of the shop, Carter was constructing a large arrangement. He looked up when I opened the door. His face lit in a momentary smile before falling back into sober lines.

I'd been pleased to hear him sounding alert and natural when he'd answered his phone earlier, though had been surprised to learn he was at his shop. I'd expected him to stay closed for at least a few more days. But he'd told me he had an important order to fill and that he was going stir-crazy at home, which I could understand.

"Those are beautiful." I halted next to the table. Blossoms in oranges, purples, and creams lay scattered across its surface. A squat rectangular metal vase containing that green spongy stuff florists use held the partially completed bouquet.

"It's for an eightieth birthday party tomorrow." Carter plucked a bird of paradise from the assortment, snipped the stem, and tucked it in place. "Good customers, both the birthday woman and the daughter who bought the arrangement. I didn't want to disappoint them."

"How are you doing?" He looked better, despite the dark shadows he still carried under his brown eyes.

"As good as can be expected, I guess." He trimmed the stem off a lily and poked it in near the front edge of the vase.

"I can't imagine how tough this must be for you." I didn't want to upset him any more than necessary, so tried to ease into the subject. If I was wrong, I hoped he wouldn't question why I was asking. If I was right, I might have another angle of investigation into Azalea's death. "With your father, you had time to say goodbye. This was so sudden and unexpected."

He didn't reply.

Fair enough. I hadn't asked a question. "What was he like? Your dad."

"He worked a lot." He jabbed the leafy green fan of a fern into the grainy foam with more vigour than necessary. "Didn't see him much when I was a kid. Mom was busy, too, had lots of responsibilities. But she always made time for me."

Azalea's loss echoed in the space between us.

"How did they meet?"

"He worked at one of the family businesses. Mom said her parents used to invite promising employees over for dinner. As a thank you and a way to scope them out, see if they were ready for a bigger role. He was one of those guys. They married three months later."

"Must have been love at first sight. How romantic." I wasn't being sarcastic. I was hoping it was the truth.

Carter dropped the small shears onto the table with a clatter and strode into the large cooler at the back of the shop. Open metal shelving lined three walls, laden with buckets filled with loose stems in all colours, shapes, and sizes. In the middle, a large stand constructed like a flight of stairs with distressed wood risers and tiled treads held completed bouquets. He disappeared behind this display for a few moments, reappeared with several gladioli clenched in his hand, and returned to the table.

"He wasn't my biological father." He placed a blossom with fierce precision, then another, without sparing me a glance. "But you knew that, didn't you?"

"No," I said gently. "I was wondering, though."

While it wasn't impossible for two blue-eyed parents to have a brown-eyed child, it was unlikely. If Azalea was expecting a baby fathered by someone who either couldn't or wouldn't marry her, Warren's appearance at the family table that night might have been a godsend. For his part, taking on another man's child might have been an acceptable trade off for marrying the boss's daughter.

"Have you always known?" I asked. "I mean, maybe not when you were young, but did your mother and father tell you when you were old enough to understand?"

He shoved aside the unfinished arrangement and began gathering stem ends and discarded leaves, his jerky, uncoordinated movements hinting at distress. I wished I wasn't the cause of it, but I needed to know more. At least, I hoped I needed to and wasn't doing this for no good reason.

"My dad—Warren—developed a blood disorder. Like leukemia, only rarer. He fought it for a couple of years, but none of the treatments worked for long. A few months before he died, I thought maybe I could donate my blood or bone marrow, whatever he needed, so I got myself tested." His cheekbones stood out pale and stark in his sharp face. "They couldn't lie to me after that."

"It must have been a shock." That was putting it mildly. Learning the truth as a child would have been difficult. Discovering it as an adult must have cracked the foundation of his world.

"You think?" The sarcasm was unexpectedly biting for the Carter I knew. He got a grip on it, though, and his next words were accompanied by a tight smile. "It took a while to get over it, that's for sure."

I had my doubts he *was* over it, but I smiled back. "Who else knows? Coral, maybe? Not that it matters. It doesn't change who you are."

"That's not how it felt. My whole life turned inside out." He tossed the refuse he'd collected into a bucket under the table and pressed his palms flat on the surface. "Mom said no one else knew. Not even my real dad." His gaze bore into mine with desperate intensity, as if he was trying to communicate telepathically.

"Don't worry. I won't tell anyone either." I wanted to ask if he knew who his father was, if Azalea had revealed everything. But I'd put him through enough today. I could always ask later, if I came up with compelling evidence it was connected to Azalea's death.

I couldn't see how it did, not yet. Still, I had few other leads to follow.

By the time I left Carousel, it was half past three. Nothing much would be going on at the agency. Friday afternoons were often quiet—our busiest days were Monday and Tuesday, when there was still time to make plans for the weekend—even when business was going well. Which was definitely not the case at the moment.

No one would blame me if I went straight home. If I did that, though, I'd have nothing to prevent me from confronting my feelings about Seth. Not ready for such soul-searching, I headed back to the office.

I was glad I did, because Indra popped in the moment I was settled behind my desk.

"I'm still going down the list of events." She sat in my visitor's chair and despite keeping her feet on the floor gave the impression of curling up, settling in for a cozy chat. The ability to focus on you and you alone was one of her superpowers. "But I've discovered one thing you might want to know."

I blew across the mug of tea I'd made on my return and wriggled my eyebrows in a go on motion.

"The charity Azalea was most involved with was the Canadian Cancer Society."

Which made perfect sense, given Warren's diagnosis and death.

"As I'm sure you know," she continued, "they do several fund raisers throughout the year. Azalea's special project, though, was the one in December."

"The Illumination Celebration." Connaught Hill Park was a park—obviously—on top of a small hill—ditto—that bulged up in the middle of downtown. Volunteers set up enormous light displays and visitors paid a fee to drive the circuit and gawk at the twinkling animations.

Indra nodded. "It's a huge undertaking. It takes days to set up, then is open all of December and doesn't close until the weekend after New Year's Day. When it's over, all the volunteers are invited to a wrap party as a thank you for their hard work. Azalea has sponsored that shindig since her husband died."

"So not just anyone can go? You can't buy tickets to it?"

"No. I talked with this year's co-chair. She says there was a dust up between Azalea and the other co-chair. She's not sure what it was about. The only reason she knew it happened was she came across the two women in a hissing match. They stopped arguing as soon as they saw her."

"I have trouble seeing Azalea in a 'hissing match.'" I sipped my tea thoughtfully. "She always seemed so imperturbable and cheerful."

"Well, according to my source..." Indra beamed with delight. "I've always wanted to say that. According to my source, it was pretty heated. Flushed faces, bared teeth, raised voices, that sort of thing."

"And it was with the co-chair, you said? Who was that?"

Indra's smile was smug and distressed at the same time. "Coral Loughty."

Wasn't that interesting.

"That's one of the people you mentioned to Piper, right?" Indra asked.

"Yes. Supposedly she's Azalea's best friend. Carter used to call her Auntie Coral."

Indra's eyes widened. "Oh. So why would they be fighting, then?"

"That's a very good question." I tapped my fingers on my desk in a slow tattoo.

"Well, I hope it helps." Indra rose from her seat. "I'm heading home. Do you want me to keep at it over the weekend?"

Piper had left while I was at Carousel and Maeve would be well into her closing routine by now. "No, that's fine. Leave it until Monday. Have a good one." I was already asking my team to go above and beyond. As much as I wanted to get all the information I could as quickly as possible, I couldn't ask them to give up their personal time too.

She nodded and bustled out. A few minutes later I heard her call goodbye to Maeve. The back door clanged behind her.

I swivelled my chair back and forth, back and forth, fingertips pressed together like a Vaudeville villain, and thought. By the time Maeve poked her head in and said her own goodbye, I had a plan.

CHAPTER TWENTY-FIVE

THE FIRST THING I noticed when I pulled into Coral Loughty's double-wide driveway was the For Sale sign propped crookedly in the crusty snow of her front yard.

While her home was by no means on the same scale as Azalea's, it was more than twice the size of mine, though only average for the neighbourhood. Three-car garages were the norm on this street, along with million-dollar motorhomes and six-figure ski boats, most of which were tucked up for the winter under protective coverings.

The sign gave me pause. I kept the motor running as I pondered.

What would happen to Azalea's house now? Would Carter move in or sell it? I assumed he was the main beneficiary of her will. I should probably confirm that.

I turned off the ignition, skirted an unfamiliar Toyota sedan, traversed the drifts garlanding the path to the front door, and rang the bell.

Coral hadn't been especially welcoming when I'd invited myself over. I couldn't blame her—I'd been at my most professionally pushy, insisting it had to be this evening. But it was amazing what people would agree to if you simply refused to take no for an answer.

I shifted from foot to foot. Wind twisted powdery snow into tiny tornadoes and licked its icy tongue down the collar of my jacket. Just as I was beginning to think she'd refuse to answer, I heard the clunk and click of a lock.

"Come in, come in. It's so cold out." Coral's voice and smile were bright and welcoming. The contrast with our earlier conversation—and the delay in answering the door—was a bit startling.

She took my coat as I peeled off my boots, chattering pleasantly about the weather, her regret she hadn't booked a tropical vacation this winter, and other inconsequential matters.

Her non-confrontational manner defused some of my edginess. If she could play nice, I could too. I scanned the wide hall cluttered with curio tables and watched over by large works of art for something I could compliment.

"That's a beautiful piece." I pointed at a twisted column of blown glass, waves of blues and greens swirling through it, so delicate it seemed to float above the round table supporting it.

"Isn't it just? Azalea and I went to Venice a few years ago. I saw it and fell in love." Coral caressed it with a light fingertip, as if it were a soap bubble. "Azalea insisted on getting it for me. She always spoiled me rotten." Her voice trembled. Whether over the loss of future gifts or her murdered friend I couldn't tell.

She led me to the rear of the house, where a large living room already had an occupant. Belva.

I'd assumed the two women were friendly only because of their mutual connection to Azalea, but maybe her disappearance and death had brought them closer together.

Belva offered a minuscule nod in greeting, her expression unyielding. She was once again dressed in shades of black. I wondered if she owned any other colours and imagined her closet as a strictly organized greyscale rainbow.

"Have a seat." Coral gestured to a wing chair with its back to the window and joined Belva on the couch opposite.

"Thanks for agreeing to see me." Might as well keep things pleasant as long as I could. "I wanted to explain why I was asking so many questions at Carter's yesterday."

They regarded me silently.

"You see, Carter asked me to help." With the kidnapping, not the murder investigation, but I figured the little white lie couldn't hurt. I added a layer of humility to sugar the admission. "I know the police have it well in hand, but I couldn't say no to him. He was so distraught. If you'll just answer a few questions, I can tell him I tried."

I didn't say I'd stop investigating, but hoped they would believe that was the implication.

Belva and Coral shared a glance I couldn't quite interpret. Whatever passed between them, though, it led to Belva saying, with great reluctance, "I suppose we could do that."

I'd been prepared for a longer battle, so was nonplussed at such a quick surrender. I refocused, intent on not wasting a moment of this détente.

"Do either of you still think my dating agency had anything to do with what happened?" It wouldn't hurt if they thought I had a personal agenda for my nosiness, one I was hiding from Carter. People who thought they knew your secrets often gave away their own by accident.

Coral smiled. "I don't. I mean, it wasn't even Azalea's idea to sign up. We both know Carter convinced her to do it."

"I never understood why she agreed." Belva sniffed. "Just the week before, she told me she wasn't ready to date seriously again. Then all of sudden she's signed up with *you* and out with a different man every night."

Her tone was more sour than usual, but that wasn't what caught my attention. "Azalea only went on three dates arranged by Blynde Dating. Was she seeing other people as well?"

"No," Belva answered sullenly. *Bang* went the hope I had new names to add to my list of suspects. "Haven't you heard of hyperbole? I just meant that Azalea never had a shortage of men interested in her."

"It wasn't just men." Coral slid her a glance, as if debating whether to say more, and continued after a short pause. "Women liked Azalea too. And not just as friends."

Belva stiffened, her expression set in the disapproving lines of an old-fashioned maiden aunt. Had the thought never occurred to her?

"And what was her response to that?" I had visualized Azalea's murderer as male, though the caller's mechanized voice hid any hint of gender. How had I not considered this angle?

Coral flapped a hand. "She thought it was sweet but amusing. And she wasn't interested, of course. But she liked to be liked."

Belva remained silent, her rapid inhales and exhales betraying an internal turmoil.

"I do know one reason she agreed to go with your agency." Coral's mouth twitched down at the corners. "There was a man who tried to get her to invest in his business.

He got nasty when she said no. Carter convinced her your company could weed out the jerks."

That sounded promising too. "Do you remember his name?"

The women shook their heads. "It was months ago," Coral said. "But I think it made her gun-shy."

I filed that for now and prodded the conversation toward the main reason for my visit. "Azalea was wealthy and well-liked. Had a devoted son and loving husband. She must have been devastated when Warren got sick. I can understand why she put so much effort into her charity work."

"She wasn't perfect, you know." The words were projectiles, propelled from between Belva's pinched lips. "Her life had been too easy. When things didn't go her way, she could be mean. Even cruel."

Coral's laughter had a jagged edge. "You're exaggerating. Azalea might have been a little short once in a while but never mean. And certainly not cruel."

This was too interesting to ignore. I put a pin in the topic of charities and directed my attention to Belva. "Was she ever mean to you?" Her mouth flattened and I could have kicked myself. *Too soon, Ginnie, too soon*. I hastened on, hoping to mitigate my mistake. "Did you witness her being mean to anyone?"

Belva glared past me into the darkened night outside the living room's huge windows. I'd pressed too hard. She had no intention of continuing the subject.

Well, I could use Coral's defence of Azalea to get back on track. "You would know best," I said innocently to Coral, hoping to butter her up. "You spent a lot of time with her, not just as a friend, but on several committees too."

"I did. We enjoyed working together. Not that we didn't have the odd difference of opinion, but she usually saw it my way once she'd had a chance to think things through."

Belva snorted. "Are you sure? You gave in to Azalea far more than the other way around."

Coral narrowed her eyes. "Azalea respected my opinion."

"About decorations and menus, maybe. But not the important things."

Coral's chest swelled with indignation. "Like money, you mean? I wouldn't be so smug if I were you. Azalea had so much of it she could let you play around. She never gave you more than she could afford to lose. We laughed about it together."

Belva's pale cheeks bloomed with red blotches. "She trusted my advice. She knew I was working in her best interests."

"She managed you so well you didn't even notice. Think about it. You'll realize you never did anything she didn't want you to. She gave you rope but always reeled you in before you went too far."

"Well, at least I'm not a jealous leech." Belva's thin fists clenched in her lap. "You couldn't afford the things Azalea could, so you'd act all sweet and self-sacrificing until she felt sorry enough to give you what you wanted. But I saw the truth, even if she didn't. You were using her."

Coral sat back sharply, as if slapped by an invisible hand. For a moment the only sound was the swift breathing of the two women staring at each other.

Belva recovered first. She glanced at me, as if only now remembering I was there. "I'm sorry," she said stiffly, her gaze on her feet. "That was uncalled for."

I wasn't sure if she was apologizing to me or Coral.

"And not true." Coral's head swivelled my way. "It's not true. Azalea was generous, sure, but because we were friends, not because she thought I was some pathetic hanger-on." Her eyes filled with tears and her lips trembled.

Something in her attitude rang false, but I didn't have the chance to poke at it as she stood abruptly. "I'm sorry. I can't bear this any longer. My best friend is dead. I need to be alone."

So much for broaching the topic of her argument with Azalea or hinting at Carter's parentage to see if she knew anything about that. Her glittering stare and pressed mouth gave evidence she was done talking. I wasn't the only one getting the bum's rush either. She swung her gaze to Belva and jerked her chin, and then ushered us both to the door, closing it firmly behind us.

Without so much as a nod goodbye, Belva climbed into the sedan parked next to mine and drove away. I got into my own vehicle and sat for a moment, thoughts whirling, before putting it in gear, my headlights sweeping the For Sale sign as I reversed out of the driveway and headed home.

My conversations with Carter, Belva, and Coral accomplished one thing. They distracted me from my misery over Seth. Not one hundred percent, and not every moment, but some.

What with one thing and another, I spent a restless Friday night. My brain wouldn't turn off, no matter how many sheep I counted or Hail Marys I muttered. My thoughts swirled endlessly between Azalea and Seth and the kidnapper and Carter and Seth and the investigation and back to Azalea. At two-thirty in the morning I grabbed my phone and sought distraction dropping down internet rabbit holes. Nothing I learned made sleep any easier, so after half an hour I forced myself to put it aside. Lying with my eyes closed had to be more restful than doom-scrolling. And on that thought, I finally fell asleep.

In the morning, I made an extra-large pot of coffee. I mainlined the first cup, gulped the second, and had just poured my third when Tam called.

"I'd like to go over a few things with you." He sounded even gruffer than usual, as if he was losing his voice, and I wondered if he'd had any downtime since Azalea's body had been found. "Is your office open on Saturdays?"

"Not to clients."

"Let's meet there. I'd like to take a look at your member list."

Damn it. The RCMP hadn't given up on the idea the agency was somehow involved. The sooner I could disabuse him of that notion so he would focus in other directions the better.

"I can be there in thirty minutes." I was still in my robe, hair uncombed, teeth unbrushed. With Saturday morning traffic, the office was little more than ten minutes away, and another ten would have been enough to get presentable. But I needed to feel and look more than presentable to deal with

Tam on the few hours of sleep I'd had. The extra ten was a necessity.

"I'll be waiting." He hung up.

CHAPTER TWENTY-SIX

TWENTY-NINE MINUTES later, I parked in the office lot and went in through the rear entrance, turning off the security system as I passed.

I unlocked the front door, poked my head out, and waved at Tam. I'd seen him in his car, waiting as promised, when I'd driven past. He hauled himself out and lumbered inside. I relocked the door.

"Coffee? Tea?" I offered.

"Tea. Herbal if you have it. Doctor says I drink too much caffeine."

"I thought that was part of the job description."

Tam waited politely in reception while I went to the breakroom, filled the kettle, and plugged it in. I rejoined him and led the way to my office. "Come on in. You might as well take off your coat. I assume we're going to be a while." He followed my suggestion as I logged into my computer and navigated toward our membership database. "What are you looking for?"

"Carter Bickersley told us you arranged several dates for Mrs. Bickersley. We know about the one with Seth Updike. Who were the others?"

At the mention of Seth's name, fresh hurt rang hollowly in my chest. It had taken me years to unmask myself and I'd been rewarded by being lied to. But Tam didn't need to know all that. "It was only three dates in total. Let me call them up."

SUSPECT ATTRACTION

I loaded the profiles and gestured Tam to my side of the desk. The kettle whistled. "I'll get our drinks. Take my seat while you read. Cream? Sugar?" He shook his head.

In the breakroom, I waited a few minutes for the tea to steep and then returned with two mugs of Lemon Zinger. I placed one near his hand. He grunted an acknowledgment but didn't look away from the computer. I sat in the visitor's chair. It was disconcerting to see my office from this angle. As if it didn't belong to me.

"What kind of vetting process do you have for your members?"

I walked him through it—online application, in-person interview, Google search, social media profile review. "We're not hunting for deep dark secrets. We just want to make sure the person is who they say they are, that there are no obvious red flags."

"Personal finances?"

I shook my head. "If something odd drew our attention, maybe. Otherwise, as long as they pay our membership fees on time, that's none of our business."

"What if a guy says he owns a company. Do you look into that?"

Of the three men I'd matched Azalea with, only Seth ticked that box. "We would make sure such a company existed, check with the Chamber of Commerce or Better Business Bureau. But it's all surface stuff. We like to assume our members are honest and above board." And look where that had got me.

"Uh huh." He clicked the mouse, scrolled the wheel.

I waited for him to finish reading, doing my best not to

pick a hangnail as my patience frayed. Was he looking for something specific? Or just on a fishing expedition?

Finally, Tam swung away from the screen. "Thanks for your cooperation." He shifted as if to stand.

I had to stop him from leaving. I doubted I'd get another chance to discuss the case with him, and I had questions. Lots of questions.

"Was Azalea in the storage unit since she went missing?" I blurted.

Tam hesitated, studied my face, and then settled back into his—*my*—chair. "I can't share details of the investigation."

"I need to know." I twisted my fingers in my lap. I'd had nightmares of Azalea slowly dying of dehydration and exposure in that icy windowless cell. "What would it hurt to tell me?"

I don't know what he saw in my expression, but he unbent enough to answer obliquely. "The unit wasn't rented until well after her disappearance, and security cameras at the facility have given us no additional information."

I took that last admission to mean Azalea had not walked into the unit under her own power and that the police knew or suspected she'd been dead when brought there. If so, how had the killer transported her body? A large suitcase? A wheeled trolley? The indignity of it made me sick.

I swallowed. "You must know when and how she died."

"Yes." He sipped from his mug. The tea must have been cold by now, but he didn't seem to mind.

I waited, hoping he might add more. He remained silent.

It occurred to me that he was indulging my curiosity on the chance *I'd* reveal something to *him*. It was a game of cat-and-mouse I was pretty sure I couldn't win, but as he made no further motion to leave, I continued my questioning.

"Then where was she before the unit was rented?"

"Knowing that might answer a lot of questions." It was entirely possible the police *did* know. His tone remained non-committal.

"Given the glimpse I had when the unit was opened," I said slowly, watching him for any reaction, "Azalea had been dead for more than a few hours. Maybe even more than a day. But she must have been alive Monday evening, when the kidnapper allowed Carter to talk to her on the phone."

He nodded. "That seems logical."

Did he emphasize *seems* just a tiny bit? "It does. And yet... If she was kidnapped for ransom, why not call right away? Or at the very least, within twenty-four hours? Something happened that stopped the kidnapper from making contact sooner. Something that forced him to regroup and caused the delay." Or forced *her,* I reminded myself, thinking of Coral's comments yesterday.

Tam blinked and then narrowed his gaze. "And what might that be?"

"I think Azalea died the night she disappeared. Very shortly after being taken."

His expression remained impassive, yet I sensed a heightened awareness in the set of his shoulders. "Then how do you explain the first phone call Carter received?" he challenged. "He swears he talked with his mother. And her son should know."

My midnight internet searches hadn't been completely fruitless. "I read about this new technology kidnappers are using. They sample their victims' voices in order to create fake conversations."

"I wouldn't know anything about that."

Again, I wondered if his ignorance of technology was genuine or a smokescreen. I took the statement to mean he wouldn't answer any further questions on that topic, however, and switched to another. "I checked out the storage facility. Turns out you can rent units online, as long as you've got a credit card. You must have looked into that by now. Whose credit card was used?"

"I can't tell you that."

I now expected nothing less, but it would have been silly not to ask. "If you knew, I think you'd have made an arrest. Or at least taken someone in for questioning. But you haven't, have you?"

He made no reply, audible or otherwise. And yet something in his absolute stillness told me I was on the right track.

"Which leads me to believe that it was a company card. Which was why you were asking me about members who own businesses." Which would keep Seth square in his sights.

"You have been doing a lot of thinking, haven't you?"

It wasn't admiration I heard in his tone. The surliness made me grin, though my heart wasn't in it. The subject was too painful for levity. "I have. Why did you ask if we check our client's finances?"

He hesitated but must have decided it did no harm to answer. "Criminals often use a ransom to bankroll other activities, such as drug running or human trafficking. Amateur kidnappers, though, can need money for almost anything. For example, paying off debts."

In the pocket of my cardigan, my phone buzzed. I took it out as I reflected on what Tam was implying. The lock screen displayed a text from Carter, asking to talk. I put it back in my pocket, making a mental note to respond as soon as I could.

"Seth is the only member I matched with Azalea who owns a business. We did the checks we always do. Nothing alerted us. It's well-established, well-respected." Those checks were Maeve's department. I had no doubt she'd done them as efficiently as she did everything else, but maybe I should have followed up with her.

"He's had a couple of bad years." Tam picked up one of my pens and fidgeted with it. "His wife died. A drug overdose that was ruled suicide. He tell you that?"

Learning about Priya Jatt the way I did had been a shock. But it was nothing compared to how I would have felt if I'd learned it from Tam at this moment. I wouldn't have been able to hide my reaction, and his suspicions of Seth would have gone through the roof.

"Yes," I said calmly. "He did tell me." I wouldn't share the details of when and why unless pushed.

He appeared vaguely disappointed at my lack of drama. "The business suffered after that. Pulled far fewer permits than the year before, despite the building boom."

"That's understandable. He was grieving."

"Maybe." He replaced the pen on my desk and did his own quick conversational U-turn. "What do you think about the kid, Carter? Seems a little nervy to me."

"His mother's been murdered," I protested. "Surely there are no rules as to how he should be acting."

"With Mrs. Bickersley dead, he inherits a healthy pile. Other than a couple of smallish bequests to charity and such, he gets it all."

I sucked in a breath. "Are you seriously looking at him for this?"

"I've seen worse for less money. Much worse. Much less."

I didn't doubt it. But Carter? "I was with him when the kidnapper called. Do you think he has an accomplice?" Everything I knew about Carter made him out to be a loner. I couldn't see him working with a partner at the flower shop, let alone to kidnap his own mother. And I certainly couldn't see him committing matricide. It was beyond belief.

Tam crossed his arms and rested his elbows on my desk. "Ever hear of robocalls?" he asked with faint sarcasm.

My heart sped up. The memory of the spam call I'd received the morning Azalea's body was discovered floated to the surface.

"I'm not saying that's what happened." Tam leaned away, as if regretting his earlier openness. "I don't want you going around telling people that's what the perpetrator did."

Mind whirling, I did my best to regroup. "Whether the calls were live or scheduled, how did the kidnapper get our numbers?"

"Other than being someone who knows one or both of you?"

I respected his bluntness. That didn't mean I was comfortable with it. "Other than."

He waved a dismissive hand. "My geeks tell me it's possible, but don't ask me how."

A thought struck me. "I talked with the kidnapper the evening of the ransom drop. Those calls couldn't have been prerecorded and automated."

"Ask any questions?"

I nodded.

"Get any answers?"

The robotic voice had been aggressive and demanding, often interrupting me. Looking back, I supposed that could be explained by a recorded call that had artfully placed pauses. "No."

He shoved to his feet and joined me on my side of the desk. "I want you to think about what we've talked about. Think very carefully." His gaze held a message I was afraid to put into words. "Be careful, Mrs. Blynde. Don't do anything stupid."

I let him out the front door, locked it, and returned to my office. I gathered the used mugs and took them to the kitchenette. As I washed them, I did as Tam had asked. I thought.

Thought hard, about so many things.

I dried the mugs and put them in the cupboard. Phone in hand, I sat in the chair recently vacated by Tam. After a few missteps, I found the recording I'd made of the ransom call Carter had taken at my house. I listened to it closely. Could it have come from an automated system? Were there clues in the message that I'd missed?

I closed the recording and dialled Maeve's number.

She answered after one ring. "Ginnie? Is everything okay?"

Everyone was on tenterhooks. "Yes, everything's fine. Sorry to bother you on your weekend."

"No problem. Do you need me to come in?"

"No, no. I just wanted to ask you a couple of questions."

"About what?"

"When you were doing the background checks on Seth Updike, did anything come up? Some little nugget that seemed harmless but now, after Azalea..." I trailed off, not exactly sure where I was going with this, but hoping she'd fill in the blank.

She didn't hesitate. "He was clean. No flags at all."

"What about his business? I heard he might be having some problems."

"He's a member in good standing with both the Chamber and BBB. Someone I talked to at one of those places—I can't remember who right now, but it will be in my notes—said he'd done fewer projects in the last year or so but mentioned he'd had some personal troubles."

This detail wasn't something I would have expected Maeve to light the bat signal for. It was confirmation of Tam's comment, however.

"I know you...like...him," she said cautiously. "Are you worried he's hiding something from you?"

I almost said "Not anymore" but stopped myself. If he'd lied about his wife, what else might he be keeping secret? "Something Tam mentioned set me wondering. It's all good."

"You've been talking to the police again?" The pitch of

her voice shot up an octave. "We've told them everything we know. Haven't we?"

"It was nothing. Just more routine questions." Mostly. "Have a good rest of your weekend. See you tomorrow."

We disconnected. I leaned back in my chair and closed my eyes.

The theory that the kidnapper had used robocalling changed everything. Automated messages were ubiquitous these days. I wondered why I hadn't thought of that myself.

Maybe because it meant I could trust no one. Not Carter. Not Seth. Not my team.

No one could be eliminated. Absolutely no one.

CHAPTER TWENTY-SEVEN

SUNDAY AFTERNOON, I did laundry. Dirty linen doesn't stop piling up just because you're tangled in criminal mayhem or suffering from a battered heart.

I was throwing a load into the dryer when my phone rang.

"Mrs. Blynde? This is Night Owl Security. We wanted to let you know the alarm at your office was triggered about twenty minutes ago. We sent a patrol car and there is no exterior damage. Still, you might want to come and see if anything has been disturbed."

I slammed the dryer shut—probably with more force than necessary—and promised to be there as soon as possible. Racing out the door while zippering my jacket, I fondly remembered the good old days, boring and uneventful and structured. When had my life gotten so complicated?

In our parking lot, the Night Owl guards climbed out of their vehicle when I pulled up beside them. Their name tags designated them Smith and Weston, which I misread as Wesson at first. Considering they weren't allowed to carry firearms, that would have been ironic.

Smith, who I guessed was in her thirties, was short, blond, and muscular. She looked like she'd have no trouble handling trouble. Weston, a twenty-something man with tawny skin and the lithe build of a gymnast had the same no-nonsense attitude. They greeted me and the three of us went into the office via the back door, which I had to unlock.

"The main door is secured as well," Weston said. "We noted that when we walked the perimeter of the building."

"We looked in the front window," Smith added. "Nothing seems out of place. But we couldn't see into the inner offices."

I checked Indra and Piper's rooms first. Both were in their usual states. If anyone had gone through them, they'd been neat about it. Ditto for Maeve's area.

"What exactly triggered the alarm?" I asked.

Weston answered. "The interior motion detector went off. Like what would happen if you forgot to disarm it when you arrived."

If it had been one of my team, they would have called either me or the security company to explain. "Let me check the fob logs." Even as I said it, I remembered my as-yet-unfulfilled promise to look into the glitch Maeve had noticed. It was too late to wish I'd made the time to deal with it.

I led the guards into my office. A large manila envelope containing something flat but bulky lay in the centre of my desk.

All the hairs on the back of my neck shivered to attention. That hadn't been there yesterday when I was here with Tam.

I circled around, picked it up, lifted the flap, and peeked inside.

My cheeks tingled. I blinked back a rush of light-headedness.

"Anything unusual in here?" Smith stood with her hands

on her hips, her gaze sweeping the tidy room. Weston had grown progressively more restive as we'd toured the undisturbed office. His toe tapped impatiently, ready to declare a false alarm.

I placed the package back on my desk and worked moisture into my mouth, making sure my voice wouldn't give anything away. "No. Everything looks good in here too. There's no need for you to stick around. I'll check the fob logs and talk to your supervisor if I have any further concerns."

Weston was already heading for the hall leading outside. Smith and I followed. "Sorry for the trouble," I said.

"No problem, ma'am." Smith tipped an imaginary hat and she and her partner left the building.

I confirmed the door locked behind them, repeated the process with the front door, and then walked slowly back to my office. I rounded my desk as if the package lying on it might explode at any moment.

With a shaking hand, I picked it up, opened the flap, and reached inside. Broken glass tinkled and grated as I partially extracted the wooden frame. I shook it to detach any remaining fragments, allowing them to fall into the envelope. Then I removed it completely and laid it face up on my desk.

The portrait of Peter and me. The one taken at our wedding. The one that had gone missing from my mantel more than a week ago.

While the glass was in splinters, the frame was intact. Sharp dents punctured the photo, one in Peter's shoulder, the other in my abdomen. My gut clenched, as if experiencing the blow.

I sat in my chair and ran my finger along the edge of the frame. Gingerly, as if it might dissolve at a touch.

And then just about jumped out of my seat when my cell phone chimed with a text.

It was another message from Carter. We'd had a long chat yesterday evening, once I had time to give him my attention. He seemed to be coming to grips with Azalea's death—as much as could be expected—but felt compelled to discuss it. It was obviously his way of processing events, so I let him talk, offering what consolation I could.

I didn't tell him about Tam's visit to my office. I didn't mention robocalls or my theory his mother had died the night she was taken. Tam's warning had echoed in my thoughts while suspicion clawed at my heart. I was guilt-ridden for even entertaining the possibility Carter might be involved.

My thumbs hovered over the phone screen, ready to extend an invitation to meet later today. Then my gaze fell on the portrait.

No. Not today. I needed some time to absorb everything that had happened in the last twenty-four hours.

Something's come up. Can we get together tomorrow? My place, about six-thirty?

He replied with a thumbs up emoji. I laid my phone down and studied the ruined photo.

So...I hadn't lost my mind the night I'd sensed an intruder in my home. Someone *had* been there. Had taken the portrait. Had smashed the innocent memento with a violence that made me shudder and then returned it. Was it a warning? And if so, of what?

Bringing it to the office in such a state meant the burglary hadn't been random. It'd had a purpose.

But what?

Even more disconcerting was how the thief had gotten into the agency. The doors hadn't been forced. How had the system been bypassed? For all I knew, you could buy spy gadgets that would accomplish such a thing on Amazon. Or maybe I was dealing with a technical wizard who could out wizard Piper.

Then a much simpler solution occurred to me.

I pulled open the bottom drawer of my desk. Inside, three little white sticky hooks held our spare fobs.

One was empty.

I sent a group text to Maeve, Piper, and Indra. They each confirmed they had their own fobs and hadn't taken a spare. Then I told them about the break-in and asked everyone to meet me first thing Monday morning.

We all had time in our schedules, as the agency hadn't yet recovered from the effects of the two scurrilous Facebook posts. Indra was the busiest, organizing Hopeful Hearts for Valentine's Day next week, but requests for tickets had dried up. Given the dearth of new clients, I hoped we didn't have to cancel.

Maeve beat me into the agency as usual. She peppered me with questions, but I told her she'd have to wait. I barely had time to check my emails before Piper and Indra arrived, and the four of us settled into my office. I spun my visitor's chair in order to face Piper and Maeve on the sofa and Indra roosting on the edge of my low filing cabinet.

I gave it to them straight. No embellishments, no suppositions. Just the facts. When I finished, their faces were a mixture of cautious, concerned, and confused.

Indra's button nose scrunched up. "It doesn't make any sense."

"Why on earth would someone steal a photo from your house and return it ten days later, all in pieces, to the office?" Maeve reached for the bun at the back of her neck and patted it. Making sure that part of her world could still be trusted, I suppose.

Piper's knee jiggled up and down and her fingers drummed on the arm of the couch, as if the thoughts spinning in her brain needed a physical outlet. "Let's leave the *why* out of it for now. Let's look at the *when* and *how*."

I'd spent the remainder of my Sunday trying to determine exactly those two things. "I don't go into that drawer very often. The last time I remember seeing all three was after New Year's, when Indra needed to borrow one because she'd misplaced hers."

"I only had the spare for a couple of days and then returned it. I know I did." She nodded vigorously.

"Yes, I remember. So, they were all there in early January."

"I'm afraid to ask," Maeve said, "but was it...?"

"Yes." I sighed in frustration, mostly at myself. "I checked the security logs. The same fob was used on Wednesday night."

This development needed to be explained to Piper and

Indra.

"It was a dry run," Piper said thoughtfully. "Whoever took it wanted to make sure it worked. Maybe even test if and when a security patrol would appear."

My thoughts exactly. It didn't make me feel any better about not following up on Maeve's report the moment she'd made it. If I'd only opened the damn drawer, we would have known to deactivate the missing fob. Except, then, I wouldn't have gotten my portrait back. But why had the thief decided to return it to the office?

I had circled back to the beginning of the conundrum. Argh.

"It had to be someone with access to my office," I said. "Since the new year, I've met with dozens of clients, and I often leave them alone to get them something from the breakroom."

"But you don't think it's a client, do you?" Piper's gaze was shrewd. "You think it's too much of a coincidence that you are suddenly involved in two mysteries. And I agree with you."

"What are you saying?" Indra wasn't dumb. She knew exactly what. Maybe she was hoping she was wrong.

I answered for Piper. "She's saying Azalea's murder must be connected to the portrait. Which means both are connected to me. Personally." I'd worked out that much last night. Still, it was eerie releasing the words to the universe. There was no taking them back now.

"If that is true," Piper said, "it narrows the suspects for our fob thief to those also connected with Azalea."

"Yes." The syllable sliced at something inside me that was

already tender and sore.

"As far as I can remember, Carter Bickersley and Coral Loughty were both in your office alone." Maeve regarded me, compassion heavy in her eyes. "And so was Seth Updike. He's been alone in it more than once, including a significant stretch of time the morning Azalea's body was discovered, when you both came here to tell us what was going on."

I'd known she'd remember. She didn't miss anything. "Yes," I repeated, keeping my voice steady. I'd also left Corporal Tam alone for a few minutes on Saturday, but if we couldn't eliminate him, we were in bigger trouble than I thought.

"How did anyone even know we used fobs in the first place?" Indra paused and then answered her own question. "I suppose whoever it was could have snooped at the back door and seen the flat boxy thing we hold the tag up to. It's rather obvious what it is, especially if you've seen one before. Why would they assume we have spares, though?"

"Everyone has spares," Maeve said. "The company that installed it insisted we have them."

"Still, they could have been stored anywhere." I waved my hands to indicate the entire building. "My office may seem logical, but none of those people were alone long enough to do a complete search."

Piper lifted one shoulder. "Your desk would be the first place to check. You only have, what, four drawers?"

I still didn't want to believe it. For a minute, we sat in glum silence.

"We'll need to deny the missing fob access." Maeve straightened in her seat. I could tell she was pleased to have something concrete to do. "That will make it useless in future, at least. And we might as well have the whole system checked while we're at it."

Piper snapped her fingers, drawing our attention. "All this fob business distracted me. I did some more poking around online and discovered something interesting about Coral Loughty. You're going to want to hear this."

CHAPTER TWENTY-EIGHT

"**WHAT IS IT?**" I asked. At this point, I doubted anything would surprise me. Nothing was what it seemed anymore.

"Did you know she's broke?" Piper's smile was slightly smug. "For a small fee you can do an online search of bankruptcy and insolvency records. I found nothing on Azalea—she's as flush as she looks—so I figured I might as well check out the others. Coral filed for bankruptcy a few weeks ago."

I recalled the For Sale sign in her yard and the mid-range sedan in her drive. Oh, wait. That had been Belva's car, not Coral's. Hmmm. "If the ransom had been picked up, that might mean something. But it wasn't."

"Is it possible Coral killed her in the hopes she'd inherit something?" Maeve offered. "And the ransom was an attempt to get more, a kind of double dipping, that failed?"

What a horrible thought. "According to Tam, Carter gets it all except for a little to charity." I also shared his not-quite-an-admission that Azalea was dead when she was brought to the storage facility and my own theory about her voice on the first ransom call. "Which means we don't know when she died. I assume the police do, from the postmortem, but that doesn't do us any good."

"Her car wasn't found until a few days after she went missing," Piper said. "What if she went somewhere voluntarily those first days and was only snatched later?"

Indra pleated her skirt with anxious fingers. "I suppose that's possible. But then why didn't she get in touch with

Carter?"

"Did you do this bankruptcy search thingie on anyone else?" I asked Piper.

"All the major players." She paused, considering me with narrowed eyes. "Are you wondering about Seth?"

My breath whooshed out. *Busted.* "Yes. Tam said something about his company being in trouble."

"I only checked personal finances. I could look into businesses if you like. Not just Seth's. Azalea had fingers in lots of pies."

"We might as well be thorough." I tightened my ponytail and tugged the cuffs of my sweater. "Well, if anyone thinks of anything else let me know. Maeve, you'll handle the security stuff?"

She nodded.

"All right." I rose, and my team rose with me. "That's enough for now. Let's get to our real jobs."

Carter showed up on my doorstep seven minutes early that evening. I let him in, the brisk scent of snow following in his wake.

"I'm sorry I couldn't meet you yesterday." I took his coat and hung it in the closet.

"It's fine." His smile was half-hearted. "Coral came over and kept me company."

"That's good. Would you like tea? Or something stronger today?"

"Not that brandy." He gave a mock shudder as he lowered onto the sofa. "It's obviously an acquired taste.

What about vodka? I'd have that with soda if you have it."

While I poured Carter's cocktail and a Malbec for me, I kept a cautious eye on him. Something seemed different, though I couldn't put my finger on what.

When I was back in my chair, we sipped in silence for a minute or two. My gaze drifted to the mantel where I'd replaced the portrait—still in its now glassless frame—of Peter and me.

After his death, I'd kept it there as a reminder to never trust anyone with my heart again. And as a punishment. Maybe I hadn't wished the hit-and-run into reality, but that didn't erase the fact I'd wanted Peter to suffer.

So much had changed since it had disappeared. And some of those changes had helped me make peace with his betrayal and my response to it. But it had felt right to return it to its place, at least for a little longer. Soon I would say goodbye, though. For good.

Carter choked, as if his drink had gone down the wrong pipe. I pulled my attention away from the past.

His gaze was directed at the row of photos on the mantel, as mine had been. He coughed again and noticed me watching. "I'm good. It's just...I wish my mom had told me." He waved a hand at the pictures, as if they were an explanation. "Had told me Warren wasn't my real dad without being forced into it. I wished she'd been honest with me. It would have changed everything." Grief saturated his voice and glistened in his eyes.

"Maybe she didn't because it didn't matter."

"Of course it mattered." A flame of anger licked at the grief.

"Let me rephrase." I sipped my wine and considered my next words. "I just meant that, to Azalea, who your father was didn't change how she felt about you. She loved you for you."

"Yeah, well, I loved her too. But I deserved a chance to get to know my real father. I'll never get that now." He stared into his tall glass, swirling the clear liquid with short, sharp movements, bubbles swirling in the depths. "You and Peter never had kids. Why not?"

The question didn't shock me. We were talking about family, after all. But that didn't stop me from wishing he hadn't asked it. Still, if hearing about my own personal misfortune helped him cope, I would share what I could.

"I had endometriosis. The severity of my condition made it impossible to conceive." Along with extremely painful periods and other fun stuff I had no intention of mentioning.

He frowned. "Aren't there treatments?"

"Yes. But some are very invasive. That wasn't a route we wanted to take." When my infertility had been confirmed, we'd been disappointed rather than devastated. Peter had even joked he had enough of kids at his day job. It was only recently that I'd begun to wonder if we'd made the right decision, if we should have researched other options.

As if picking up on my thought, Carter asked, "You never considered adoption?"

"No." Before I could dig deeper into why he was so curious about my childlessness, my phone rang, clamouring from the kitchen counter where I'd left it. I rose from my seat. "Sorry. Let me just check who that is."

It was Seth.

This was the first time he'd reached out since I'd learned about Priya. I'd been thankful he was honouring my wish for privacy, until a more disturbing conclusion had crossed my mind.

Maybe he hadn't called because he didn't care enough to try and fix things between us.

Aware of Carter watching me, I laid the phone down. Privacy was required for my next conversation with Seth. The ringing stopped. I wondered if he would leave a voice mail.

"Who was it?"

Remembering Carter's dislike of Seth—unwarranted as it was, he was entitled to his opinion—I told a little white lie. "No one." I smiled. "Want another drink?"

He said no to more beer but accepted a glass of water. "The cops asked me about Belva. Asked if Mom had ever complained about how her accountant handled her money."

I accepted this change of topic with relief. As much as I liked Carter, I would never be comfortable discussing my marriage with him.

"Financial advisor," I corrected. His words sparked a memory. It slipped and slid away from my grasp, like a goldfish in a pond. "What did you tell them?"

"I said no. She hadn't ever complained. Not about the money. She said that was the one thing she could trust Belva to handle."

"Do you mean she *couldn't* trust Belva to handle other things?"

"I don't know." He wiped the condensation off his glass

with a slim finger. "Sometimes she acted a little weird. Belva, I mean. I'd catch her watching Mom with an odd expression."

I tried to recall if I'd seen something similar the night I'd visited Azalea. All I remembered was Belva's scandalized look at the suggestion she join Coral and Azalea on a triple date.

Speaking of finances, though... "What about Coral? Was Belva her financial advisor too?"

"I have no idea. She was divorced a long time ago and I'm pretty sure she was getting alimony. Mom used to tease her about it, said Coral would never remarry because she enjoyed her free ride too much."

That sounded rather catty. I wondered, not for the first time, if Coral's claim to being Azalea's best friend was more wishful thinking than the truth. Belva had accused her of preying on Azalea's generosity. Maybe Azalea had decided she was tired of being used, had told Coral it was over, and Coral had retaliated.

Of course, there was a universe between ending a friendship and ending a life.

Every time I thought the vista of Azalea's abduction was clearing a fog rolled in and I lost sight of it again.

Carter and I talked of nothing important for another half hour or so before I chivied him out. He was reluctant to go, and I hoped he didn't see how eager I was to have him leave. But I couldn't wait to check my voice mail any longer.

Nothing.

SUSPECT ATTRACTION

Disappointment tightened my chest. I reminded myself I was the one who had asked for space, for time to think. And yet, I missed Seth. I wanted to hear his voice, smell his scent, feel his warmth.

If there had been no link between Priya and Peter, I could easily understand hiding her death from me. I hadn't talked about my husband until pushed, either. But if the only reason Seth had come to the agency, had expressed interest in me, had *made love* to me, was because of our spouses' connection...well, I didn't know if I could handle that.

I futzed around until such time as was reasonable to call it a night. After locking and securing the house—another reminder of Seth, damn it—I prepared for bed and slid under the covers. My mind tumbled with facts and suppositions, fantasies and stratagems. I closed my eyes, resigned to another restless night.

The next thing I knew, my phone ah-oo-gahed like a submarine dive alarm.

I flailed under the comforter, cursing the twisted sense of humour that had chosen that racket as the default notification. My first grab sent my phone skittering off the nightstand, dangling from the charging cord. I swept it up and turned off the alert.

Silence. Except for the blood racing in my ears and the breath sawing out of my throat.

I checked the time. 3:33 am. I didn't bother appreciating the symmetry of the number.

When Seth had installed my system, he'd put contact sensors on the exterior door to the garage, the door from the deck where I kept my barbeque, and the front door. His kit hadn't included enough for any windows, but he'd said I could add them later if I wanted. At the time, I'd felt secure enough with the doors monitored.

Someone had opened one of those doors and broken the contact. Had they heard the alarm? It would depend on which door they'd breached, I supposed.

I felt exposed and vulnerable, so slid off the mattress onto the floor. If someone looked in my room, they'd see the empty bed, but at least I would be hidden.

With ears alert to any creak of floorboards, I swiped to the system's app and pulled up the live camera feeds. There were three, covering the exterior approaches to the same doors that had contact sensors.

Too late to regret not putting any inside the house.

Nothing jumped out at me—haha—as I switched from feed to feed. All the doors were closed. The intruder could have run away when he heard the alarm.

Or he could have closed it behind him once he was inside.

I was going to have to look for myself. Again.

I rolled to my knees, stifling a groan, and crouch-walked to the end of the bed. Don't ask me why. It felt right at the time.

I snagged a pair of yoga pants from the stool where I piled my discarded clothing. No way was I reconnoitering in just a T-shirt and robe. To put on the leggings, I would have to either lie flat on the floor or stand up.

Screw it. I took a deep breath and stood up.

Throughout all of this—and the wriggling that followed as I pulled the tight fabric over my hips—I heard nothing to agitate me. Easing toward the open door, I peered around the jamb.

At the far end of the hall, a shadow fell out of the living room and slid across the floor.

Christ Almighty. Someone *was* in my house.

Fear evaporated, rage taking its place. I'd been burgled, entangled in a ransom delivery, discovered a dead body, had my office infiltrated, and was now being burgled again. I was done with it. So damn *done*.

With a guttural roar, I raced down the hall and skidded around the corner, pivoting with one hand on the wall.

A dark shape stood frozen in front of the large window, silhouetted by the glow of the streetlamp outside. The instant I barged into view, it turned and charged for the front door.

The carpet runner betrayed me. My toe caught on the edge and down I went, twisting one knee and bashing the other against the leg of a long narrow side table. By the time I struggled to my feet, spouting curses I hadn't thought I'd known, the intruder had the door open and was sprinting down the driveway.

Even so, I shoved my feet into a pair of boots and limped off after him. Not that I knew it was a him. All I could tell was they weren't abnormally tall, short, heavy, or slim. And they were fit enough to run. Fast.

My house occupied a pie-shaped lot on the outer bend of a crescent. I could see no movement on the street straight ahead of me, but as I stood at the end of my driveway an engine fired up a few houses to my right. A nondescript vehicle pulled out from the curb and drove away, easy and slow.

It might have been my intruder. It also might have been one of my perfectly innocent neighbours heading off to a perfectly innocent early morning shift at work.

I braved the chill a little longer but saw nothing more than a cat hotfooting it across the road, something dangling from its mouth. I trudged back inside, wincing with every step, my knee already swelling.

Enough was enough. It was time to wrap this up. And I didn't only mean my knee.

CHAPTER TWENTY-NINE

BELVA GINSBERG DIDN'T seem to be associated with any national or international firm. The sign on her office door simply read Ginsberg Financial Services in a bold font, along with her full name followed by a rather impressive list of credentials in more discreet letters. It was on the third floor of one of the smaller downtown buildings, not that far from the agency. Downtown being the size it was, the proximity wasn't surprising.

What was surprising was the luxuriousness. The reception area boasted uncomfortable looking but obviously expensive seating, an area rug I was afraid to walk on in my snowy boots, and a sharply dressed young man sitting behind a heavy dark wood desk.

"Can I help you?" His smile was blindingly white.

"I'd like to speak to Ms. Ginsberg, please." I hadn't called ahead, not wanting to give her a chance to avoid me.

It was nine on Tuesday morning, and my determination to put an end to the turmoil of the last several days hadn't waned. A quick text to Maeve had explained I might not make it to the office, but not to worry. She'd replied with assurances all would be well without my presence, adding I deserved a mental health day.

Which, in a way, was what I was doing. I would certainly feel better once everything was resolved.

"Do you have an appointment?" The young man remained polite, but it was clear he knew the answer and wasn't impressed.

"No. But if you tell her Regina Blynde is here, I think she'll see me." If she refused, the suite wasn't that big. Her slender, pampered gatekeeper looked like he spent more time at a spa than a gym. In the mood I was in, I would enjoy bowling him over on my way to find her inner sanctum.

I didn't get a chance to put my badassedness to the test. He hung up the phone and pointed down the hall with another glittering smile. "First door on your left."

Belva was standing behind her desk when I entered, her hands clasped at her waist. Like the first time I'd met her, she wore a long-sleeved white blouse buttoned up to her throat, a black pencil skirt, and a short rope of pearls. She regarded me with haunted eyes. A French aristocrat watching peasants build a guillotine might have had a similar expression.

I swallowed back sympathy. She wasn't the only one who'd had a bad week. "Thanks for seeing me."

"Did I have a choice?" She tried to sneer, but a tremble in her lip defused it.

"I'm not the police," I said. "Of course you have a choice."

"Refusing wouldn't stop you from sticking your nose where it doesn't belong."

"True." She hadn't offered me a seat, but I took one anyway.

After a pause she sank into her own, the tendons under her jaw stiff with tension.

"How long have you been in love with Azalea?" I asked.

It was as if I'd pulled a release cord. All the muscles in her body loosened and she sagged back, eyes closing, hands dropping to her lap.

I waited. She showed no sign of answering or even acknowledging my question. Yet somehow the silence was soft, accepting.

"It's okay, Belva." I crossed my legs, felt both knees twinge from last night's adventures, and uncrossed them. "I believe you would never want to hurt Azalea. I just need to get a few things sorted."

Her eyelids raised and her usual grim expression slackened, erasing years from her appearance. She looked vulnerable, fragile.

"How long?" I asked again.

"Since the day I met her." Her voice ached with longing. "It was what Coral said, right? That's what clued you in?"

I nodded. That, and Carter's observations. I wondered if I should warn her that he might know as well.

"I admit it was a shock. Coral is so self-centred. I didn't think she'd ever notice, even if I slipped once in a while." She rubbed her knuckles against her breastbone. "You probably think I'm silly. No one cares if you're a lesbian, not these days. At least in the abstract."

Light began to dawn. "But not in the specific?"

"My parents are devout Catholics. They love me. They want me to be happy. But they do *not* want me to be gay." The corner of her mouth wrenched in a wry smile. Had she just made a *joke*?

Huh. Belva had hidden depths. Depths I might appreciate.

Still, I needed her to tell me the truth. "Did Azalea know how you felt?"

Her chin lifted. "I told her. We met for lunch on the day she had her date with Seth."

The day she disappeared remained unspoken but glowed like neon.

I searched my memory. "You told me you'd talked to her that day, but you said it was about her investments."

She looked down at her hands. "Yes, well, that wasn't the truth. We talked, all right. But it was about us. When she suggested I go on a triple date with her and Coral, I couldn't bear it any longer. I'd thought maybe she'd just, I don't know, figure it out. But she hadn't. She wasn't going to. I needed to tell her how I felt. To let her know she had someone who loved her right in front of her, didn't need to look for anyone else."

"What was her reaction?"

Belva lifted tragic eyes, face pale with anguish. "She laughed. I told her I loved her, and she laughed."

Yet more proof Azalea was as flawed a human as the rest of us.

"Had she ever led you to believe you might get a different reaction?" Belva wasn't stupid. She wouldn't risk baring her soul to Azalea if there was no evidence her feelings were reciprocated.

I was wrong. She had.

"No. It didn't matter. I had to tell her. I expected her to let me down. But I didn't expect her to *laugh*. She patted my hand and said it was sweet, but I wasn't her type. She thought it was *funny*." Her voice cracked and she swallowed hard.

Coral had been right. I kind of hated that.

I gave Belva a few moments to collect herself before continuing. "That first night at Azalea's, I parked next to two vehicles. Fancy, expensive vehicles. Neither of them was the Toyota you drove away from Coral's the other night."

"I have two cars. One for everyday, one for fun." She answered listlessly.

"So business is doing well? No troubles? Nothing for your clients to worry about?"

Some of the starch returned to her spine. Her eyes narrowed. "No matter what Coral says, I am an excellent financial advisor. Not that *she* trusted me with her money. Azalea's finances are in better shape now than they were when I took over. And she's not my only client. I make money for everyone, myself included."

Unrequited love must be good for business, I thought facetiously. Maybe breaking up with Seth would help my agency.

I didn't want to break up with him. But I had things to do before we could clear the air between us.

From my car, parked on the street outside Belva's office building, I called Corporal Tam.

"I thought you should know about a couple of things that have happened since I last talked with you."

When I finished my recital, which included details of both the break-ins at my home and the unnerving package left at my office but not my conversation with Belva, there was a long silence. My right knee throbbed under its elastic bandage. I eased my foot forward between the brake and gas pedal to give it a stretch.

"For god's sake." His burly voice held more than irritation. He was angry. "Why am I just hearing all this now?"

"When the photo went missing, I honestly thought it was a mistake, that I'd imagined the intruder and misplaced the picture. When it was returned, I needed time to think about what it meant. As for last night, what would you have done if I'd called you? He was gone, whoever it was. And he hadn't touched anything inside the house that I could see."

"How did he get in?"

I heard the beeps that indicated another call and Carter's name appeared on my dash screen. I was going to have to talk to him again but now was not the time. I tapped the red X and answered Tam's question.

"The person door to my garage was pried open." It still shut but couldn't be locked. I'd barricaded it with heavy boxes supplemented by a few sandbags I'd found lurking in a dark corner. Getting it repaired was also on today's agenda. "That might explain why he came inside. He would have been too far away to hear the alarm go off in my bedroom."

"Did you check the system recordings? Can you see anything on it?"

"I did, but it doesn't help. You can see a figure, but no face. Nothing identifiable."

"Still, you should have called me."

"Would you have pulled out all the stops for either break-in?"

He didn't deign to reply to that accusation. "What the hell was he looking for this time?" Not waiting for an answer, for which I was grateful, he continued. "Anything else happens, you tell me, and you tell me right now. Get it?"

"Got it. What about you?"

"What about me?" His tone was suspicious.

"Anything you can share with me?" I don't know why I bothered. Sheer stubbornness, I guess.

Unfortunately, he didn't surprise me. "Our inquiries are proceeding."

And so were mine. Coral was next on my list.

As with Belva, I didn't want to give Coral a chance to avoid me, so I didn't call ahead.

Unlike Belva, she didn't have a regular work schedule, so I wasn't sure where I would find her.

The logical place to start was her house, so I went there. She didn't answer the first ring of the doorbell. Remembering her slow response on Friday, I gave her plenty of time. When the wait proved fruitless, I pressed the button until the tip of my finger throbbed, hoping the sheer annoyance would drive her out of hiding.

Still nothing.

I climbed back in my car, turned on the engine to get the heater going, and called Maeve.

"Are Piper and Indra in?" She replied in the affirmative. "I'm trying to track down Coral Loughty. I'm hoping one of you might have an idea where I could find her."

"I thought you were taking the day off."

I could hear her frown. She was worried for me and didn't even know about the most recent break-in. Maybe I should have felt guilty for not telling her, but I didn't. I'd only told Tam because he was official. "Just ask them. Please."

Her sigh whooshed through the speaker, and then I heard staticky rustling, as if she was holding the phone against her chest.

I blew on my chilled fingers. A couple of minutes later, Maeve spoke, once again crisp and clear. "I'll text you a list of possibilities. Piper has some places she found during her financial search. Indra's suggestions are the charities Azalea supported. She says since they both volunteered for the Canadian Cancer Society, maybe they worked together on others."

"Good idea. Thanks. I'll be in touch if I need anything else."

"Be careful, Ginnie. I don't know what you're doing, but be careful." Her concern was real, despite the scolding tone.

I disconnected, my gaze sweeping over the For Sale sign on Coral's snow-covered lawn and back again. I hesitated, and then, in the spirit of leaving no stone unturned, I called the number of the Realtor listed.

A woman answered with exaggerated good cheer. "Trudy Kozar, Sunshine Realty. How can I make your day better?"

I stared at the dash screen. I was all for polite and eager, but this was too cutesy for me.

"Hi, Trudy. I'm a friend of Coral Loughty." Yes, I know that was a lie. Bees with honey, etc., etc. "This is an odd question, but do you happen to know where she is at the moment?"

"Hi, friend of Coral! I'm afraid I don't. Have you tried

calling her?"

I'd describe her tone as irritatingly chipper. Well, when in Rome... I trilled out a giggle. "Silly me. That's why I need to find her. I forgot my cell at her house. I'm calling from my land line. And while I can remember my childhood number, I can't remember Coral's for the life of me."

"Isn't that the way it is? I have it here. Just let me put you on speaker while I call it up."

I dutifully repeated the digits back to her as if I were writing them down and thanked her for her help. While I was going through that charade, I heard the beeps indicating a text had arrived. I disconnected from Ms. Sunshine with relief.

Maeve's message was just the list, no other nagging instructions. I didn't know whether to be grateful or disappointed. It was kind of nice having someone worry about me.

The list wasn't long—only nine names. I had warmed up since my assault on Coral's front door, so I turned off the engine. If I called from here, I could lie in wait at the same time.

CHAPTER THIRTY

I REACHED OUT TO the Canadian Cancer Society first. Even if Coral wasn't there, I might be able to learn more about the argument she and Azalea had had at the Illumination Celebration wrap up party.

No luck on all fronts. The woman who answered the phone knew Coral and seemed sincerely dismayed she couldn't help. She was sorry, but Coral wasn't in the office. No, she herself hadn't been at the thank you party. Yes, she knew who the co-chair was, but also knew she had left that morning for a two-week Caribbean cruise.

Scratch that one off.

I had similar bad luck at the second charity. And with the next three Indra had suggested.

I did learn something interesting from all five, though. Coral had recently resigned from each of them. And by recently, I meant since the new year. Indra couldn't have known that little tidbit or she would have passed it on to me. She had been asking about Azalea, not Coral, so it was understandable why no one had mentioned it to her.

The non-charities on the list were a spa, a gym, a bank, and a lawyer. I doubted I'd get far with the last two. I mentally flipped a coin over the others. The gym won.

The chill had returned to my toes and nose and my butt was sore from sitting. None of this discomfort drowned out the ache in my knee. Deciding I wasn't cut out for surveillance work, I started the engine and backed out of the driveway.

Coral's gym, according to Piper, was an expensive boutique health club in a small mall about ten minutes from her house. I pulled into the parking lot and stepped out of my car. I'd only taken a couple of steps when she emerged from the building.

She didn't see me. A rolled yoga mat with straps and a small bag hung from her shoulder, bumping against her hip with each hurried stride. Head down, she crossed the parking lot, wiping her eyes with her fist.

"Coral!" I strode after her. "Coral, wait."

She threw a quick glance over her shoulder and walked faster. I broke into a trot, my knee protesting with every jolt. "Please. I just want to talk."

Her destination was an older-model grey sedan with a dent in the rear fender. She opened the driver's door, tossed her mat and bag onto the passenger seat, and slid behind the wheel. Before she could shut me out, I grabbed the window frame and held tight.

"Leave me alone." She tugged half-heartedly, giving up easily when I refused to let go.

I caught a glimpse of her face. Her eyes were red and swollen and glistening tracks snaked down her cheek. "Are you okay? Have you been crying?"

"No." She sniffed. "I'm sweating. I was working out."

That might explain the moisture on her skin but not the irritated eyes. "I'm not buying it. What upset you?"

Her laugh was derisive. She gripped the steering wheel

with both hands and glared out the windshield. "What upset me? What *hasn't* upset me lately? This is the last straw."

"What is?" She didn't answer. I said cajolingly, "It's cold out. Let me in and we'll talk."

I thought she was going to refuse, but then she reached for the unlock button and the door behind her clicked. I grabbed for the handle before she changed her mind. Our doors slammed shut in unison.

I slid to the middle of the back bench and leaned over the console, wedging my shoulders between the front seats. She still refused to look at me. "What's going on? Maybe I can help."

She snorted. "Right. Like you'd help me. You think I had something to do with Azalea's death."

"Why would you say that?"

"Why else are you stalking me? I doubt you just happened to be in the area and accidentally"—she made air quotes around the word—"ran into me."

Maybe bluntness would shake something out. "Are you having financial troubles? Your house is for sale and this isn't the vehicle you had at Azalea's."

"Wow. Sherlock Holmes in a skirt."

I didn't bother pointing out I was wearing jeans. "Did something happen at the gym to upset you?"

"Not really. I just...I had to cancel my membership."

I had the feeling she hadn't cancelled it voluntarily. I'd shed plenty of angry tears of my own. I should have recognized them sooner.

"Azalea and I used to come here together." She sounded defeated, beaten down. "It was her favourite."

"It looks expensive," I probed.

"Yeah." It was barely a breath. "Azalea was generous. When she wanted to be. She took care of my monthly membership. They heard she died and told me I'd have to change the payment method. I can't afford it."

"I'm sorry about that."

"I'm losing everything." Her voice was plaintive. "My house, my car, now my health club. My life sucks."

I noted Azalea wasn't included in that list of losses but decided not to point it out. "What happened?"

She picked at the cracked vinyl of the steering wheel, her gel-polished fingernail tick-tick-ticking. "I had some investments that went bad."

When she didn't offer more, I asked the only logical question, certain I knew the answer and equally certain it would galvanize Coral. "With Belva?"

She spun in her seat and glared at me. "No. She wouldn't have me, even if I wanted her meddling in my affairs. I was too small a fish for *her*."

This didn't quite jive with what Belva had told me, but given their adversarial association, it was probably a bit of both.

I had one more thing to ask and hoped it wouldn't dam the flow. "You told me you'd talked with Azalea on the Tuesday she went missing. Do you remember what time that was?"

"Of course I remember. It was the last time I spoke with my best friend." Her voice caught on a sob. As complicated as I suspected her relationship with Azalea had been, I did believe she missed her. "It was eight o'clock. Maybe a couple of minutes before."

"Did she say what she was doing?"

"I told you all this before. All I know is she said she was going to meet the love of her life." Derision tainted her voice. "I assumed she was on her way to her date."

"I see." I was beginning to see a few things. Whether I was right about any of them remained to be, well, seen.

My stomach growled as I left Coral sitting disconsolately behind the wheel of her beat-up second-hand car. I'd skipped breakfast for a third cup of coffee and now my gut was gnawing itself in a search for sustenance. My favourite sushi place was nearby, so I ordered takeout and headed home.

I'd done what I'd set out to do today and a good boss would have gone to the agency to help with things there. But I wanted some quiet time to cogitate.

Tam had neither confirmed nor denied my theory that Azalea had died the night she disappeared. And I didn't know when she had been brought to the storage facility. But if I was right about her time of death, whoever had killed her—intentionally or not—must have had a place to hide her body while he or she arranged the rental of the lock-up.

That ruled out literally no one. I could think of dozens of possible locations. The trunk of a car, another storage locker, a basement. It was winter. A garden shed would be colder than a morgue body drawer.

I also couldn't eliminate abduction for profit as a motive. Just because the ransom hadn't been picked up didn't mean it hadn't been the intended prize all along. There were lots of reasons the kidnapper might have been unable to retrieve it.

As for her death—maybe Azalea had put up a fight and died in the struggle. The abductor might have tried to recoup some of his losses by sticking with the original plan, albeit belatedly.

On the other hand, maybe her death had been the goal all along and it was the ransom that had been impromptu.

I surfed Google and learned far more about 'interactive voice response systems' than I ever wanted to know. The main fact I gleaned was that pretty much anyone could do it from pretty much anywhere from pretty much any device. Providers made it sound simple enough that even I might be able to do it.

My suspect pool was small. If the perpetrator wasn't someone in Azalea's inner circle, it would be up to the RCMP to find them. I didn't have the resources to widen my investigation.

Investigation. What a fancy word for being nosy and asking irritating questions I didn't have the right to ask.

In between all these musings and ponderings, I thought about Seth.

My anger at his deceit had faded. As for how authentic his feelings were, he was the only one who could tell me. Which meant I'd have to ask.

I wasn't as averse to conflict as many people were. In my career before Blynde Dating Agency, I had dealt with it daily. I knew several techniques for helping others navigate the confusing maze that emotions and misunderstandings could create.

It was totally different when I had to use those

techniques on myself.

I leaned back in my chair and rubbed my eyes. As often happened since I'd returned it to the mantel, my gaze settled on the wedding portrait. There was another mystery. Why had it been stolen and returned, glass splintered but mostly unharmed? How did it tie into Azalea's murder? I was certain it did.

Rising to my feet, I went to the fireplace and picked it up. Peter and I had chosen Rainbow Park, a popular location with photographers, for our not-quite-formal shots. We stood on an arched white bridge over a dry creek, beaming with delight.

I returned to my chair and traced Peter's smiling lips with my fingertip. God, I'd loved him so much. His first affair—the one I'd thought his *only* affair—had seasoned us, forged our commitment to each other. For almost thirty years, it had been just the two of us. We'd been each other's world. Or so I'd thought.

The closest I'd come to recapturing that feeling of love and surety had been in Seth's arms. I missed him. A lot more than I should, given the briefness of our relationship.

No matter how uncomfortable it made me, I had to talk with him. I needed to know the whole truth. Why had he sought me out? Why had he pursued me?

The eight by ten photo was set in a larger frame, allowing for a double matte. For the first time, I noticed the picture was slightly askew. I laid it face down on my knees and pried open the tabs, intending to realign it. I lifted the back off, revealing a piece of paper between it and the reverse side of the portrait. I plucked it out and unfolded it with idle curiosity, assuming it was scrap I'd used to keep the photo wedged in place.

The page was old and flimsy, with an ornate blue border and an official looking stamp in the lower corner.

A birth certificate.

Carter Humphrey Bickersley's birth certificate.

I absorbed the details with one swift glance. Birth date. Birthplace. Mother's name. Father's name.

My cheeks prickled as if I'd drunk too much wine. My vision blurred. The paper crinkled as my fingers clenched around it.

I'm not sure how long I sat there, trying to unsee what I'd read. Trying to figure out how and when Carter's birth certificate had been secreted in my wedding portrait. I do know I was cold and stiff by the time I picked up my phone and dialled.

Carter answered on the second ring. "Ginnie? I'm so glad you called. I feel like I'm always calling *you*." He sounded genuinely pleased.

I didn't let the pinch of guilt derail my purpose. "I wanted to apologize. I feel like I might have rushed you out yesterday. That wasn't what I intended. You're important to me and are welcome in my home anytime." That was the truth, but not the whole truth. A little soft soap would smooth the way toward the favour I was about to ask.

"Please, don't apologize." His voice trembled. "You've been nothing but good to me. Whenever I remember I'm never going to see Mom again, hear her voice, I think of you."

As uncomfortable as I was with the responsibility this sentiment laid on my shoulders, he'd given me the opening I needed. Feeling only slightly remorseful, I said, "Would you like me to come over tonight? To make up for cutting our visit short yesterday?"

"Would you?"

His gratefulness had me doubting my conclusions, but I soldiered on. "And maybe you could ask Belva and Coral too."

"Why?"

No way was I going to answer that honestly. "I think it would be good if we were all together tonight."

I waited through a lengthy pause. "Fine." His tone was resigned. "I'll call them."

Now for the tough one. "I'd also like you to invite Seth Updike."

"No." This reply was swift and decisive. "I won't have that man in my house."

"Please, Carter. I wouldn't ask if it wasn't important."

"He upsets me. You know that. Why do you want him to come?"

I stuck to my guns. "You wanted me to do some sleuthing into your mother's disappearance, remember?" Not that he'd ever followed up on that conversation. Maybe he'd forgotten all about it in the maelstrom of recent events. Maybe he had other reasons for not asking what I was doing to fulfill my promise. "I've found out some things and I want Seth to be there when we discuss them."

It took some more wheedling, but he finally agreed, and

we settled on seven o'clock.

I found a notepad and pen in my kitchen junk drawer and returned to my chair. There was a lot I was going to unpack this evening, and I wanted to make sure I didn't forget anything. Writing it down would help me organize my thoughts.

CHAPTER THIRTY-ONE

AT TWO MINUTES TO seven, I turned into the parking lot at Carter's apartment, aware of a white pickup following me in. Similar vehicles were as thick as January snow in Prince George, but I knew who owned this one.

I climbed out and shut the door, the clunk echoing as Seth did the same. Pulse thumping, I sidled between the two vehicles and met him at the tailgate.

"Hi." The single syllable was all I could manage. *Smooth, Ginnie.*

"Hi." Blue eyes searched my face, as if seeking out any changes the last few days had wrought. "How have you been?"

"Fine. You?" He looked good. Really good. He hadn't shaved recently, and silver scruff roughened his jaw. My fingers itched to run over it, feel the tickle on my palm and between my legs. Even more, I ached to lean into his strength, have him wrap his arms around me, accept the comfort in his warmth. But that wasn't why I'd insisted Carter invite him.

Seth's next words followed on the heels of my thought. "Carter wouldn't tell me what's going on." He shoved his hands in the pockets of his parka and hitched one shoulder. "He just said you wanted me here."

A questioning cadence revealed he wasn't sure whether that was a good or bad thing. "Yes. I'm glad you could make it." God, this was more awkward than I'd thought. A strand of hair blew across my face, driven by the icy breeze, and I shivered. "We should go in."

We walked side by side toward the entrance, my skin prickling with awareness.

"Are you limping?" he asked.

"It's nothing," I assured him. "I hurt my knee a little. I'll explain later." I intended to explain a lot of things later.

In the vestibule, I buzzed Carter's apartment, and he let us in without fanfare.

Seth headed for the elevator. I grabbed the sleeve of his jacket.

"Just a minute." My gaze swept the lobby. Spotting a sign indicating the stairwell, I dragged him toward it. We would find some privacy there. The door clanged shut, reverberating off the concrete steps and walls.

"What's going on?" Instead of tugging out of my grip, he laced our fingers together.

"I need to know something." This was *not* the right time to have this out, but I couldn't wait any longer. My belly twisted and I licked my lips, mouth dry. "Did you sleep with me because of Priya and Peter? Was it some sort of twisted way of getting back at my husband? Were you faking your attraction?"

He stared. "What? No. Is that what you thought?"

I closed my eyes briefly. "Maybe. Yes. Why else would you have lied to me about Priya?"

He yanked me forward, his free arm wrapping around my waist, and slammed his mouth on mine. His kiss was bruising and forceful and reassuring. Even through several layers of heavy clothing, his heat enveloped me. I clung to his waist and responded with enthusiasm.

"Faking it, was I?" He muttered the words against the skin under my ear, nudging the wool of my scarf out of his way. "Does this feel fake to you?" He grabbed my ass and pressed me against his hips. The hard rod of his erection was unmistakable.

"Then why?" I did my own exploring, nipping his bottom lip hard in erotic punishment. "Why sign up for the agency? Why seek me out after that first day?"

"I admit, it started because I was curious." He pressed his forehead against mine. "Can you blame me? I'd just learned about Priya and your husband. I wanted to get a look at you, see if you knew who I was. But the minute I walked into your office..."

"What?" I inhaled his sandalwood scent, feeling as if I'd come home. "What happened then?"

"I saw you." He pulled away, his hands gripping my shoulders, his stare fierce and direct. "It was insane. I could barely breathe. I had to get to know you better because of *you*. Not for any other reason."

Warmth suffused my cheeks. Still— "You could have fooled me. Did fool me. You looked so calm, so relaxed."

"Trust me. I was anything but calm."

I needed to know it all. "Everything you said about wanting a companion, researching other dating sites, appreciating the references on my website...that was all a lie? A cover story?"

"I did look up your website. I wanted to be prepared. As for the rest..." Shamefaced lines creased his cheeks. "Whether you recognized me or not, I was going to say I'd changed my mind, that I wasn't interested anymore, and get out of there. But I was so shaken by my reaction I went along, let you set me up with Azalea. You don't know how much I wish I'd been honest with you from the start."

I wasn't sure whether to be flattered or annoyed. I knew I'd be second-guessing my people skills for a long time because of his deception. "We'll have to talk more before this is wrapped up once and for all. But it will have to be later. Carter will be wondering where we are."

In answer, he pressed his mouth to mine in another penetrating, fiery kiss.

I had no desire to fight the passion raging between us, but after several moments I dragged my mouth away, panting. "We can't. We have to go."

He groaned and let me ease out of his hold. "Let's take the stairs. I need a minute before I'll be presentable."

Carter welcomed us with a brusque nod, the corners of his mouth pulled tight. I could tell he hadn't forgiven me for coercing him into inviting Seth.

We hung up our coats and followed him into the living room. Belva and Coral sat in the squat white chairs on opposite ends of the long low table, as isolated as if they were trapped under bell jars. Neither of them looked me in the eye and both acknowledged Seth's introduction with stiff politeness.

Carter dropped onto one of the sofas and crossed his legs in a casual gesture. "Have a seat."

Seth and I took the couch opposite. He pressed close

enough I could feel the heat of his body. The trek up the stairs had made my knee ache and I stretched my leg to ease the pressure.

I wished we could leave, go to my place to finish our conversation. And complete our reconciliation. But I'd engineered this evening, and it took precedence.

"Well, Ginnie. Why have you gathered us all here tonight?" Carter's tone was faintly mocking, and the look he slid my way held none of his usual friendly openness. Even if I was wrong, nothing would be the same between us after tonight. Regret pinched the back of my nose.

I drew in a deep breath, preparing myself. "I've discovered a few things I wanted to discuss with everyone." Belva's eyelids fluttered and Coral's upper lip sneered at the corner. Carter remained impassive. "To start, we need to tell them about your real father."

"No." He frowned, a shadow flitting across his face. His resistance was automatic, a knee-jerk response to a long-kept secret.

"I don't understand." Coral's scorn faded into confusion. "What are you talking about? Carter's *real* father?"

I didn't shift my attention from the young man. "It would be best if you told them, but if you don't, I will." For several moments our gazes battled. In his, suspicion dawned. Still, he couldn't *know* I'd discovered the truth.

The lines on his forehead smoothed. He had decided to bluff it out, as I'd suspected he would. "It's quite straightforward, Coral. My mother was pregnant before she met Warren Bickersley."

The other woman's puckered expression deepened. "I

knew she was already expecting when they married. It was simple math. But she would have told me if he wasn't—"

"She wouldn't have told you. She never trusted you." Disdain glowed in the amber embers of Carter's deep brown irises. Irises the same rich shade as Peter's.

"His birth father was already married when Azalea got pregnant." All eyes swung to me. "Isn't that what she told you?"

He nodded, his eyes narrowed. Calculations were going on inside his head. I couldn't give him time to think.

"And you told me her lover didn't know she was pregnant." Stress sweat beaded in the hollows of my elbows. This, almost more than anything else, had been occupying my mind since I'd discovered the birth certificate.

"That's what Mom said." He sat straighter. "She wanted him to leave his wife because he loved her, not because he felt responsible for me. But he wouldn't. He stayed with his wife. He stayed with *her*."

The last word shot accusingly across the low table, aimed directly at me. I held back a flinch as Carter's eyes scorched into mine with an intensity he'd disguised until now. That answered another burning question. Carter *did* know who his real father was.

If I'd pressed him the day he told me about Warren, would this scene be playing out differently? Or would it have been avoided entirely?

Belva's attention flashed from Seth to me and back to Seth, yet her question was intended for Carter. "Is that why he's here?"

Coral gasped as the incorrect penny dropped. "*He's* your

dad?"

Carter was contemptuous. "Not *him*. Of course not."

"No, not Seth." I swallowed around the stone in my throat. "Carter's father was Peter Blynde. My husband."

Carter's eyes, so familiar even before I'd known why, stretched into round circles. If he'd realized I'd discovered the truth, he hadn't thought I'd confess it. Belva and Coral stared in silent fascination.

Seth took my hand, pressing my fingers. I gripped hard and focused on Carter. "I know you found out Warren wasn't your biological father only after he got sick. When did you find out who *was* your dad?"

"A month or two after Warren died." He answered easily, still in shock at my revelation of his secret. "Mom refused to tell me at first. She said it was in the past, that it didn't matter. Well, it mattered to *me*." The last words were almost a cry.

"What did you do after you found out?"

"I tracked him down. You still have a land line. The number's in the phone book. It was dead easy." He puffed out his chest as if expecting praise. And maybe he deserved it. To his generation, a land line was archaic, a phone book the stuff of legends. "I followed him to work one morning. When school was over, I found him in his classroom."

"What did you want from him?"

"I wanted him to be my dad. I'd always known, deep inside, that Warren wasn't my father. He never liked me. I never liked him. All I wanted was a dad." His tone was childlike, his expression wistful.

But only for a moment. His face hardened. "Peter

refused. Said it was a lie. I showed him my birth certificate. He wouldn't look at it, wouldn't even touch it. Fine, he said, maybe it's the truth. But I'll never acknowledge you. My wife can never know." He bared his teeth in a vicious mockery of a smile. "He chose you over his own son. But I wouldn't have given up. I was going to change his mind. And then he was killed."

A soothing wave swept over me. Peter hadn't hidden the birth certificate behind our portrait. I hadn't wanted to believe he could have been so insensitive and was glad I'd been right about that, at least.

Earlier, I'd worked out the timeline. There was a gap of about six months between Warren Bickersley and Peter's deaths, and Carter would have been hounding him for several of them. Also during that time, Peter had been having an affair with Priya.

No wonder he'd seemed abstracted on occasion. In retrospect, I felt sorry for him. I had loved him too long not to have some sympathy at the predicament he'd found himself in.

Right now, however, I had more important issues to deal with.

CHAPTER THIRTY-TWO

BEFORE I COULD continue, Carter stood abruptly. "I need a drink." He added, rather ungraciously, "Anyone else?"

I hated to lose the momentum I'd been building, but I was parched and could use some liquid courage. I requested white wine, Belva a gin and tonic, and Coral a Caesar. Seth asked for water.

"Come now." Carter's smile held an edge. "As your host, I insist on something more than that. What can I get you?"

Seth upped his order and unbent enough to provide a reason for it. "A club soda is fine. With lime if you have it. Alcohol and I don't agree."

Carter's eyes widened. "Oh, that's right. Ginnie mentioned you have an allergy."

"An allergy to alcohol?" Coral's attitude thawed enough for her to show faint curiosity. "Is it serious?"

"Yes." Seth softened his curt reply with a wry smile. "Serious enough that I never touch it."

Carter moved toward the kitchen. "I'll be right back."

It was so quiet in the living room I could hear soft clinks and glugs and rattles as an invisible Carter prepared our drinks. The only time I recalled mentioning Seth's allergy in Carter's presence was the night Tam and his officers had been at my house. Was it odd that he'd taken note of that fact while he'd been distraught over his mother's kidnapping?

Maybe. Maybe not.

He returned several silent minutes later with a laden teak tray. Belva took her drink and downed a large gulp. Coral sipped daintily. They continued to pretend the other didn't exist. Any truce Azalea's death might have inspired hadn't survived last Friday's clash.

Carter dropped onto his sofa, holding his glass high to avoid spilling. It was a tall tumbler, filled with clear liquid fizzing over ice and a wedge of lime and looked much like Seth's. "How's your drink, Seth? Watery enough for you?" If he intended to sound teasing, he missed by several degrees.

"It's fine, thanks." Seth took a swallow and set the glass on the table, shifting closer to me as he did so.

Coral watched Belva like a hawk. Belva regarded Carter with a wrinkled brow. Carter's eyes flicked from Seth to me and back again. I couldn't see where Seth was looking, but his thigh was taut where it pressed against mine.

I placed my drink next to his, gripped his hand again, and took the next step.

"One thing puzzles me, Carter," I said. "Your birth certificate. You must have seen it before. School registration, passport application, something. Did you never notice your father's name on it?"

"I have two certificates. One is wallet-sized with only my name, birth date, and ID number." He scowled. "After I made Mom tell me the truth, she showed me the complete one. She told me Warren allowed her to include my father's name as long as she kept it hidden."

And she'd honoured that promise until after his death. "Carter." I spoke slowly, carefully. "Did you break into my house? Was it you that took my wedding portrait?"

Seth's fingers tightened painfully around mine and then relaxed. He had to have questions of his own, but he was

283

letting me handle this my way. I appreciated his forbearance.

"What portrait?" Belva asked.

"Yeah, what portrait?" Coral echoed, a fraction later.

Carter wasn't surprised by my accusation. Instead, he seemed pleased to have the chance to explain. "When Peter died, my mother wanted me to forget about him. It was over, she said. He was gone and there was nothing I could do. I just had to live with it. And I tried to. I really did."

"You started Carousel, found a girlfriend," I said.

"She left me." His face crumpled. "She *left* me. Said she wanted to have kids, but didn't think I was mature enough to be a father. It was all my mother's fault. If she'd told me the truth, if I'd had a chance to know my real dad, things would have been different."

The last words were a plea for understanding. Ripples upon ripples, reaching out to touch everyone in this room.

Tiny muscles twitched under Carter's eyes as he continued. "Then I got an idea. I convinced Mom to sign up for your agency. She was supposed to become your friend. If she couldn't give me back the time I should have had with my dad, she could give me time with the next best thing. You."

"What did she think of that? You were asking her to befriend the wife of the man she'd had an affair with. The man she'd had a *child* with." Knowing what I now did coloured every interaction I'd had with Azalea. I'd replayed them in my head, over and over. Yet I couldn't see one instant where she'd treated me with anything other than gracious cheerfulness.

Carter looked puzzled, as if he'd never considered the

possibility his request might have bothered his mother. "She didn't care. Why would she? She was the one that kept telling me the past was the past."

Maybe that was true. Maybe it really hadn't mattered to her, not after all the years between. It wasn't like I could ask her myself, though, could I? I'd have to make peace with not knowing.

"Besides," he went on. "We were certain Peter hadn't told you about me. Mom said it was obvious her name meant nothing to you during her first interview. We decided I would be the one to tell you, when I thought it was right."

It was important to keep him focused on his parentage, so he didn't see what else was coming. "You didn't break in until after Azalea went missing. Why then? It's been years since Peter died."

"I'd lost—" He broke off, the corner of his mouth quivering. "I told you. I couldn't forget him. I wanted to spend some time in his house. I asked if I could come over that night, but you refused. I had to find another way."

I recalled the sensation of being watched in the parking lot. "Were you following me?"

A crafty smile twisted his lips. "Yes. I told you I followed Peter. After he died, I followed you a few times. You never noticed." His pale brows drew together. "I thought I might feel closer to him in the place he'd lived. I didn't. It was like he had never existed. Then I saw the portrait. It was the only thing that spoke to me. I had to have it."

"And you concealed the birth certificate in it."

"Birth certificate?" Shock sharpened Coral's exclamation. "In the portrait?"

I watched her closely. "Yes. I found it wedged in the back after it was returned to me."

She looked a little green around the gills. I let it go and turned my attention back to Carter.

"I wanted it to be with him." He rested his elbows on his knees and leaned forward, his glass clasped in his hands. "And then, last night, I saw the portrait at your house again. I thought maybe you'd had a copy made, so when I got home, I looked for mine. It was gone."

"Which meant I now had your birth certificate. You broke in a second time to retrieve it. My alarm system woke me, and I chased you out of the house, but I fell before I could catch you."

Seth heaved in a rasping breath as my reply to his question about my limp suddenly made sense.

I went on. "Earlier today, I noticed the photo was out of alignment in the frame and decided to fix it. That's when I found the document."

Carter was still puzzled. "How did you get it back, though? And when?"

"I think Coral can answer that."

"Me?" She'd had time to recover from her surprise and blinked, wide-eyed and blameless. I wasn't fooled. "Why on earth would I know?"

"Because you're the one who stole it from Carter. You're the one who destroyed it and then returned the remains to me this past weekend. What I want to know is why."

Her innocence melted away like a mountain icecap in summer, replaced by indignation. "I don't have to explain myself to you."

"From the start, you've been angry about Carter's relationship with me. An anger out of all proportion to the situation." Maybe she truly cared for him as a person, as someone she'd known since he was a baby. Maybe she wanted him to replace Azalea as her benefactor. I doubted I'd get an honest answer if I asked.

"I was his mother's closest friend. He should have come to *me*, not a stranger." Her declaration shimmered with resentment.

"Ginnie's not a stranger," Carter said. "She's my stepmother."

Stepmother. It was an echo of how I'd started to feel about him, the son I'd never had. But that relationship was impossible now. More regret layered on top of my already complicated emotions.

"Well, I didn't know that, did I?" Coral said. "If I'd known about your real dad, maybe I would have understood. But I didn't. All these years, and Azalea never—" She cut herself off, fury blazing in red flags on her cheeks. Huffing air out her nostrils, she continued, slightly calmer. "When I saw that photo, it made me furious. I took it away and smashed it. Then I left it where *she* would find it, hoping she'd think you'd done it. That you were rejecting her. Like you'd rejected me."

Her distress sounded sincere, even if it stemmed from selfishness. It wouldn't stop me from pressing on with my agenda. "From your earlier reaction, I assume you didn't know the certificate was in the back."

She answered without looking at me, her attention all on Carter. "Of course I didn't. I still can't believe Azalea never

287

told me the truth."

"Believe it. My mother might have liked you fawning all over her, but it didn't mean she trusted you." Carter took a slug of his drink. "That portrait was in my bedroom nightstand. You couldn't have seen it unless you were snooping around. But that's what you do, isn't it? Poke your nose where it doesn't belong. It's what makes you the sneaky, lying bitch you are."

I was stunned silent. I'd never heard him speak so cruelly, so bitterly.

Belva recovered before I did. "Carter! That's uncalled for."

More shock held my tongue. Belva, sticking up for Coral?

"Don't scold me. You're not my mother." Carter's smile was nasty. "Oh, but you wanted to be, didn't you? You wanted to be my second mommy."

Belva hissed in a breath. Beside me, Seth stiffened.

Coral laughed, a spiteful tinkle. "You really thought that was such a big secret? Everyone knew about your pathetic unrequited love."

Carter turned on her, quick as a striking snake. "At least she loved my mom. Not like you, you vampire."

Wow. Things were unravelling fast. "Carter—" I began, but I was his next target.

"You." His tone was low and biting. His eyes glittered with fury. "You were the reason I never knew my father."

My cheeks flushed. "That's not fair," I replied quietly. "I didn't know about you."

"You want to talk about not fair?" He slammed his glass

down on the low table, making Belva jump. "Me, living a lie all my life. My mother tricking me into calling a stranger 'Dad.' My real father not acknowledging me because he didn't want to hurt your feelings."

His voice hitched and he fell back against the cushions, eyes closed. I waited, tense and frozen, expecting another outburst.

It didn't happen.

Cautiously, I regained control of the conversation. "Coral, when did you take the portrait from Carter?"

She stared at the floor.

"Was it the day you and Belva were here after Azalea's body was found? You insisted he take a tranquilizer, so he probably slept a lot."

"If you think it was then, why don't you accuse *her*?" She jerked her chin at Belva, lips pressed tight with animosity. "She had the same opportunity."

Carter opened his eyes but remained in his slumped position.

"Because it was returned to my office by someone using one of our spare security fobs. A *stolen* security fob. Belva never came to the agency so she couldn't have taken it. You were in my office, though. I left you alone long enough for a quick search through my desk. What I don't understand is why you took it in the first place. Why would you want access to my office?"

Few people could resist showing how smart they were, especially to someone they considered their enemy. Coral was no exception.

"I'd seen the Facebook post that morning. The one

warning people about your agency. If I could discover other scandals, it would prove to Carter he shouldn't trust you. I needed a way to come back when no one was around so I could search your files." She smirked. "I thought I might find a key. Instead, the spare fobs were in the first drawer I opened."

"What if I'd notice one was gone, and we'd change the codes?"

Her lip curled higher. "It was worth a shot. I knew you hadn't by Wednes—" She snapped her teeth shut.

"By Wednesday. Because you tested it that night, didn't you?"

She glared but remained silent.

"We noticed a fob had been used, but we put it down to a glitch. In retrospect, I should have checked the spares then, but I didn't." I'd had other things on my mind, but that was no excuse.

"I can't believe it," Belva said with disgust. "I always knew you were meddlesome, suspected you were conniving. But this?"

"Screw you." The crudity fell oddly from Coral's full, pouty mouth. "I don't have to stand for this. Carter, thanks *so* much for the invitation"—her sarcasm sizzled the air—"but I think I'll be going."

"Don't you want to find out what happened to Azalea?" I asked.

CHAPTER THIRTY-THREE

SILENCE.

Carter sat up slowly. Speculation twisted Belva's mouth. Coral, who had lifted her butt off the seat, hovered for a long moment, and then sat back down. I took a sip of my wine, wishing it was water so I could chug it.

Seth took a long swallow from his own glass, lowering the level from mostly full to less than three-quarters. "Tell us, Ginnie. Tell us what you know." It had been several minutes since he'd spoken, and his voice was low and hoarse.

Maybe I should have gone to Tam with my suspicions, even though I didn't have any real proof. Maybe I shouldn't have attempted this on my own. But it was too late now. The doors had blown wide open, and I couldn't close them again.

I checked my mental notes and forged on. "Here's what I've sussed out. Azalea and Seth went on their date two weeks ago this evening. They met at six-thirty and spent a little over an hour together."

Seth cleared his throat. "That sounds about right."

Our eyes met and I begged silent forgiveness for what I was about to do. "How did your date go?"

Maybe he knew where I was heading. Maybe he'd figured it out himself before I had. Whatever the reason, he went along with my questioning. "We had a lovely dinner. But I had to tell her that I'd met someone else, that I wouldn't be interested in seeing her again."

"How did she take that?"

He shrugged. "Calmly. She even laughed a little about it."

"Who was the woman you rejected Azalea for?"

"Rejected seems a harsh word." His voice roughened and he coughed.

"Who was she?"

His gaze bore into mine. "It was you, Ginnie. The woman was you. *Is* you."

Locked in the blue of his stare, I was only faintly aware of the others shocked reactions—quick drawn breaths, restless movements. I blinked and dragged myself back on track.

"Coral, you called Azalea on her cell just before eight o'clock that night. Supposedly, you'd forgotten about her date. Personally, I think you were jealous and wanted to disrupt it, especially if it was going well."

Coral's suspicious stare snaked from Seth to me and back again before she answered, chin raised haughtily. "Why would I be jealous? Belva was the one in love with her."

I'd needed Seth to confess his feelings for me, but it wasn't my place to disclose Belva's declaration to Azalea and its humiliating consequences. "People are jealous for lots of reasons other than romantic love. Your reaction to Carter's friendship with me, for instance." Coral flinched but I felt no compassion. "Also, you've insisted you were Azalea's best friend. Often. Almost as if you were trying to convince yourself."

"It's the truth. Why would I lie about being friends?"

"Oh, I don't doubt you were friends. It's the degree that's under debate." Especially given Carter's interpretation of his mother's bond with Coral. "I imagine you grew closer after

Warren died. You wouldn't be happy she was starting to date. If Azalea found someone else to love, you'd be relegated to the back seat again."

Coral's chest swelled and her mouth opened.

I raised my voice, heading off what was sure to be an outraged response. "Let's leave that for now."

Aware of Carter, focused and intent, in my peripheral vision, I switched my attention to Belva. "I believe the ransom calls were sent by an automated delivery system, though I can't prove it. Corporal Tam gave me the idea, so I'm sure the police are looking into it. And as you've probably heard, the voice was unrecognizable. It had been run through some sort of changer and could have been anyone."

Belva nodded, her spine stiffly erect.

"When I thought Azalea was being held for ransom," I continued, "you were my top suspect. Maybe you were embezzling from her. Maybe your business wasn't as lucrative as it seemed, and you had to cover some bad decisions. I can think of several other financial reasons you might need a sudden infusion of cash. But once I knew you were in love with Azalea, ransom for profit didn't make sense. You'd never steal from the woman you loved."

I drew in a long soothing breath and let it ease out before addressing Carter. "Your mother gave you everything you ever wanted. This apartment, your business—it all came from her. If you needed money, all you had to do was ask. So, if a botched kidnapping was the reason for Azalea's death, you were out. That left Coral."

"You think *I* kidnapped her?" Coral's voice jumped in

pitch as quickly as she jumped to a conclusion I wasn't going to make. "I told you. Azalea was generous. I might not have had as much money as she did, but she never left me out."

"Exactly. Fancy health club memberships, impulsive vacations, expensive gifts...if you were no longer Azalea's best friend"—Seth cleared his throat again even though I had kept all cynicism out of my voice—"you risked losing all that. And your financial troubles added to that stress."

"You're crazy." She waved her hands emphatically. "You're crazy if you think I killed her."

"No, I don't think you killed her. I did wonder if you'd kidnapped her, in order to solve your financial woes, and then the kidnap went bad." The fact she'd used the office fob on the same night I'd delivered Azalea's ransom hadn't eliminated her as far as I was concerned. "What I'd like to know is...what were you arguing about at the Illumination Celebration wrap up party?"

She froze, jolted by the rapid change in topic. "The Illumination Celebration?" she repeated warily.

It took some doing, but I finally weaseled it out of her.

"December was tight for me. So many gifts to buy, and I couldn't be any less generous than usual or people would know I was having...ah...difficulties. It was bad enough I couldn't afford my usual winter vacation." She crossed her arms over her chest and pouted. "I borrowed some of the donation money. Azalea found out, I don't know how. She was angry. Furious, really. Demanded I pay it back right away. I couldn't, so she did for me."

"What did she want in return?" I was pretty sure I knew the answer. Azalea might have covered up her friend's theft, but she wouldn't let her off scot-free.

"She insisted I resign from all my volunteer activities. Said I couldn't be trusted, and she wasn't going to let me steal from anyone else. Steal!" She was insulted at the accusation. "I wasn't stealing anything. I was just borrowing."

Her acceptance of this unearned entitlement left me dumbfounded. I let it go and returned to the night of Azalea's disappearance. "When you called her the evening she and Seth went out, where did she say she was going?"

"I told you this already. She said she was on her way to see the love of her life." Coral shot a sullen glance at Seth. "I thought she meant him."

"But their date was already over when you talked with her." I tightened my gut, tangled my fingers together, and looked directly at Carter. "She was going to meet you, wasn't she?"

He shrugged, unruffled. I imagine he'd seen it coming for a while now. The warm yet immature young man he'd played was in abeyance, a cold confident creature now in control. "Maybe. What's so surprising about that?"

"Nothing. What is surprising is how long it took me to realize I had asked everyone else about the last time they saw or spoke with Azalea, but never you. So...Carter, when was your last contact with your mother?" My stomach juddered and roiled.

He stared at me, unblinking.

"It's not a difficult question." I tried a smile, hoping to coax the answer out of him. "But maybe I should start earlier. Where were you Tuesday night, during Seth and Azalea's date?"

Another lengthy pause. Belva shifted as if about to interrupt and I shot her an insistent glance. She subsided.

I pressed harder. "What did you tell the police about that evening? I'm sure *they* asked you about it."

The quiet intensified, heavy, unrelenting. Finally, Carter spoke. "I told them I was at Carousel. Working late."

"And what about your mother?"

"I told them I hadn't seen her all day."

"I think you lied, Carter. Not about where you were, but about your mom. I think Azalea went to Carousel to report to you. After all, she had something extra juicy to share. She knew you'd want to hear about Seth's confession, his attraction to me."

No reaction.

I went on. "Only you know what happened after that. But this is what I think. I think she said she wouldn't be your spy any longer. She was having fun meeting new people. I believe she respected what Blynde Dating Agency does. Maybe she'd started to feel guilty about all the false pretenses."

Carter drained the last of his drink, placed it on the table, and draped his arms insolently along the back of the sofa. But his careless attitude was betrayed by a jittery knee. "What if she did? I wouldn't have cared."

"But you did care. Very much. You cared enough to convince her to join the agency in the first place, to break into my home and steal Peter's portrait. I think you would have been angry. Very angry." A new thought struck me. "Or maybe she told you she was going to come clean, tell me who she was, who you were. And that wasn't part of the plan."

"There was no plan," he scoffed.

"You told us you and Azalea had agreed *you* would tell me when the time was right. And it was too soon, wasn't it? You convinced your mother to befriend me as a consolation prize for not knowing your father. But what if that wasn't the real reason?" I met his stare as the final pieces clicked into place. "You wanted revenge. You blamed me for Peter rejecting you. Ruining my business, my reputation, might have seemed...logical." Warped, but logical.

He smiled. It wasn't a nice smile.

"What happened, Carter? What happened that night?"

For several moments I thought he'd refuse to answer. Then his eerie smile faded, and his expression crumpled. His arms pulled in and he hugged himself, rocking back and forth. "It was an accident. It was an accident, I swear. She fell. She hit her head."

To my right, Seth inhaled sharply and shifted in his seat. A choked gasp escaped Coral. Grief emanated from Belva in silent waves.

I released a long breath. "You didn't call an ambulance?"

The pace of Carter's rocking increased. "She was dead. I could see that. She was dead and I was all alone. I'd lost the only person I ever really loved. I didn't know what to do."

"So, you put her in your cool room." Sometimes the right solution was the simplest one. Carter had the perfect place to store a body. It had been staring me in the face from the beginning.

"There's an empty space, under the display shelving. I needed time to think. I didn't know what to do, so I put her there so I could think."

297

"What did you do with her car?"

"I parked it in the shed behind Carousel."

I'd never considered Carter a viable suspect. But when I'd listened to the recording I'd made of the kidnapper's second call, trying to determine if it was a robocall or live, I'd noticed something. Something that had been flickering just outside my consciousness but that I only managed to grasp after reviewing it several times.

The distorted voice had said "Your mother has it. Go to her accountant. Get it from her." I'd taken the final pronoun to refer to Azalea. But who knew her finances were controlled by a woman? And who always called Belva an accountant?

Carter.

My second reason for discounting him had been his apparently genuine confusion and deeply rooted fear for his mother's safety. It boggled my mind that he'd been a good enough actor to hide the truth from everyone.

Then it had struck me. He *hadn't* hidden it. Even before Azalea's body was found he talked as if she was dead. I'd assumed he was being pessimistic and melodramatic.

When all he'd been doing was speaking the truth.

I doubted I'd ever understand fully, but I needed some sort of explanation. "The whole time we were searching for her, dealing with the kidnap threat, you knew she was dead?"

"It didn't seem real." He huddled tighter into himself yet kept up his rhythmic rocking. "Once I hid her, it didn't seem real. It was easy to pretend it hadn't happened. At least at first. But she wasn't coming back. She was never coming back. I couldn't leave her where she was. Couldn't discard her body on the streets or in the woods. I needed to do something."

"Which was when you decided to frame Seth."

His swaying stopped. A sly expression erased the misery on his face. "It was brilliant. It should have worked."

Belva and Coral's heads swivelled toward Seth. He stiffened and straightened his spine. "You didn't know who I was. The police only told you after." His breathing was tight and wheezy, as if fury was choking him.

"Of course I knew about you." Carter was scornful and unrepentant. "My mother told me everything. I only pretended not to know so I had an excuse to call Ginnie. I wanted to find out if Mom had spoken with her before she came to see me that night. Then, a couple of days later, I was driving around, trying to figure out what to do, and I saw your name on the signage at the construction site. By then, the police knew you were the last to see her. It was too perfect. I drove Mom's car down Saturday morning and parked it, then walked back to Carousel. The police were already looking for it since it wasn't at her house. All I had to do was wait for them to find it."

Seth rose to his feet. At first, I thought he was going to launch himself at Carter, take out the frustrations of the last two weeks on the man who deserved it. Instead, he turned to me.

"Ambulance." He pounded his chest as if to dislodge something. "Allergy."

And collapsed to the floor.

CHAPTER THIRTY-FOUR

HE FELL BETWEEN the sofa and the coffee table, his head barely missing the sharp glass edge.

"Seth!" I shoved the couch out of the way—it slid easily on the glossy hardwood floor—and dropped to my knees beside him.

"Interesting." Carter's tone was clinical, detached. "I didn't realize it would be so dramatic."

"What did you do?" I loosened the buttons on Seth's shirt, hoping to ease his struggle for breath.

"I must have mixed up our drinks. Both soda with lime. With the addition of vodka in what was supposed to be mine."

"You bastard." He hadn't made a mistake. He'd done it intentionally. But to what purpose? Fury rose, hot and fast. I'd deal with him later. "Seth! Do you have an Epi-Pen with you?"

He lay flat on his back, heaving in short wheezing breaths with determination. Flat red blotches dotted his neck and upper chest. "Coat. Inside. Pocket."

I rose to my feet, crouching like a runner at the starting line, though not as athletically balanced. Carter stretched out and shoved me. I fell onto my bad knee and let out a pained yelp.

"Carter!" Coral screeched.

I scrambled out of his reach and levered to my feet. Knee screaming, I turned to the front hall.

Carter stood in my way.

"You ruined everything." He spoke through clenched teeth, his fists bunched at his sides. "You were right. I did want revenge on you. And then I got to know you and I wanted it even more. You and your condescending attitude."

"Get out of my way." I sidestepped. He blocked me. Seth's tortured breathing sawed in and out, and I could hear Belva on the phone with 911. God knows what Coral was doing. "Seth needs help. Get out of my way. Now!"

"This is your fault. If you hadn't brought him tonight, I wouldn't have thought to do it. But I saw how you looked at each other when you came in, saw how close you sat, how you held hands right in front of me. You're screwing him, aren't you? You're replacing my father with him."

Seth's breathing grew more laboured, with long pauses between each gasp. We couldn't wait for the ambulance.

"If you don't let me get his Epi-Pen, he could die." My voice cracked. "Let me by, Carter, please."

He spread his arms wide. "I don't think I will. I didn't know what would happen. I only put a little vodka in, as an experiment. But I like seeing you like this. I like knowing you're hurting. You deserve it, after all the misery you caused me."

Time Seth didn't have was wasting away. I stopped trying to reason with Carter and sidestepped again. This time, when he blocked me, I dodged past and sprinted for the front hall.

A searing pain scorched my skull, and my headlong dash was cut short. Carter forced my head down, my long ponytail wrapped in his fist. I reached up with both hands, trying to relieve the pressure, tears blinding me.

"Why does everyone like you so much, Ginnie? Why are they so loyal to you? You couldn't give Peter a child, and still he refused to be a father to me, the son standing right in front of him. My mother liked you so much she said I should make friends with you instead of snooping around behind your back. And Seth..." He shook me by the hair, lightning bolts of pain crackling from my scalp. "Seth takes one look at you and decides my mother isn't good enough for him. He chose you over her, just like Peter did."

"I'm sorry." I could see nothing but the floor and our feet. "I mean it, Carter. I'm so sorry. Let go and we'll talk. We'll figure this out." I had no intention of talking and every intention of doing whatever I had to get that Epi-Pen.

He shook me again and I bit back a shriek. "Seth is the reason my mother died. If he hadn't admitted he liked you, she wouldn't have decided we had to tell you the truth, and I wouldn't have gotten angry with her. I can't let you help him."

He dragged me deeper into the living room. Ignoring the agony blazing from my skull, I anchored my weight and tugged, hard. It pulled him off balance and he staggered, his grasp loosening just enough. Stars of pain and dizziness spangled my vision as I yanked out of his hold and straightened. Planting my feet, I used none of the grace but all the strength my dance lessons had imparted and kicked him in the balls.

He dropped with a grunt. I spun on my toes and raced to the front closet.

Willing Seth to stay alive, to just keep breathing, I tossed coats to the floor, searching for his. Panic fluttered wildly in my belly, shortening my own breath.

I wasn't losing another man I loved.

I pulled Seth's heavy wool coat off the hanger and struggled to find the inside pocket. The red case I extracted was emblazoned with a white cross. Fingers shaking, I fumbled for the zipper tab and opened it. Two chunky cylinders rested inside.

I dashed back to the living room. Carter still lay on the floor, groaning and clutching his groin. Coral crouched next to him. I hurtled past them and joined Belva, kneeling beside Seth.

She looked up, the whites showing all around her irises. "He's still conscious. Hurry."

Someone had pushed the couch even further out of the way and covered him with a throw blanket. He no longer had enough breath to speak, the skin around his mouth tinged with blue.

I shook the tubes out of the case, and they fell on the floor, along with a folded slip of paper. I told myself it wasn't wasted time to read the instructions. If I did this wrong, doing it fast wouldn't help.

Seth clutched the blanket and dragged the fabric off, slapping his thigh. His blue eyes, dark with pain, urged me to hurry.

I removed the cap, held the tube carefully upright, pressed the end to the heavy muscle of his thigh, and pushed.

1 Mississippi.

2 Mississippi.

3 Mississippi.

I gave it another second, just to be sure. Then I pulled the auto-injector away, tossed it aside, and gripped Seth's hand. His knuckles whitened as he strained to breathe.

"It says you can give a second injection in five to fifteen minutes if necessary. I've noted the time." Belva held the instructions I'd discarded. "The ambulance should be here soon. And the police."

Seth dragged his other hand across his torso and laid it on top of mine. I completed the clasp and squeezed so fiercely I felt his bones grind together. He didn't seem to mind, clutching my hands just as tightly, his strength reassuring, though the air whistled in and out of his lungs in rasping sighs.

"You're going to be okay." I disentangled one hand and brushed a lock of hair off his sweaty forehead. "You're going to be okay."

His head jerked in the smallest of nods.

I looked past Belva, realizing we were the only ones in the living room. "Where are Carter and Coral?" If she'd helped him escape, after all this...

"She took him to his bedroom. You gave him a good crotch shot."

A tiny spurt of amusement leaked through my anxiety at her satisfied tone. "Do you think it's okay, leaving the two of them together?"

"I don't know, and I don't care. They deserve each other. Spiteful, selfish, deceitful." She rubbed a hand under her nose. "Do you really believe he killed his own mother?"

"Yes." Was it my imagination or was Seth breathing more easily? "Time?"

"Three and a half minutes from injection." Then she echoed my own thoughts. "He doesn't seem to be struggling as much. Do you think it's working?"

Seth's voice, though weak and thready, had never sounded better. "It's working."

Paramedics arrived before I had to decide about giving a second injection. A different set of blue uniforms followed on their heels. Belva, calm yet urgent, directed the officers down the hall.

I released my grip on Seth's hand with reluctant relief. I didn't want to let go of him ever again, but now the professionals were here, I could allow reaction to overtake me.

My legs had gone numb from kneeling on the floor. I hobbled to my feet, sat on the couch, and pressed my trembling hands under my arms. In my mad struggles with Carter, I had forgotten about my injured knee, but now it throbbed viciously, demanding attention. And as if conjured up by a demon, a hot flash swept through me.

I sat quietly aching and sweating and watched the paramedics give Seth a thorough assessment, including another shot of something. He had recovered enough to resist being put on a stretcher, though he did agree to being monitored at the hospital for a few hours. He was arguing about his mode of transportation when Tam appeared at the door.

He waved me over, glowering. I told Seth I'd be right back and went to meet the irritated corporal.

"Want to tell me what the hell is going on?"

Limping, I led him to the kitchen, which blocked my view of Seth but allowed me to keep an eye on the hall to the exit. If they left before Tam finished with me, I'd see them.

I kept my report as concise as possible, though I'm sure it was garbled in places. Nevertheless, he didn't interrupt, just stood, stolid and square, and listened.

"Seems you brought things to a head just a few hours before us," he grumbled. "We were lining things up to bring Bickersley in tomorrow."

"You were?" Maybe I sounded more skeptical than I should have. His glare grew fiercer.

"We've been looking at him from the start. Too much in his story didn't add up. We've been waiting for full access to the account that made the robocalls. Just got it a couple of hours ago."

"What did you learn?" Remembering his earlier reticence, I added, "If you can tell me, that is." If he resisted, I was too tired to argue.

Maybe because Carter was in custody, he didn't hesitate to answer. "To start, we confirmed it was his account. Then we reviewed the logs. The very first ransom call, when he said he talked to his mother?" I nodded. "It only lasted about ten seconds. Not nearly long enough to include everything he says it did. We think he was testing the system. He would want to be sure the next calls would go as planned. Especially the second one, when he was with you. You were to be his alibi."

"What about the calls on Wednesday, though? The first was supposed to come at noon and go to Carter. But it didn't come until five and was sent to me. If he'd set everything up ahead of time, how did that happen?"

"We determined those calls, and any following, were rescheduled and redirected. Pretty sure he decided not to risk them coming to him while we were there."

"I thought you were monitoring his phone. How did no one catch him at it?"

"He didn't use his phone. Probably a laptop or tablet he didn't admit to having. I imagine it's in this apartment somewhere, but wherever it is, we'll find it."

My muscles went watery, and I braced myself against the counter. "I didn't want to believe it was him. He seemed sincerely desperate to pay the ransom and too terrified to call the police because it would risk her life. Yet, all that time she was dead. And he knew she was dead because he'd killed her."

"Mrs. Bickersley died from a head wound consistent with a fall—he told you the truth there—though we may never know if she was deliberately pushed. We also know the credit card on the storage unit rental links back to that flower shop of his." He leaned his hips against the counter, lifting the holster on his utility belt out of the way and crossing his arms. "You'll be interested to know he was behind the Facebook posts too. The ones slamming your agency."

I hadn't thought about those posts for days. "He was? Why? How?"

"How is being tracked by the tech team. As for why? That's a question we'll be asking. I'm guessing it was a smokescreen, like the ransom. One more thing to confuse the investigation. And maybe to mess with you. From what you said, I can't decide whether he loves or hates you."

Maybe ruining my business had been part of his revenge plan all along. He could have been waiting for Azalea to tell him of a situation he could manipulate. Then when she died...

My throat burned. Swallowing didn't ease it. "All because he wanted to know his real father. I wonder if Azalea would still be alive if she had told the truth sooner. To Carter and to Peter." How would my life have played out if I'd known Peter's first affair had resulted in a son? Would he and I have stayed married? Would he and Priya have become lovers? Would *they* still be alive?

Would I have ever met Seth?

"Speaking of your husband." Tam's gun belt creaked as he uncrossed his arms. "I want you to know the case isn't closed. There are a few things in the file I want to look into deeper."

"What things?"

He shook his head. "I can't say. You'll be the first to know if I learn anything new."

I shifted my weight more heavily onto my good leg. "I won't hold my breath. But thank you."

Seth appeared in the hall leading to the front door, shepherded by the paramedics but walking under his own power. He glanced into the kitchen and halted. One eyebrow quirked up in question.

I smiled and made a shooing gesture. I knew he'd interpret that as I'd follow him to the hospital as soon as I could.

As soon as Seth and his escort had departed, a uniformed officer entered the kitchen. "Sir? We're ready to take Mr. Bickersley to the station."

"Be right there." Tam heaved himself away from the counter. "You have anything else to tell me before I go?"

I shook my head, relieved to be telling the truth. I was done with secrets.

CHAPTER THIRTY-FIVE

I DIDN'T STICK around to see Carter escorted out. Any softer feelings I'd had toward him had been incinerated by his confession. I never wanted to talk to him again.

The only person I wanted to see was Seth. I waited as Tam clumped down the hall to the bedrooms and then slipped out the front door. The outer foyer was empty, an elevator waiting invitingly, so I took pity on my knee and rode it down.

The ambulance was just exiting the parking lot. Seth's truck was still next to my car, so the paramedics had won that battle. We could arrange to get it back once the dust had settled.

I sent a text to Maeve with an edited version of the events of the evening, leaving out the rigamarole with the portrait, and promising to share the whole story as soon as I could. I ended it with a warning I was shutting off my phone for the night, hit send, and went incommunicado.

At the Emergency ward, I inquired for Seth at the reception desk and after a bit of back and forth was allowed in. I found him in a bed behind an ugly orange curtain, lying on top of the covers fully dressed, eyes closed, his forefinger clipped into one of those monitoring things. He still looked pale and dishevelled, but there was no oxygen tube, no intravenous line.

No gasping breaths and blueish lips.

Something deep inside me kicked. *Hard*. I clutched the

stiff fabric of the drape, making the rings on the rail rattle. His eyes sprang open and fastened on me.

"Ginnie." He held out his hand.

I leapt to take it. "You're okay." I meant it as a statement, but the tremor in my voice betrayed me.

"I'm okay. Come here." He shifted his hips to one side of the narrow mattress and gave me a tug. I crawled up willingly and laid my head on his chest, my sore knee bent over his thigh. Not that I would mention the pain. It was nothing compared to what he'd been through.

"I was so scared." I whispered the words, half hoping he wouldn't hear them but needing to acknowledge my fear.

His arm tightened around me, and his lips brushed the crown of my head. "Me too."

His heart thudded, reassuringly steady, under my cheek. I splayed my hand on his ribs, revelling in the rise and fall as air moved without effort in and out of his lungs, and slowly relaxed.

We lay like that for a long, long time. The sounds of the ER washed over us—the squeak of wheels, quiet murmur of voices, a distant baby's wail, intoxicated muttering from the cubicle next door. Once a nurse poked her head around the curtain, but at Seth's assurance he was fine, she vanished, presumably in search of others more in need of her attention.

At one point, I asked, "Have you told Grace what happened? I mean, maybe not about Carter, but about your allergic reaction?" His daughter wouldn't be pleased to hear how close she'd been to losing another parent, but she deserved to know.

His shoulder moved under my head. "It's too late

tonight. I'll call her tomorrow."

Several hours after he was admitted, Seth nudged me out of a doze. I yawned, propped myself up on one elbow, and looked down into his face.

"They're letting me go." The lines around his mouth were deep with fatigue.

"I didn't hear anyone come in." Sheepishly, I wiped at a small damp spot on his shirt.

"You're exhausted."

"We both are." I swung off the bed. "Come on. Let's go home."

Seth put up a half-hearted resistance when he realized I meant *my* home, but I rolled over his protests. I wasn't ready to let him out of my sight.

It was almost dawn, the sky indigo velvet. Our breaths floated from our lips in clouds as we walked hand in hand to my car. I drove through the empty streets, dazed from fatigue and stress, yet at peace. Seth was beside me. He was coming home with me. All was as it should be.

When we reached my house, I led him to the bedroom. We undressed each other with slow, undemanding movements. I couldn't resist dropping kisses on his bare pecs, shivering as he swept his hands over my breasts and belly.

I giggled when his cock swelled and rose. "You've got to be kidding me."

His laugh huffed against my cheek. "I'm always half-hard near you. But I don't have the energy to do right by you. Not tonight."

When we were naked, I kissed his chin, drew back the covers, and crawled to the centre of the bed. Seth curled around me and pulled the comforter over us.

"Sleep," he whispered. "We'll finish fixing the world in the morning."

So, I did.

I woke up in much the same position I'd gone to sleep. Stiff yet rested, I held back a groan as I wriggled to my back, draping my knees over Seth's stacked thighs. Our heads lay on the same pillow, so close our noses brushed. I pulled back a bit and studied him.

His beard was thick with silver. Pale lashes fanned his cheeks, and a tuft of hair stuck up at his temple. I couldn't resist a sentimental urge to smooth it down. When my fingers touched his skull, his eyes drifted open.

"Morning," I said.

"Morning." His voice was hoarse, but not with the struggle to breathe.

I repressed a shudder of remembered terror. "Sleep well?"

"Mm-hmm. You?"

I nodded. The platitudes, instead of creating a zone of comfort between us, felt awkward. Ignoring morning breath and my craving for caffeine, I jumped in with both feet.

"I talked with Tam yesterday. While you were with the paramedics."

"I saw. Was he congratulating you on solving his case for him?" His sleepy eyes sparkled. "You were amazing. You know that, right?"

I would have to fill him in on everything the RCMP had

discovered, but that wasn't what was hanging over me like a blade. "I just about got you killed!"

His fingers had been gliding tantalizingly over my hip. At this, he gripped my flesh tight. "No, *you* didn't. That bastard Carter is the one who poisoned me."

"But you wouldn't have been there if I hadn't insisted. I didn't really need you present. I could have told them what you confessed to Azalea."

"It was better, coming from me."

"Still..." I drew in a deep breath. I wondered if I'd ever do so again without thinking of his struggle last night.

"Don't do this, Ginnie." He sat up, the comforter falling from his shoulders. "Don't blame yourself for what a mad man did."

I hitched a pillow behind me and leaned against the headboard while tugging a sheet up to cover my breasts. "I can't get it out of my head. I felt so helpless."

He pushed back on the mattress, so we were shoulder to shoulder. "You were anything but helpless. I was a little busy at the time, but Belva told me you kicked Carter's ass."

My giggle at his self-deprecating description trembled with tears. "Well, his balls, but I get what you're saying."

For a few moments we sat in silence. Then, stomach clutching, I took a step toward the future. "We're here. Together, even after all the drama. I guess that means something."

"It means more than I can say." He reached around me, scooped me up, and plopped me on his lap. "It's been a crazy couple of weeks, hasn't it?"

"Yes." Heart racing, I ran my fingers through the silver

curls on his chest, delighting in the springy texture. "But we made it through."

He hugged me tighter and I tucked my head under his chin. His voice reverberated under my ear. "You forgive me, then? For not telling you the truth the moment we met?"

"Yes. I even understand. Kind of. But don't ever do it again." I tugged a small handful of hair in punishment, and he sucked air through his teeth. "No more lies. No more deceit."

"If it's honesty you need, then there's one more thing you should know."

I lifted my head so quickly I bashed my skull against his jaw. Blinking away stars, I stared at him. "What now for god's sake?"

He laid a palm on my head and searched for a lump, flattening my sleep-ruffled strands. Finding nothing, he slid his hand down my cheek and cupped my chin. "I love you." His eyes shone with amusement and heat and just enough apprehension to convince me he was telling the truth.

Warmth suffused my chest and swept up my cheeks. Was I ready for this? A quick search of my heart gave me the answer. "Seth."

He must have heard the longing I couldn't hide, because he gave me the confirmation I needed. "I love you, Ginnie Blynde. I never thought I'd say those words to another woman, but as you said...here we are."

Any doubts I'd had about my own feelings had been swept away watching Seth fight for his life on the floor of Carter's living room. Emotion choked me, trapping my own declaration inside. I would have to show him.

I pressed my mouth to his and he opened eagerly. Our tongues twined and twisted as we burned away all the fear, all the uncertainty, all the anxiety until it was just us.

Seth and I. Naked. In my bed. With nothing keeping us apart, emotionally or physically.

Without breaking our kiss, I wriggled carefully off the hard hot erection rising under my buttocks. Released, his cock slapped against his belly. I straddled him and pressed my breasts against his chest, my nipples pointed and aching.

He groaned into my mouth and clamped one hand on my ass. The strong, taut muscles of his thighs spread my hips as his other hand slipped between us. Calloused fingertips dipped inside me. I jolted, throwing my head back, arching away.

"Yes." Even with my eyes closed, I could see him, cheeks flushed, eyes sparkling darkly, expression intent. All his focus on me. Pressure built as he stroked my inner walls and flicked my clit.

Wanting him to share in my pleasure, I gripped his shaft. The rhythm of his caresses stuttered as my thumb swept the tip. Tension spiralled inside me, tightening every cell in my body. The scrape of his teeth on the slope of my breast before he drew the nipple into his mouth threw me over the edge. Desire drenched me. I gasped and shuddered and screamed with abandon.

"Again." Seth's fingers dove deeper, stretching me, filling me.

I sobbed, riding his hand, and peaked so quickly I had no time to prepare, my defences already breached.

Collapsing against him, I heaved deep cleansing breaths,

searching for the remnants of my sanity. His hands stroked up and down my spine, toyed with my hair, his heavy whiskers catching as he rubbed his chin through the strands.

"I love the sounds you make when you come," he said.

Limbs still trembling, I pushed back so I could see his face. "I haven't said it yet, have I?"

His eyelids fluttered. "You don't have to. Not if you're not ready."

There was only one answer to that. "I love you, Seth Updike." With my fingertip I traced the shell of his ear, blushed red with heat. "I know it's only been a couple of weeks, and it should be too soon. For either of us. But we've been through more in those weeks than some couples experience in a decade."

"And we're not naïve twenty-year olds, either." He cupped my breasts and brushed the sensitive nipples with his thumbs, making me twitch, though I didn't move away. His gaze never left mine. "We know how short life can be. Why waste it when we know what's right?"

"Exactly." His touch rekindled cinders that were never fully doused in his presence. I slid out of his hold, down between his legs.

"Ginnie."

I nuzzled the musky hollow where his hip met his body. "I love when you say my name like that. Full of wonder and excitement."

His cock jerked against my cheek, and I accepted the invitation. When my mouth closed around him, his hands settled on my head.

I took him to the edge with lips and tongue and fingers,

revelling in his taste, his scent, his texture. His whispers grew disjointed, fractured syllables of encouragement but no longer words. I grazed my fingernails in sensitive places and delighted when he whimpered. I wanted to wreck this man, as he had wrecked me, and then put him back together again with my love.

With a tearing moan, he gripped my shoulders and muscled me to my back. More than ready, I widened my legs in welcome. "Condom. Nightstand."

He wasted no time protecting us and then knelt before me and eased home. His head dropped to my shoulder, his breath panting on my skin, and for long luxurious moments I gloried in the sensation of being part of a whole, of two bodies joined as one.

"Ginnie."

"Yes." Hooking my calves into the notches of his knees, I circled my hips.

He pulsed into me, insistent and demanding. Over and over again, until my skin dissolved and I had no limits. There was only him and me and us.

CHAPTER THIRTY-SIX

A WEEK LATER, Seth and I celebrated our first Valentine's Day together by helping to host Blynde Dating Agency's Hopeful Hearts. I'd tried to talk him out of coming, explaining it would be a working evening, but he'd insisted. I'd been happy enough to give in. We'd spent very little time away from each other since the showdown at Carter's, and I wasn't ready for that to end.

I surveyed the crowded room. Apparently, Blynde Dating's association with a scandal was forgiven—maybe even celebrated—now the murderer had been caught. Sometimes humanity's ghoulishness astounded me.

We stood in the corner of the banquet room where Indra had banished me. "I've got this," she had scolded. "You're here only as the pretty face behind the name. Now get out of my way."

It wasn't that I didn't trust her. But I wasn't completely over the dramatic events of last week, and micromanaging had become my therapy of choice.

Seth nudged me with an elbow. "Not that I've ever been to a singles event, but this one looks like a success."

"It is. Indra is good. Very good."

No formal seating arrangements constricted mingling. Instead, Indra had decided on a walking dinner. Several tall tables, sans chairs, were clustered near the sumptuous buffet set up in one corner. In another, cozy looking couches provided an intimate conversation area. At the farthest end, her carefully curated playlist of ballads interspersed with more upbeat tunes oozed from a wireless speaker near a tiny dance floor.

The casually inviting atmosphere was working. Two couples were already dancing, while most participants were chatting in pairs or groups. Those that weren't were being expertly corralled by Indra and introduced to the gathering she thought would suit them best.

Maeve monitored the buffet and bar, while Piper lurked nearby in case of technical issues. This wasn't her scene, but it was an all-hands-on-deck evening and, while she'd fussed at having to be here, she'd shown up, reliable as always.

The three of them had been shocked and horrified when I'd finally filled them in on everything. But as they hadn't witnessed Seth's poisoning or Carter's arrest, it had been easier for them to accept and move on.

I'd become hyper-vigilant over what Seth consumed. I'd watched the bartender pour his soda and lime with an eagle eye and had chosen a soft drink as well. In fact, I hadn't had a glass of wine, or any other alcohol, in over a week. I'd lost the taste for it.

"You're wound up tighter than a spring." Seth rubbed my back with a large warm hand. "What's going on?"

"Nothing." He quirked an eyebrow and I surrendered. "Everything that happened seems so long ago and, at the same time, as if it was just yesterday. I'm giving myself whiplash trying to deal with it. I just wish things would get back to normal."

Carter was being held for psychiatric evaluation. Tam, who was obligingly keeping me in the loop, seemed certain his lawyer was going to plead diminished responsibility in Azalea's death. "But even if the judge goes for that," he'd said, "we've got him cold on indignity to a human body, wasting police resources with the false ransom claim, the two break and enter charges, and assorted other crimes."

I hadn't bothered making a complaint against Coral for her part in the portrait theft. In the end, it didn't seem worth it. I doubted she would thank me, though, should we ever run into each other again. I had no plans to seek her out and was confident she felt the same way about me.

As for Belva—well, she stood at one of the tall tables, conversing stiffly with Lillian, home from Vancouver. Both of them were here as my guests, though neither were members. Yet. It was the first time Lillian had accepted my invitation since her divorce. She didn't seem to mind Belva's prickly attitude, flashing bright smiles as she chattered.

I'd reached out to Belva a few days after Carter's arrest. Her loneliness was tangible, and I'd convinced her one night at a singles event wouldn't betray her principles. She'd lightened her usual black and white palette with a leaf-green scarf, so I had hope for her yet.

"Grace is excited to meet you," Seth said.

I focused on him. "Are you sure it's not too soon?" We had a trip to Edmonton planned for the upcoming Family Day long weekend. He had given her an edited version of what had happened, and she had insisted on the visit, wanting to see for herself her father was okay. Somehow, I'd been included in the demand.

"Of course not." I'd left my hair loose and he tugged a lock. "There's no need to be nervous."

"Me, nervous?" I scoffed, but the butterflies in my belly knew the truth.

His hand drifted from my hair to grasp my palm. I squeezed it in solidarity. "I never hid from her that I joined Blynde Dating, so I think I'll stick with the surface truth—that I was ready to meet someone new, got tangled up in a kidnap/murder, and came out unscathed. There's no need to mention her mother or Peter."

I agreed wholeheartedly with that. "What does she know about Carter and Azalea?"

"None of the details. I want to tell her face-to-face. As for us...I told her what we have is the real thing."

Thrilling at his assured, confident tone, I placed my glass on a nearby table and snuggled into his arms. "I knew you were trouble the moment you walked into my office."

Completely comfortable with my PDA, he wrapped me in an embrace. "You did?"

I nodded, my cheek rubbing the smooth lapel of his suit. "Big trouble." I leaned my hips into his, shoulders back, so he could see my face. "But it's a trouble I don't ever want to live without."

Also by Brenda Margriet

Bendixon Sisters
Allegro Court
Gateway Crescent
Crossroads Corner
Taking His Measure: The Complete Bendixon Sisters Series

SILVERBERRY SEDUCTION Seasoned Romance
Secrets Under the Covers
Loving Between the Lines
Turn the Next Page
Strictly by the Book
Too Good for Words
Silverberry Seduction: The Complete Series

TIMELESS Seasoned Romance
After Words
Richly Deserved

Standalone
When Time Falls Still
No Life But This
Mountain Fire
Reserved for You
The Promise of Frost
Suspect Attraction

Watch for more at www.brendamargriet.com.

About the Author

Brenda Margriet writes savvy, slow burn, contemporary romances with ordinarily amazing characters. In her own ordinarily amazing life, she had a successful career in radio and television production before deciding to pilfer from her retirement plan to support her writing compulsion.

Readers have called her stories "poignant," "explicit and steamy," "interesting, intriguing and entertaining," and "unlike any romance you've read before" (she assumes the latter was meant in a good way).

Join Brenda on social media—she is most active on Facebook and Instagram. And don't miss any of her writing news by signing up for her newsletter!

Find out more on her website, www.brendamargriet.com